THE GOOD SISTER

Also by Drusilla Campbell

Bone Lake

Blood Orange

The Edge of the Sky

Wildwood

THE GOOD SISTER

Drusilla Campbell

GRAND CENTRAL PUBLISHING

NEW YORK BOSTON

This book is a work of fiction. Names, characters, places, and incidents are the product of the author's imagination or are used fictitiously. Any resemblance to actual events, locales, or persons, living or dead, is coincidental.

Grand Central Publishing
Hachette Book Group
237 Park Avenue
New York, NY 10017

www.HachetteBookGroup.com

Printed in the United States of America

First Edition: October 2010
10 9 8 7 6 5 4 3 2 1

Grand Central Publishing is a division of Hachette Book Group, Inc.
The Grand Central Publishing name and logo is a trademark of Hachette Book Group, Inc.

Library of Congress Cataloging-in-Publication Data
Campbell, Drusilla.
The good sister / Drusilla Campbell.—1st ed.
p. cm.
ISBN 978-0-446-53578-6
1. Sisters—Fiction. 2. Family secrets—Fiction. 3. Postpartum depression—Fiction. I. Title.
PS3603.A474G66 2010
813'.6—dc22

2010004910

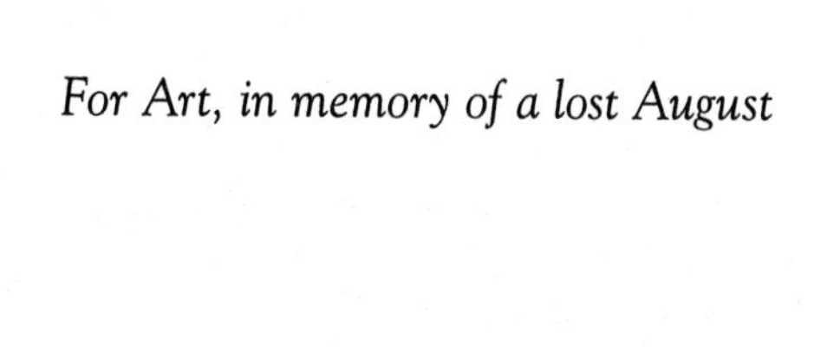

For Art, in memory of a lost August

Acknowledgments

The writing and production of a good novel take the hard work and cooperation of dozens of men and women. My full gratitude list would cover a dozen pages and even then be incomplete because the truth is, anything and anyone can inspire me. Twenty years ago I saw a woman wrench her three-year-old from aisle to aisle in the supermarket, scowling and snarling as he wailed louder and louder. Her spirit lives in *The Good Sister* as does the memory of exhaustion written on the faces of my son and daughter-in-law as they learned to manage life with a newborn. I wish I could thank you all, but for now let me name just a few.

First, and always, my immeasurable gratitude goes to Art, who makes me laugh and keeps me steady.

To Margaret, my own good sister. The best.

To my mother for a lifetime of love and encouragement.

To Nikki, my daughter-in-law, for her courage and her

always honest answers to my often ignorant and intrusive questions.

To my excellent sons, Rocky and Matt. Who'd have thought those little boys would grow up to be my rudder and compass.

To my agent, Angela Rinaldi, who has shown repeatedly that she can talk me down off the ledge and up off the floor.

To my stellar editors at Grand Central: Karen Kosztolnyik and Beth de Guzman, for their patience, insight, and high standards. Karen deserves special kudos for her diplomacy in the face of terrible first drafts.

At Grand Central, my thanks go to Bruce Paonessa, Chris Barba, Karen Torres, Martha Otis, Harvey-Jane Kowal, and Jamie Raab, who are responsible for turning *The Good Sister* into a book we can hold in our hands. Thank you also to Liz Connor for her haunting cover and to Celia Johnson for nagging me gently.

Many women shared with me their deeply personal experiences of motherhood and depression. Your trust and honesty moved me deeply. My heart goes out to the millions of mothers who for centuries have suffered from the gradations of postpartum depression alone, misunderstood, and often condemned.

Finally, thank you to the Ladies of the Arrowhead Association, the mothers, sisters, and friends who make it all possible.

Home—the private journal where we learn who
we are by recording who we love.

—Judith Tate O'Brien

THE GOOD SISTER

Chapter 1

San Diego, California
The State of California v. Simone Duran
March 2010

On the first day of Simone Duran's trial for the attempted murder of her children, the elements conspired to throw their worst at Southern California. Arctic storms that had all winter stalled or washed out north of Los Angeles chose the second week of March to break for the south and were now lined up, a phalanx of wind and rain stretching north into Alaska. In San Diego a timid sprinkle began after midnight, gathered force around dawn, and now, with a hard northwest wind behind it, deluged the city with a driving rain. Roxanne Callahan had lived in San Diego all her life and she'd never seen weather like this.

In the stuffy courtroom a draft found the nape of her neck, driving a shudder down her spine to the small of her back: she feared that if the temperature dropped just one degree she'd start shaking and wouldn't be able to stop. Behind her, someone in the gallery had a persistent, bronchial cough. Roxanne had a vision of germs floating like pollen on the air. She wondered if hostile people—the gawkers and jackals, the ghoulishly curious, the homegrown experts and lurid trial junkies—carried germs more virulent than those of friends and allies. Not that there were many well-wishers in the crowd. Most of the men and women in the courtroom represented the millions of people who hated Simone Duran; and if their germs were half as lethal as their thinking, Simone would be dead by dinnertime.

Roxanne and her brother-in-law, Johnny Duran, sat in the first row of the gallery, directly behind the defense table. As always Johnny was impeccably groomed and sleekly handsome; but new gray rimed his black hair, and there were lines engraved around his eyes and mouth that had not been there six months earlier. He was the owner and president of a multimillion-dollar construction company specializing in hotels and office complexes, a man with many friends, including the mayor and chief of police; but since the attempted murder of his children he had become reclusive, spending all his free time with his daughters. He and Roxanne had everything to say to each other and at the same time nothing. She knew the same question filled his mind as hers and each knew it was pointless to ask: what could or should they have done differently?

Following her arraignment on multiple counts of attempted murder, Simone had been sent to St. Anne's Psychiatric Hospital for ninety days' observation. Bail was set at a million dollars, and Johnny put the lake house up as collateral. He leased a condo on a canyon where Simone and their mother, Ellen Vadis, lived after her release from St. Anne's. Her bail had come with heavy restrictions. She was forbidden contact with her daughters and confined to the condo, tethered by an electronic ankle bracelet and permitted to leave only with her attorney on matters pertaining to the case and with her mother for meetings with her doctor.

Like Johnny, Roxanne visited Simone several times a week. These tense interludes did nothing to lift anyone's spirits as far as she could tell. They spent hours on the couch watching television, sometimes holding hands; and while Roxanne often talked about her life, her work, her friends, any subject that might help the illusion that they were sisters like other sisters, Simone rarely spoke. Sometimes she asked Roxanne to read to her from a book of fairy tales she'd had since childhood. Stories of dancing princesses and enchanted swans soothed Simone much as a lullaby might a baby; and more than once Roxanne had left her, covered by a cashmere throw, asleep on the couch with the book beside her. Lately she had begun to suck her thumb as she had when she was a child. Roxanne faced the truth: the old Simone, the silly girl with her secrets and demands, her narcissism, the manic highs and the black holes where the meany-men lived, even her love, might be gone forever.

A medicine chest of pharmaceuticals taken morning and night kept her awake and put her to sleep, eased her down from mania toward catatonia and then half up again to something like normal balance. She took drugs that elevated her mood, focused her attention, flattened her enthusiasm, stifled her anxiety, curbed her imagination, cut back her paranoia, and put a plug in her curiosity. The atmosphere in the condo was almost unbearably artificial.

Across the nation newspapers, magazines, and blogs were filled with Simone stories passing as truth. Her picture was often on television screens, usually behind an outraged talking head. Sometimes it was the mug shot taken the day she was booked, occasionally one of the posed photos from the Judge Roy Price Dinner when she looked so beautiful but was dying inside. The radio blabmeisters could not stop ranting about her, about what a monster she was. Spinning know-it-alls jammed the call-in lines. Weekly articles in the supermarket tabloids claimed to know and tell the whole story.

The whole story! If Roxanne had had any sense of humor left she would have cackled at such a preposterous claim. Simone's story was also Roxanne's. And Ellen's and Johnny's. They were all of them responsible for what happened that September afternoon.

Roxanne's husband, Ty Callahan, had offered to put his work at the Salk Institute on hold so he could attend the trial with her, but she didn't want him there. He and her friend Elizabeth were links to the world of hopeful, optimistic, ordinary people. The courtroom would taint that.

The night before, Roxanne and Ty had eaten Chinese takeout; and afterward, while he read, she lay with her head on his lap searching for the blank space in her mind where repose hid. They went to bed early and made love with surprising urgency, as if time pressed in upon them, and before it was too late they had to establish their connection in the most basic way. Roxanne should have slept afterward; instead she got up and watched late-night infomercials for computer careers and miraculous skin products, finally falling asleep on the couch, where Ty found her in the morning with Chowder, their yellow Labrador, snoring on the floor beside her, a ball between his front paws.

"Don't look at me," she said, sitting up. "I'm a mess."

"You are." Ty handed her a mug of coffee, his smile breaking over her like sunlight. "The worst-looking woman I've seen this morning."

She rested her forehead against his chest and closed her eyes. "Tell me I don't have to do this today."

He drew her to him. "We'll get through it, Rox."

"But who'll we be? When it's over?"

"I guess we just have to wait and see."

"And you'll be here?"

"If I think about leaving, I'll come get you first."

In the courtroom she closed her eyes and pictured Ty with his postdocs gathered around him, the earnest young men and women who looked up to him in a way that Roxanne had found sweet and faintly amusing back when she could still laugh. She knew how her husband worked, the care he took and the careful notations he made in his lab notebooks in his precise draftsman's hand. With life falling apart and nothing certain from one day to the next, it was calming—a meditation of sorts—to think of Ty at work across the city in a lab overlooking the Pacific.

Attorney David Cabot and Simone entered the courtroom and took their places at the defense table. Cabot had been Johnny's first choice to defend Simone. Once the quarterback for the San Diego Chargers, he had not won many games but was widely admired for qualities of leadership and character. His win-loss statistics were much better in law than in football. He had made his name trying controversial cases, and Simone's was definitely that.

Simone, small and thin, her back as narrow as a child's, sat beside Cabot, conservatively dressed in a black-and-white wool dress with a matching jacket and serious shoes in which she could have hiked Cowles Mountain. In her ears she wore the silver-and-turquoise studs Johnny had given her when they became engaged. As intended, she looked mild and calm, too sweet to commit a crime worse than jaywalking.

Conversation in the gallery hushed as the jurors entered and took their seats. One, a college student, looked sideways at Simone; but the others directed their gazes across the courtroom to the wall of rain-beaten windows. Among the twelve there were two Hispanic women in their mid-twenties, one of them a college student; three men and a woman, all retired professionals; a Vietnamese manicurist; and one middle-aged black woman, the co-owner of a copy shop. Roxanne tried to see intelligence and tolerance and wisdom in their faces, but all she saw was an ordinary sampling of San Diego residents. For them to be a true jury of Simone's peers at least one should be a deep depressive, one extravagantly rich, and another pathologically helpless.

Just let them be good people, Roxanne prayed. Good and sensitive and clear-thinking. Let them be honest. Let them see into my sister and know that she is not a monster.

Chapter 2

August 1977

Roxanne's mommy said they were going for a long trip in the car, and that it would be an adventure; but she wouldn't say where they were going or how long they would be gone. When Roxanne asked questions she just walked away, sat at the table in the kitchen, and smoked cigarettes.

In less than two weeks Roxanne would begin first grade in Mrs. Enos's class at Logan Hills Elementary School in San Diego, and she wanted to stay home and get ready. Mrs. Enos's classroom was on the edge of the playground in a temporary building that didn't look like it had ever been painted. Mommy called the building a portable and said it had been around since Jesus Christ wore diapers. Roxanne didn't know who Jesus Christ was, but she liked the portable classroom because it seemed like a clubhouse and the door opened right onto the playground. She didn't care that there were no trees on the playground and barely any equipment to climb or swing on, and she didn't care if Logan Hills Elementary had mice and roaches shiny as black olives because in the first grade she was going to learn about numbers.

She was already a good reader. Her mother and Mrs. Edison said it was spooky the way she had taught herself. They asked her how she did it, but she couldn't tell them. She just paid attention to words like the ones in Mrs. Edison's recipe book and the sounds that went with them until the squiggles on the page started to make sense. Plus she watched *Sesame Street* at Mrs. Edison's house. That was also how she had learned to count, but any dummy with fingers and toes could do that.

While Mommy went to work Roxanne stayed next door with Mrs. Edison, a soft, blond woman who had no children of her own and appreciated the extra cash. It was she who had walked Roxanne to the elementary school, shown her the portable classroom, and introduced her to Mrs. Enos. The teacher was tall and had brown skin and frizzy orange hair. She crouched down to say hello, eye to eye. "You're going to love this one," Mrs. Edison said, wagging her eyebrows; and Roxanne's face got hot because she knew Mrs. Edison was talking about her.

When she said good-bye Mrs. Enos gave Roxanne a silver pinwheel that spun blurry-fast.

Mrs. Edison's husband and Daddy were both in the Marines, but that didn't mean they were best friends. On his own time, Daddy played poker and pool across the street at the Royal Flush. Mr. Edison's nose was always stuck in a copy of *Popular Mechanics.* Mommy said he was going places in the Marines, and Daddy said big effing deal.

Grown-ups spoke a peculiar language full of words and mystery phrases like *big effing deal* that Roxanne didn't know. One day Mrs. Edison took her to the library, and she looked up *effing* in the big blue dictionary. It wasn't there, and that got her started worrying how she would ever learn the meaning of all the words people spoke. On television children talked to their parents and their parents talked back. Questions and answers were called conversation; and while no one ever said it, not exactly, Roxanne knew Mommy and Daddy didn't want to have conversation with her.

If Mrs. Edison was in a good mood she answered Roxanne's questions but she told her to watch out, curiosity killed the cat. Mrs. Edison had a yellow cat named Tom but he'd be hard to kill because he had nine lives. Roxanne talked to other people and knew the postman had been bitten by a dog and got ten stitches in his arm, and the woman at Von's market was having a baby and she hoped it was a girl so she could call her Rashida. Up and down the street she spoke to everyone, including the woman on the corner who always wore a scarf. All this talking, the words she didn't know and the contradictory things that people said, confused her. She had decided there must be rules for what was right to say and feel, rules for when to talk and when to listen, and sometimes she was afraid of what would happen to her if she never learned these rules. She didn't want to be like the homeless woman who wore a red wool cap even in the summertime and talked gibberish to herself as she pushed her shopping cart along the sidewalk in front of Roxanne's house.

Roxanne's world was full of dos and don'ts—don't cross the street on a red light or touch a hot stove, do lock the doors at night, and don't talk to strangers—so it made sense that there must be rules that applied to how people talked and what they did. Maybe if she read enough books and learned all the words in the dictionary and if she never stopped watching and listening, she would understand why mothers on television loved their daughters, but hers didn't.

At dinner Mommy said, "You're going to stay with your grandmother for a while."

This was the first Roxanne had heard of a grandmother.

"We'll leave tomorrow after breakfast. Put what you need in that pink backpack and don't forget your toothbrush." Mommy went into the bathroom and closed the door.

The questions lined up like Marines in Roxanne's

logical mind, a platoon of them beginning with *why* and *who* and *when* and what would happen if she missed the first day of school.

She heard the sound of water running into the tub. In a minute steam would seep out from under the door like smoke. Mommy must be nervous. She always took a bath when she was nervous. The medicine cabinet opened and clicked shut; the lid of the toilet seat hit the tank behind it. These were normal sounds and nothing to worry about. But if everything was normal, why did Roxanne feel like something big and mean and cold as a polar bear had walked in the front door and was right now standing in the middle of the room, staring at her?

"Are you mad at me, Mommy?" They sat at the card table eating spaghetti.

"Why? What have you done?"

This trip to her grandmother *felt* like trouble.

"Eat your dinner. Let me think." Mommy twirled the spaghetti around the fork in her right hand; she held a cigarette in her left.

Her mother's name was Ellen and she was prettier than most of the moms on television. Mrs. Edison said she had hair to kill for. At the roots it was dark brown like Roxanne's but every few weeks Mommy washed it with something stinky that came in a box and turned it a silvery-yellow color. She wore her hair in long loose curls and looked like one of Charlie's Angels. Her face reminded Roxanne of the kittens in cages at the pet store when they pushed their noses against the wire and mewed at her. Roxanne wanted to take them all home, but Mommy said over her dead body.

Roxanne hated when she said that.

"Are you?"

"Am I what?"

Mad at me.

"You know."

"No, I don't know."

"How long are we going to be there?"

"You mean how long are *you* going to be there. I'm not staying one minute longer than I have to. I gotta work, you know." Mommy worked at a Buick agency on the National City Mile of Cars. The ads on television said it was the biggest dealership in San Diego County. "Mr. Brickman's letting me use a good car."

"Am I going to sleep there?" The polar bear was ready to swallow her up now, and there was something heavy in her stomach like a thousand ice cubes bunched together. "I don't want to sleep there. I want to stay in this house." One bedroom, a kitchen with space for a table, a bathroom with a tiny window over the tub, and a screened porch at the back where Roxanne slept. "I like our house."

"You need your head examined."

Mommy put her bare toe on the pedal of the garbage can, and the top sprang up and clanged into the side of the stove. She dumped most of her dinner. Mrs. Edison said Mommy didn't eat enough to keep a bird alive.

"What if she doesn't like me?"

Roxanne's mother sighed as if she had just that minute put down a bag of rocks and been told to pick up another. "Look, I know you don't want to go up there, but believe me, I've got my reasons and they're plenty good. Someday you'll thank me. But we're not going to talk about it and that's final. And I don't want you calling me up and whining on your grandmother's dime. She'd make me pay for those calls and like I've said to you about a thousand times only you don't seem to get it, I am not made of money."

After dinner Roxanne pushed a stool up to the sink and filled a square plastic tub with hot water. She washed two plates and two forks and the spaghetti pot. She rinsed her glass and sudsed away the milk scum, rinsed it again in the hottest water she could bear and set it in the drainer. As she worked she thought about her mother's words. Some of the things grown-ups said were ridiculous. But not all. The trick was figuring out when Mommy meant what she said and when she didn't.

Hair to kill for.

Made of money.

Roxanne wiped down the counter and the stove top. She emptied the brimming ashtray on the table and put the beer cans in the garbage and swept the kitchen floor, careful to poke the broom into the space between the stove and the refrigerator where the greasy dust bunnies lived. She imagined people with dollar bills for arms and legs and eyes made out of coins. The children would have Indian faces like the nickel she once found in the gutter.

Roxanne set the timer on the stove for one hour, the length of time she was permitted to watch television after dinner. Mommy didn't like Roxanne to sit close; but the yearning to lean against her shoulder, to press her body against her mother's hip, was so intense Roxanne's skin tingled the way it did when she knew the oven was hot without touching it. On television she had seen mothers and daughters with their arms around each other, kissing and hugging. Was she meant to believe this or was television like a fairy tale, a made-up story no different from the fantasy about children with heads like Indian nickels?

There was so much Roxanne didn't know.

Mrs. Edison baked pies and cakes to earn extra money, and she had taught Roxanne to read the recipes. Roxanne liked cooking because when Mrs. Edison followed the directions Roxanne read to her, the desserts turned out perfectly. But life wasn't like cakes and pies. Even when she did exactly what she was supposed to do, Roxanne was still afraid when she heard Mommy and Daddy talk and laugh and fight at night. Though their words went by too quickly to understand and she pulled the blankets over her head, making a tent full of her own familiar breath, their mixed up angry-happy voices filled the darkness. She thought about the homeless woman in the red wool hat and wondered if she had ever been in the first grade.

Roxanne and her mother lived on a street where the traffic was noisy until late at night. There were two bars on their block. One had a name Roxanne could not read because it was in Spanish. Mommy often left her in bed at night and walked across the street to the other one, the Royal Flush; and when he was home from the Marines, Daddy made money playing pool there.

Roxanne tried to remember when she had last seen her daddy. She remembered asking her mother where he was, but she had forgotten the answer. She raked through her memory for something she had forgotten or done wrong that would explain why Daddy wasn't home, and Mommy was making her live with a grandmother she'd never met or even heard about until that day. At home she didn't talk too much or whine for candy in the supermarket or ask even half of all the questions in her mind. She hardly ever forgot to do her chores. In fact, she enjoyed making the kitchen orderly after dinner; and in the morning she made her bed and swept the porch before she went to Mrs. Edison's. It gave her a safe feeling when all the chores were done.

In the car the next day she asked, "Are we almost there yet?"

"We're not even to Bakersfield."

Roxanne imagined a field full of Mrs. Edisons and all of them rolling out pie crust and making cakes.

"How long till we get to Bakersfield?"

"Stop with the questions, Roxanne. I'll put you out at the side of the road, I swear I will."

From the car window she saw a sad part of the world, run-down buildings and vacant lots, broken-down fences and hardly any trees, just bushes that looked like dried-up spiders, and paper litter, fast-food wrappers and coffee cups blowing up from the dirt at the side of the road as cars and trucks rushed by. How would she live out there?

A dry wind blew grit into the car, and Roxanne's hair flew up and around her face in tangles that made her skull hurt. She held up her silver pinwheel and watched it whirl into a blur. She thought about nice Mrs. Enos, and wondered if she would look around her first grade class and worry because there was no Roxanne.

The Buick loaned to Mommy by the dealership was shiny and almost new-looking, but the air-conditioning didn't work. When Mommy realized that, she said a lot of the bad words forbidden to Roxanne, who had no idea what they meant anyway. In the heat Roxanne's bare legs stuck to the car seat. Already she knew she would be unhappy in Daneville. She imagined her grandmother had a nose that curved down and almost touched her chin.

"I don't want to stay alone with her."

"I've got a job, Roxanne. Mr. Brickman depends on me."

Mr. Brickman, the manager, called Mommy all the time and sometimes at night he drove her to meetings about serious dealership business. She got dressed up for her job as his secretary and was always excited when the day began; but by the time she fetched Roxanne from Mrs. Edison in the afternoon, her mood had soured and she couldn't wait to pop open a beer, sit on the couch, and watch television.

"What about my toys?" There hadn't been room for much in her pink backpack. "And my books?"

"Your grandmother's got a whole roomful of books."

This was the first good news Roxanne had heard.

"What kind of books?"

"Book-books. How should I know?"

She had seen her mother read only magazines and sometimes the newspaper. "You don't like books."

"What I don't like is being told I have to read them or else I'm stupid."

"You're not stupid, Mommy."

"Well, thank you very much." Her mother looked at her for so long that Roxanne started to worry she would crash the car. "Sometimes I'm not so sure."

Mommy said, "Watch for the signs to Visalia."

"Is that where we're going? Are we going to Visalia?"

"Jesus, Rox. I told you we're going to Daneville. The turnoff's near Visalia."

Mommy put her foot on the gas and passed a truck driven by a man in a white straw hat. Roxanne smiled at him and waved her silver pinwheel and he waved back.

She risked another question.

"How come you don't like her?"

"Did I say that?"

"Is she your mother?"

"No. She's Jackie Kennedy's mother. What do you think, Roxanne? Jesus."

Mommy muttered something else. Roxanne saw her lips move, but the only sounds she heard were clicks and puffs. Back in wintertime Roxanne had had an earache and now she didn't hear very well in her left ear.

Mommy jerked the wheel, turning onto an exit.

"Is this Visalia?"

"If I don't get a Coke soon, I'm going to pass out."

Four cars awaited their turn at the take-out window at Jack in the Box. Four plus the Buick made five. Roxanne figured that without counting on her fingers. Adding and take-away were simple if the numbers weren't too big, but she worried about multiplication. Even the name was hard to say.

"What about school?"

"Oh, believe me, the old lady'll get you to school. She's big on school."

The words sounded good, but Mommy's tone said otherwise.

"Does Daddy know I'm going to Gran's?"

Mommy's face went suddenly scarlet. "Do you think that's funny?"

"What's funny?"

"He's dead, Roxanne. Remember? You must have a hole in your head."

She didn't want to remember Mommy crying, throwing kitchen pans into the wall and screaming, *What the fuck am I supposed to do now?* Later Mrs. Edison had come over, and she and Mommy drank whiskey. Mrs. Edison said, "They always leave. One way or another."

"How did he die?"

"He was a Marine. Marines die." Ellen took her right hand off the wheel and reached behind her head, lifting her long hair off the back of her neck. "Judas Priest, I hate this fucking valley."

Roxanne stared at the shiny car radio and read the name written across the top: MOTOROLA. In books and on television if a girl's father died, there was a funeral and a lot of food, and the girl cried and everyone was nice to her. But nothing like that had happened as far as Roxanne knew.

"Did Daddy have a funeral?"

"I don't want to talk about it. Just forget about it."

Roxanne pulled her legs up onto the seat and wrapped her arms around her knees. Her daddy was dead but she didn't feel sad, not even a little bit. She just wanted to forget about it.

Back on the highway, Roxanne fell asleep; when she awoke they were driving on a two-lane road, and on both sides rows of trees lined up at attention. She tried to count them but they went by too fast and made her go cross-eyed. Through the car's open window the air smelled like fruit and wine mixed up together. Weeds stood stiff and brown at the edge of the road, but beyond them the trees were dark green and cast pools of deep shade.

"Does my grandmother have a hammock?"

"How should I know? I haven't seen her since before you were born."

There was a world of lonely meaning in her mother's response, and Roxanne knew better than to ask about it.

"Will she like me?"

"If you behave yourself."

"How do I behave myself?"

"Goddamn it, Roxanne, you've gotta give me some room here, some air. I can't breathe with all these questions. She's okay, you might even like her. She's . . . orderly, like you."

Orderly and books and big on school.

"Tell me what day you'll come back."

"You think I have a calendar in my head?"

Roxanne liked calendars.

"I'm starting in first grade."

"And you're gonna be dynamite."

"I saw my teacher. Her name is Mrs. Enos and she has orange hair."

"Roxanne, please—"

"I told her I could read recipes. I know the words for milk and butter and eggs and—"

"Don't do this to me, Rox." Her mother's voice cracked like the sidewalk in front of the house. "I'm warning you, don't push your luck."

They drove past a house with a water tower beside it, a field where people were picking something, a fruit stand with boards nailed across the front, and Roxanne waved at a boy riding a fat horse beside the road. All the questions she had been wanting to ask had joined up into one huge thing she had to know, right then and immediately.

"Will you come back?"

Her mother hunched over the wheel, scowling at the road.

"Promise?"

"What?"

"Promise you'll come back so I can go to first grade."

Her mother slammed her foot on the brake and turned the car left, across the pavement and into a driveway lined with thick-trunked palm trees like huge dusty-green toadstools. Ahead Roxanne saw a two-story house built of stone and wood with a pointed roof and a wide porch, surrounded by so many trees that she could see only three or four windows. On one side there was a water tower, on the other a long, low shed that extended the depth of the house. An old truck and a pile of rusty machinery stood off to one side of it.

Nothing looked ordinary or familiar, nothing looked absolutely safe.

"Promise, Mommy?"

Chapter 3

July 2009

Roxanne finished her second cup of coffee as she scanned the to-do list sharing space on the refrigerator door with pictures of her sister, Simone, and her family. On the to-do list more than half the items were circled—done, accomplished—but she fixed on those that weren't. There were similar lists in the bedroom and stuck to the bathroom mirror, a world of things to do before she and her husband, Ty, were due at the airport. Lists, calendars, clocks: she relied on these to navigate her world, and if Ty got this job in Chicago it would mean lists on top of lists; even the lists would have lists to keep her from getting lost.

A turquoise enamel bowl piled with nectarines sat on a counter in the kitchen of the bungalow on Little Goldfinch Street. They'd be ready in a day or two, but she and Ty wouldn't be there to enjoy them. She would take the fruit to school when she went to her meeting. They would spoil if left on the counter over the weekend and be tasteless if she refrigerated them. Roxanne never wasted anything if she could help it.

Though it was barely eight a.m., the July day was already hot and the air carried a hint of the humidity that would come in August. Roxanne was still in her dressing gown, barefoot, a pencil stuck behind her ear. Chowder, the family layabout, sprawled on the kitchen floor, panting and pleased with himself after a good run.

Roxanne was mildly irritated that Ty had taken time for a run that morning when they both had so much to do. He wore his old shorts and an MIT T-shirt thinned by a thousand washings and smelled pleasantly of clean sweat. His beat-up running shoes were only four months old but had already traveled hundreds of miles. He had a tall, lean runner's body and looks that were both homely and handsome at the same time; his was the kind of large-featured face that got better-looking with age. After she met him, Elizabeth, Roxanne's best friend, had said that by the time Ty was fifty Roxanne would have to beat off the competition with a stick.

He gestured her over to the kitchen window. "Our friend's back." He pointed to an iridescent green hummingbird dipping its spike beak into the cup of a red trumpet flower, emerging with a crown of gold dust. For half a moment Roxanne tried to see them living in an apartment in the Windy City, in what would always be to her—thanks to her grandmother's leatherbound edition of Carl Sandburg's poems—the hog butcher to the world. No trumpet vines there, no pollen-crowned hummingbirds.

It was not a happy thought so she put it aside in a part of her mind labeled LATER. In a few hours she and Ty would board a plane for Chicago, where he was interviewing for a senior position at the University of Chicago. She'd been trying for a month to accept the possibility of a major move, but she hadn't had much luck so far. He was sure to get the job and when he did, LATER would become NOW and NOW meant TROUBLE.

"Shall we eat at the airport?" Ty asked. "I know you never like to miss a chance for fast food."

That morning she wasn't amused by jokes made at her expense. So what if "fast" was her cuisine of choice? Not everyone had been fortunate enough to have a mother who made dinner every night, all food groups present and accounted for.

"Can you take Chowder to the pet sitter?" She heard her voice—crisp, efficient, a little chilly—and wanted to take the question back, start again. She knew she was being a pain but the closer they got to takeoff, the harder it was to pretend away her apprehension. Common sense told her that Ty hadn't meant his food crack as criticism, but they'd been married less than a year; she wasn't used to being teased, however lovingly.

She laid her hand on his forearm. "I'm sorry, honey, I'm just feeling the pressure. I should be out of the meeting by one but a roomful of teachers...it could go on way past that. There might not be time for dinner at all."

Roxanne had taught at Balboa Middle School for more than ten years; she knew that Mitch Stoddard, the principal, would understand if she no-showed, but she never liked to miss a meeting, especially not one where new hires would be introduced, first impressions made, and a pile of new rules and regulations presented.

Ty said, "No problem, I'll take Chow to the lab and drop him off after. Don't be nervous, Roxy. It'll all get done."

"Easy for you to say."

"Chicago will love me, love you, they'll beg us to join their elite faculty, and we'll be the belles of the ball." He put his arms around her. "Trust me, even if they hate us, it doesn't really matter."

"But it does. You want this job."

"Well, yeah, but it's not like I'm unhappy at the Salk."

Roxanne wanted to ask, *If you're not unhappy, why are we flying halfway across the country for an interview?* Ty had been a research biologist at the Salk Institute for eight years, loved the work and was good at it; but he said he was ready for a change. The Chicago job would mean a full professorship and a chance to continue his research into new antibiotics with the full weight and influence of the University of Chicago behind him. He could trivialize the outcome of this weekend's interviews and meetings, the dinner parties Roxanne particularly dreaded, but she wasn't fooled. He would be disappointed if he didn't ace the interviews and get an offer. As she told Elizabeth, she would go with him to Mars if he asked; but that didn't mean she had any enthusiasm for leaving San Diego, her job, her friends. And her sister. Mostly she didn't want to leave Simone.

"What am I going to say to these people, Ty? They're going to think you married an airhead. I don't know anything about biology—"

"Holy shit! Why didn't you tell me this before?"

He could make her laugh, make her doubts and anxieties seem unimportant.

"Just be yourself, Roxy. The only thing I worry about is you'll forget to breathe. You're like our friend the hummingbird out there. You don't dare relax."

She didn't like being compared to a bird.

Until Roxanne heard her sister's name, the radio had been background noise, muttering to itself from the top of the refrigerator.

She turned up the volume as the announcer said, "About now Simone and Johnny Duran are probably asking themselves why they decided to have kids."

"Cue screaming brats," said the cackling sidekick, and the recorded wails of half a dozen children filled the kitchen.

"God, that man is irritating," Ty said and turned down the volume slightly.

"Yesterday, San Diego police responded to a 911 call

from a girl who said her mother was trying to drown her sister in the swimming pool. At the Duran residence."

"I have to get over there!" Roxanne cried.

"Cue screaming sirens."

Chowder's head came up and he looked around. Another two seconds of this and he'd start howling.

"Seems the kiddies had learned all about the emergency call number 911 the day before—"

Roxanne was on her way to the bedroom, shrugging off her dressing gown as she went. She opened her closet and pulled pants and a shirt off their hangers. "It's probably nothing, but I've got to check. Simone'll be in a state."

"What about the meeting?" Ty stood in the bedroom doorway and watched her dress. "You want me to call Mitch?"

"Just tell him I'm at Simone's. He'll get it." By now half of San Diego would have heard the news.

* * *

The day after Merell Duran did the bad thing that made the police come, she was in her hideout between the pool house and a clump of pampas grass reading Harry Potter. Nanny Franny had taken the twins and Baby Olivia to the park, but Merell had been there about a thousand times and she knew she'd get stuck pushing the twins in the bucket swings while Nanny Franny tried to make Olivia stop crying. She had acid reflux and cried all the time. Screamed.

This was the third time Merell had read *Harry Potter*

and the Order of the Phoenix and she liked it better every time. But today the words blurred on the page because she couldn't concentrate. She kept remembering the day before: the cameras and the police and everyone telling lies while the police wrote it all down as if it were the truth. It made her mad that they all believed she was so dumb she'd call 911 for no good reason at all. Last night her father, Nanny Franny, and Gramma Ellen had stayed up late talking. Merell sat on the stairs and tried to hear what they were saying until Daddy came out of his study and told her to go to bed; they would deal with her tomorrow. Tomorrow was today. Her father had gone to work and no one had dealt with her.

She wondered if Mommy was angry with her because of yesterday. Everyone else sure was. At breakfast Gramma Ellen gave her a look like if she were a wizard Merell would be turned into a houseplant. She closed her book and went into the house and upstairs. It wasn't a good time to remind her mother of her promise, but if she waited for a good time, she'd be an old woman.

Merell Duran was not quite nine but already she knew that she wasn't beautiful like her mother or even cute as the twins were. But she was smart, even smarter than her mother, which didn't seem right to Merell. Her arms and legs were long and skinny and the elbows and knees might as well belong to a boy, they were that bouldery. Her hair was sort of mud-brown and nothing special at all, just ordinary hair made horrible by the fact that she had three cowlicks on the back so anyone standing behind her could see her pink skull. The tip of her nose bent a little to one side; and when she smiled at herself in the mirror her face looked lopsided so she tried to ignore mirrors as much as she could. Daddy said she was gorgeous, but she knew he wasn't telling the truth.

The subject of honesty and lies was of great and perplexing interest to Merell, almost as baffling as gravity and sex.

She squeezed her hand on the knob of her mother's bedroom door, opened it carefully, and stepped into the gloom. She had learned to slip into rooms and disappear into the shadowy corner spaces, becoming practically invisible. Grown-ups didn't like it if she ran into a room talking, better to enter silently and stand as she was now, next to the door and a little behind a chair, away from the light. Across the large bedroom, her mother lay buried under a blue comforter against a half dozen pillows, with celebrity and fashion magazines scattered around her. The blackout drapes were pulled, and the room was dark except for a wedge of light from her mother's dressing room. The air-conditioning was set so low that Merell got goose bumps, and it didn't smell good. When the meany-men came to call, Merell's mother got unhappy; and when she was unhappy she didn't shower and she hardly ever washed her hair unless Aunt Roxanne or Gramma Ellen helped her.

Earlier in the month her mother had a lot of good days

one after another, and Merell had almost forgotten what it was like when the meany-men were in her head. Only last week she had been happy to help Celia fold the big fitted bedsheets, and when she emptied the dishwasher she sang the alphabet song with the twins, mixing up all the letters on purpose, which Merell didn't think was a good idea. Earlier in the week Mommy and Nanny Franny, Merell, and her sisters had gone to the zoo and afterward they ate dinner at the Big Bad Cat, where Mommy gave the DJ a twenty-dollar bill so he would play "Chantilly Lace." She asked one of the waiters to dance with her, in and out and between the tables, and the other food handlers stood around chewing gum and clapping hands in time to the music. Afterward everyone cheered and Mommy made a bow like a princess. She was the only mother Merell had ever seen dancing at the Big Bad Cat. As she thought about it now, she realized the dancing might have been a warning that the meany-men were coming back.

Merell studied her mother's moods the way a sailor read the wrinkle of the wind on the face of the sea. She didn't have to see her mother to know how she felt. The air in the house vibrated with her moods.

"Why are you hovering?" Mommy sat up a little and pulled off her black satin sleep mask. Her eyes were pink and puffy and crusted with yellow crumbs. "You know I hate when you hover."

"Were you sleeping?"

"Do I look like I'm asleep?"

"I'm sorry." Merell knew that although her mother spent hours and often whole days in bed, she hardly slept at all.

"Mommy, I was wondering..."

"Merell, my head hurts."

"I've been thinking about school." She waited a moment, hoping her mother would remember on her own. "And I was thinking, I was wondering...Do you remember I'll be in Upper Primary this year?"

"And?"

"Did you forget?" She spoke softly because Mommy had sensitive ears.

"Will you get to the point, Merell?"

"You said we'd go shopping." In September Merell would start fourth grade at Arcadia Upper Primary, and she needed a new uniform because girls in fourth grade and older didn't dress like the babies in Lower Primary. "You said we'd go in a taxi."

At that moment Merell realized that she had never truly believed her mother would take her to Macy's, walk around the crowded store, and act like other mothers; and though this disappointed her, she wasn't angry, for she knew her mother never intended to break her promises. She just couldn't help it.

"I've got the meanies today, Merell. I can't do anything."

Merell had a far-off memory of a time before she knew about the meany-men, when the twins were still in their cribs and they had their own nanny. In that sweet time Merell spent hours in her mother's bedroom, where they played games and looked at picture books together. Sometimes they played Pirates of the Caribbean. Mommy emptied all her jewelry onto the bed—earrings, necklaces, rings, and bracelets, everything that sparkled—and then buried it beneath the covers, under the pillows, up inside the shams, between the mattress cover and the mattress. They wore scarves tied over their eyes and pretended to be pirates searching for treasure. Afterward they draped the booty all over themselves.

One day Mommy had found her wedding dress in a box at the top of her closet and let Merell put it on, using safety pins to pull it tight. Mommy wore a special suit called a tuxedo and held up the pants with suspenders.

"You're the princess," her mother said that day. "And this is your wedding day and all the important people in the kingdom have come to see how beautiful you are."

She turned on soupy music, made a little bow, and lifted Merell into her arms.

"Will you dance with me, my beautiful bride?"

Merell would always remember how her mother's eyes sparkled like treasure as they held each other. They couldn't dance because the wedding dress had too much skirt and veil, and everything got tangled up around them. Instead they stood in one place and hugged and swayed side to side in time to the music.

Mommy whispered with her lips touching Merell's ear.

"I love you, I love you, I will love you forever, my beautiful girl. My wife."

Soon after that the meany-men came for the first time Merell knew about, and in the months and years that followed they seemed to come and go as they wished, taking up residence in her mother's head for a few hours, days, or weeks. Once Merell had pulled back her mother's hair and looked in both her ears, hoping to see one of the little monsters. Now, of course, she knew that the evil little men weren't real, that Mommy was depressed; but *depression* was just a word like *sad* or *lonely* and she didn't understand what gave it such great power, so she continued to think of her mother as possessed by tiny, evil-minded creatures whose sole desire was to make her miserable. Since Baby Olivia was born the meany-men hardly ever went away, and Merell wondered if she was the only person in the family who could see that they were hurting Mommy, making her sick.

"When does school start?"

Merell said that city schools opened the day after Labor Day, Arcadia Academy a week later.

"It's still July, isn't it? There's plenty of time."

"It's okay, Mommy. I understand."

Simone lay back, closing her eyes again. "You're such a good girl, Merell. I wish I weren't this... way."

Merell's mother slept as much as Baby Olivia. Nanny

Franny said that babies had to sleep a lot because their brains were growing.

"Mommy"—Merell took a tentative step closer to the bed—"is your brain growing?"

"Christ, no. It's getting smaller every day." She waved Merell away. "Off you go—"

At that moment Gramma Ellen walked into the bedroom without knocking. "Your sister's here."

Mommy said, "Crap."

Merell stepped away from the bed and close to the window where the heavy drapes bunched against the wall.

Gramma Ellen said, "I just saw her drive through the gate."

"I don't want to see her."

Mommy loved Aunt Roxanne more than almost anyone else in the world, but the meany-men made her say things that weren't true.

"What does she want?"

"What do you think? I suppose she's seen the news like everyone else in this city."

Mommy groaned and pulled the comforter up over her head. "Tell her to come back when it snows."

"Very funny, but I don't think you have any choice. You know how persistent she can be."

"Say I moved to China."

"She loves you, Simone. I'm sure she's as worried as the rest—" Gramma Ellen stopped.

Aunt Roxanne stood in the doorway. "Who's moving to China?" She gave Gramma Ellen a quick kiss on the cheek.

"You might knock, you know. You could have rung the bell."

"If I did that, Simone, you'd pretend to be asleep."

Gramma Ellen began making excuses.

Aunt Roxanne held up her hand like a crossing guard. "Truth time, folks. What happened yesterday?" She had a no-nonsense schoolteacher voice and a tall, strong body. Merell thought it would take a whole lot to knock her down.

Groaning like she had a tummy ache, Mommy pushed back the comforter and sat on the edge of the bed. She wore her bra and panties and her skin was the color of skim milk. "It wasn't a big deal. I was in the pool with Baby Olivia and she squirmed out of my arms. That's all that happened. She was screaming and twisting around. You know how she is."

Perhaps Aunt Roxanne had forgotten that Baby Olivia suffered from acid reflux and was in pain more often than she wasn't. The doctor said she would outgrow it, but she'd been screaming for eight months and didn't seem ready to stop yet.

"It was no one's fault, just a terrible misunderstanding." Gramma Ellen tossed up her hands. "Honestly, I never saw such a tempest in a teapot."

"What about you, Merell? You called 911." Though she

stood in the shadows, Aunt Roxanne knew right where she was, looked right into her eyes before she could look away. "Why did you do that?"

Gramma Ellen said, "Nanny Franny had been teaching them about how to use the emergency number and Miss Merell here just had to try it out."

"Is that what happened, Merell?"

She wondered if lying would someday be easy for her, as it seemed to be for her mother and grandmother. Now it hurt, as if there were a dozen thick rubber bands around her chest. Nevertheless she nodded, agreeing with her grandmother. A moment later she slipped out of the bedroom unnoticed.

* * *

Ellen Vadis stood in the door of Merell's bedroom and watched her granddaughter where she stood at the window overlooking the back garden and the terraces down to the swimming pool.

She said, "Merell, I want to talk to you."

Ellen wondered what was going on in Merell's quick child's mind, what story she was dreaming up. Roxanne had been a deep child, but nothing like this one. This girl was the Mariana Trench, and Ellen had been dreading this conversation since Johnny enlisted her for the job the night before. If he were here he would probably gather Merell into one of his enveloping hugs to soften the resistance out of her before he said anything, but Ellen had never been able to show her affection that way. If she couldn't do it for Simone and Roxanne, this little girl wasn't going to thaw the Arctic in her.

Merell had wobbled Ellen's confidence from the day she started putting sentences together. She knew too much, read too many books, and listened in on too many adult conversations, hovering in the shadows, hearing things never meant for a child's ears. If this talk with her were not absolutely necessary, Ellen would have turned and walked out the door rather than start up.

She said again, "Merell."

The child turned and for the flash of a second Ellen saw her own mother's plain, strong features; and she was suddenly a child herself, kicking the toes of her Buster Browns into the floor, getting lectured. Merell had the same narrow, straight back and squared shoulders, the hair that was no color in particular. Her knees were bony, her arms were long, and her hands were big. All indications that she would be a tall woman. Ellen's mother had been almost six feet tall.

"I want to talk to you about yesterday," Ellen said. "There are some things I want to make sure you understand."

"Mommy's sick. I know all about it."

"She's not sick," Ellen answered automatically, without considering a more complicated explanation. Never mind how bright Merell was, a child was a child was a child. "She's sad. Everyone gets sad sometimes. And these sad times pass. You know they always do. But it's not a sickness."

"It's a sickness in her head. I went online and read about it. It's called..." Merell looked off to the right, chewing her lower lip. "Like postal depression. Only different."

"Postpartum depression."

"Yeah. It comes from having babies."

Whatever one called it—clinical depression or acute depressive disorder or postpartum depression—it was nothing Ellen was going to discuss with a nine-year-old.

"It said online there are pills."

If only it were that simple, Ellen thought.

When Simone was in her early teens, Ellen had taken her to see a psychiatrist who prescribed antidepressant drugs. But there had been side effects, and Simone couldn't be relied upon to take the medication regularly. Eventually Ellen stopped getting the prescription filled. She had been married to BJ Vadis then, and she never wanted to jar their harmony with thoughts or talk about Simone's problems. During the period after Merell was born, when Simone had one miscarriage after another and with each one sank deeper into depression, she had been given medication again; but for some reason Ellen didn't know, it hadn't worked the second time either.

Merell said, "She wanted to hurt Olivia."

"What nonsense!" Hearing the truth stated with such

uninflected candor made it all the more terrible. "She loves Olivia. You mustn't say such silly things."

"Then why..."

"I know you're smart, Merell, but this is a grown-up thing. And it must be a private thing. You can't tell your aunt what happened. Or your father. This has got to be a secret between the women in this family."

"Franny isn't in the family."

"You know what I mean."

"Isn't Aunt Roxanne part of our family anymore?"

"You can't tell anyone, Merell."

"Why not?"

"You know the answer as well as I do."

Or maybe she didn't. It was easy to forget how young Merell was. Despite her intelligence, her powers of observation, and the wonders of the Internet, she was only nine years old. "Come here and let me tell you something."

Merell did as she was told, dragging her feet.

Ellen took hold of Merell's hands, a gesture that felt awkward and unnatural to her, but seemed necessary to underscore the importance of her words. "What you did yesterday, the 911 call, I know you think it was the right thing to do. But whatever you believe you saw, you were wrong, Merell."

"Mommy tried to hurt Olivia."

"Don't keep saying that."

Merell snatched her hands away and stuck them up under her arms.

"You're a child and there are things you don't understand. People are complicated and sometimes things seem to be one way when they are really another. Your mother loves her girls, all of you. But what happened... happened. And you'll understand what I mean when you grow up."

Merell stared at her bare feet, curling the toes under.

"If those policemen hadn't been so nice and if they hadn't listened to what Franny and I told them, your mother might have been arrested."

At this point, another child would have begun to cry, Ellen thought. But not Merell. This girl had the same proud-hearted reserve as Ellen's mother.

"Imagine what it would have been like if she'd been taken to the police station and put behind bars." Exactly how much would it take to make this child show decent remorse, a little healthy shame? "And if your mother was arrested, it's even possible you girls would have been taken away from her and put into foster care."

"Daddy wouldn't let that happen."

Probably not. But there would have been the kind of public and legal trouble even a rich and well-connected man like Johnny Duran would have a hard time managing.

Ellen had been awake most of the night worrying if

she should tell him the whole truth. On the one hand, he had a right to know what had really happened. But he was most comfortable dealing with concrete things: bricks and boards, permits and easements and contracts. If he knew the full story, there was no predicting how he would handle it. Johnny had a temper, he could be mean, and none of them wanted that.

Ellen would never have chosen to live with her daughter's family but three years earlier BJ Vadis had fallen dead before her eyes at a broker's and agent's meeting, and that changed everything. BJ had been the great love of her life, late to appear but no less wonderful for the delay. After he was gone the empty rooms and silent meals, the sleepless nights and long, idle days unhinged her. She couldn't work, so she sold the business; and with that last link to BJ gone, she was even more miserable. Johnny had offered to build her an elegant granny flat over the new garage built for his vintage cars. He never said it aloud, but she understood the bargain. In return for a home with them, Ellen would help to keep his household running smoothly.

She could have declined the offer. Despite the economic downturn and the real estate slump she had plenty of money. Theoretically she could live anywhere in the world that suited her. But it had taken only one trip on her own—a miserable cruise to the Galápagos—to teach her that geography was no escape. Wherever she went she would be alone.

The night before, Ellen told Johnny the story she and Franny had agreed upon; and Simone had no choice but to go along with it. Simone had been in the water with Baby Olivia, who squirmed out of her embrace. Seeing her sister underwater for the few seconds before Nanny Franny scooped her out of the pool gave Merell all the reason she needed to try out the 911 system. It wasn't quite a prank, more like an experiment.

Johnny hadn't thrown a fit. Instead he growled, threatened to "deal with" Merell "later," and then called the police chief at home. They played tennis together and apparently the chief didn't mind taking a call from Johnny Duran during dinner. Ellen overheard some conversation about "smart-ass little girls." The chief had promised to lose the paperwork, but before he could get to it someone at the police station told a man who wrote a police blog. Now it was all over the news and the phone had been ringing since seven a.m. Johnny had been adamant before he left for work. No one was to answer the phone unless his voice came through on the answering machine. That didn't mean Ellen couldn't monitor messages left by reporters. She'd heard enough to feel confident they didn't know anything. They were just fishing and the gossip would wear itself out. In a city the size of San Diego there was always a new story to distract the public.

"Merell, what happened was a mistake but fortunately no great damage was done. Now you must give your word that you won't talk about it to anyone. Not your father, not your aunt."

"On the History Channel they said that God told Moses lying was a sin."

"We're not lying. We're just not telling all the details."

"I told the police I only called to see what would happen. That's a lie."

"Swear, Merell. God will understand."

Chapter 4

Roxanne called Ty to let him know she'd be staying awhile at her sister's, not to worry, she'd be home in time to make their flight. She lured Simone into a cloud of bubble bath and then she washed her hair and blew it dry for her. Afterward, wearing shorts and a tank top, Simone got back into bed and pulled a blanket over herself.

"You wear me out, Roxanne."

"Everything wears you out, but you'll feel better once you're up and moving. I'm going to turn off the air-conditioning and open the windows."

"I don't like drafts."

"What do you mean? Why don't you like giraffes?"

Simone giggled and pulled the covers up to cover her face, all but her huge brown eyes. "Rox, you're the only person who can make me laugh."

"So get up and I'll tell you all the jokes I've read off the Internet. Good Lord, you're skinny. Have you eaten today?"

"I had some soup."

"For breakfast? What kind of soup?"

"I don't know. Franny brought it up. I didn't like it."

Roxanne's thumb and forefinger easily encircled her sister's wrist. "You're way too thin, kiddo."

"The little monster's a cannibal."

Roxanne stared at her sister. "You're pregnant? Again? It's too soon. How old is Olivia anyway?"

Simone yawned, not covering her mouth.

"You sound like a hippo."

"Giraffes. Hippos. Is today zoo day?"

"I'm not laughing, Simone. Just answer my question. How old is Olivia?"

"I don't even remember."

Roxanne didn't have words to say how deeply this casual dismissal troubled and saddened her.

"How far along are you?"

"A couple of months, maybe three."

Roxanne sucked in her breath. "Your poor body."

"It's not my fault I have good eggs."

"Which is great if you live in a henhouse. You've heard of birth control? The pill?"

"Don't preach at me, Rox. You know how Johnny is. He's going to keep me pregnant until he gets his son. Period. No discussion."

"But it's your body. You get to say what happens to it."

Simone laid her palms across her stomach, fingertips

touching. "I think this one's a boy, it feels a little different than the others."

"You've seen a doctor?"

"It's too soon. Anyway, I knew when it happened. I felt it, like a pinch."

"When were you going to tell me?"

"Maybe if you came around a little more."

To avoid Simone's accusations of neglect Roxanne would have to move in with her and keep her company seven days a week, as she had when they were children. "You didn't tell me because you knew how I'd react."

"I miss you when you stay away."

"I wasn't staying away. I'm married, Simone, remember?" Roxanne sucked back her impatience. Being angry with Simone was pointless unless Roxanne wanted to make her more confused and unhappy than she already was. "We went up to the Bay Area to see Ty's family, we spent a weekend in Vegas..." There were not enough reasons in a lifetime to satisfy Simone when she was feeling sorry for herself. "Stop being a baby. If you won't go for a walk, at least come outside for a while. You look like you live under a rock."

Downstairs Roxanne made her sister a glass of iced coffee with milk and sugar and, like a nurse administering medication, watched her drink it. Nanny Franny, the twins, and Olivia burst in from the park, rosy-cheeked and starving. The twins were four years old, slender and dark-eyed like their mother, and identical to each other except for a wave of freckles that broke across the bridge of Valli's nose and Victoria's almost constant whining. Victoria and Valli threw themselves on their mother as if they hadn't seen her in months.

It was decided they would all eat an early lunch on the side lawn.

Roxanne wondered aloud if they should invite Ellen to join them.

"She's not here," Merell said. "She had a date. For coffee."

"A date? Your grandmother? Who with?"

"Who knows?" Simone said. "She's meeting men online."

"I've heard her talking on the phone to them," Merell said. "And she goes online late at night."

"How do you know that?"

Merell tugged on her ragged bangs.

Nanny Franny said, "You know you're not supposed to go outside at night, Merell."

"I like to look at the stars. It's interesting. Anyway, it's safe. I just go in the backyard. Once she was sitting on her balcony. I heard her talking and she said she was wearing a satin nightgown."

Roxanne, Simone, and Franny looked at one another.

"What about BJ?" Roxanne had been very attached to her stepfather.

Simone said, "He'd understand."

Maybe he would, Roxanne thought. Probably. Whatever made Ellen happy, BJ Vadis was almost always in favor of it.

Nanny Franny brought out badminton rackets and birdies and assorted balls for throwing and kicking. She and Roxanne lugged several wheeled vehicles and a full picnic basket around the side of the house to a spacious rectangle of lawn secluded from the street by a dense Eugenia hedge. Simone followed with an old quilt in her arms. Franny went back for a couple more.

"So we can sprawl," she said, spreading them in and out of the shade of a wide-branched old pepper tree.

Watching her enlist the children in the picnic arrangements, Roxanne thought that everything seemed to be fun for Frances Biddle. This pretty, take-charge girl, short and stocky with a stubbornly square Yankee jaw and a radiant smile, seemed up to any challenge.

After a lunch of peanut-butter-and-potato-chip sandwiches—"Bad for us, but delicious," Franny whispered to Roxanne—Simone read aloud from a chapter book the twins knew so well they could repeat sections from memory. Merell called it a baby story, but she seemed happy to lie with her head in her mother's lap and listen. When the girls' interest flagged, Franny enrolled them in a hybrid version of kickball and keep-away while Roxanne and Simone stretched out with Olivia between them.

The baby sucked on her binky, watching overhead as

a soft breeze stirred the long, narrow leaves of the pepper tree and the festoons of green corns hanging like grapes. She was a scrawny infant, not plump and rosy as she should be at eight months. Her bony little fingers had nails the size of baby aspirin tabs.

Simone lay back, resting her head on one hand. Beneath her thin, white wrist the purple veins branched and pulsed with life; and despite the circles around them, her dark eyes were beautiful. Roxanne saw tears.

"What's the matter?"

"I wish—" She shut her eyes. "Never mind what I wish."

"If wishes were fishes our nets would be full."

"And if cats were canaries the clouds would meow."

"Imagine the size of the cat boxes," Roxanne said.

Simone laughed. "Imagine the rain."

Later Franny brought out a Frisbee and offered to teach Merell how to throw it while the twins pulled a wagon, gathering leaves and stones for some purpose Roxanne couldn't guess. Beside her, Simone was half-asleep. The humid August heat heightened the peppery fragrance of the tree; in the blue beyond its branches, a fresh contrail zippered the sky. Roxanne watched the pinked line spread and blur and disappear. A muscle car turboed up Fort Stockton Boulevard, disturbing the quiet.

Without opening her eyes, Simone asked, "If you were a bird, what kind would you be?"

"Crows are smart and the black feathers are very chic. Plus they know everything that's going on."

"Sounds like Merell's kind of bird."

Roxanne mentioned the iridescent hummingbird she'd seen powering around the blossoms of the scarlet trumpet vine.

Simone said, "They seem fierce, don't you think? And brave." She rolled over on her stomach and rested her cheek on her folded arms. "In my next life, I get to be brave and fierce."

Victoria and Valli lost interest in leaves and stones and picked a few red hibiscuses for their mother. Simone showed them how to split the stems and link them together to make a lei.

"Tell Franny to take you around the other side of the house. Those bushes are in bloom and you can pick them all. Your aunt and I are telling secrets, none of your business."

"What kind of secrets?" Valli asked.

"I like secrets," Victoria said.

"And I like you," Simone said, kissing her round cheek, flushed with sun. "But scram anyway."

As soon as they turned their backs, Simone fell back again, groaning. "Was I like that, Roxanne? Was I that useless?"

Roxanne thought the twins could be irritating but were funny and sweet as well. She said so.

"You don't have to live with them." Simone brushed the pollen-laden stamen of a hibiscus blossom against her lip. "A hummingbird spends the whole day with its nose in flowers, sucking up pollen and nectar. Sexy, huh?"

"No wonder you're pregnant all the time."

Simone looked at Roxanne with a wicked little smile. "Do you remember Shawn Hutton?"

Roxanne had a vague memory of a skinny boy with a peeling, sunburned nose who sometimes worked at his parents' boat shop on the Shelter Island marina.

"They had the most beautiful sailboat." Simone rubbed a spray of peppercorns between her hands like a gambler warming the dice. "The *Oriole* had berths for eight or ten people, and Shawn and I had sex on every one of them. More than once."

"You're lying. You're making this up."

"Scout's honor." Simone held up her hand and the pungent fragrance of pepper filled the air between them.

* * *

Until Simone met Johnny, she had never been happier than during those summer days when she sailed on the *Oriole*, a fifty-foot ketch painted black and yellow like the bird it was named for. Even now, ten years later, she imagined she could feel the heat of the sun on her skin and smell the fresh varnish.

"The summer before I was a senior BJ decided that I needed more exercise."

Without consulting Ellen he had enrolled Simone in

a sailing day camp and every morning he drove her to Shelter Island himself and in the evening he picked her up. It had come as an astonishment to everyone that she enjoyed sailing.

"What I really loved was the reckless feeling you get when you're flying over the water."

"Maybe you should try skydiving."

"Shawn was a junior instructor at the camp. He'd been around boats all his life so there was nothing he didn't know.

"But he sure was funny-looking," Simone said, remembering. "A scarecrow with turquoise eyes and a killer suntan." She had been his first girlfriend and he could not believe his luck. "The first time he put his hand under my blouse, I thought he'd go off right then, he was so excited."

"You were virgins together."

Simone giggled.

She had been feeling miserable after yesterday's scene at the swimming pool but telling the story of Shawn Hutton and seeing Roxanne's openmouthed amazement cheered her up a little. It was good to remember that once upon a time she'd been a wild girl, that for one whole summer she had awakened every morning tingling with anticipation of the day ahead. Even her first months as Johnny's wife did not have the thrill of that summer.

"You weren't a virgin?"

"Please." Simone rolled her eyes. "Let me tell you, Rox,

I didn't waste any time once I figured out what those shiny-hair vitamins you gave me really were—"

"You knew?"

"Shiny-hair vitamins?" Just saying it made Simone laugh. "I may be slow, but I'm not a complete idiot."

Roxanne said, "Elizabeth got the prescription from her brother. The boys wouldn't leave you alone. I was sure you'd get in trouble. Does Johnny know?"

"You think he would have married me if he knew?"

"But how . . . ?"

"Roxanne, it's not that hard to fool a man who wants to be fooled."

So there, Simone thought with satisfaction. *Roxanne, you might be smarter'n me, but there's still things you don't know.*

"What about STDs? You could have gotten AIDS."

"Honest to God, Rox, I'm pretty sure the danger's past."

"I can't even think about it . . ."

Simone wished she could stand up and dance in and around Roxanne's appalled expression.

"Listen," she said. "I was dumb as dirt back then. I thought STD was something you put in the gas tank to make a car run better."

Roxanne didn't believe her and then she did. They fell against each other laughing.

After a moment Simone said, "The guys liked me, Rox. I knew that from the time I was twelve or thirteen."

Coming and going from the house at night, she had made sure Ellen and BJ never knew. "I was pretty and they didn't care if I was a whiz kid or not. Even the smart ones. And I always made them work for it but in the end...I was willing."

And I was good at it, she thought. It was like Johnny said. Her body was made for sex. And babies. Always babies.

Roxanne faced her, looking almost stern. "This doesn't make sense, Simone. You hate water. You hated water when you were a baby."

"Salt water was different. I loved the taste of it, and it feels different on the skin, kind of thick and silky. And I always wore a life jacket. Mr. Hutton wouldn't let me off the dock without one."

"Where was I when all this was going on?"

"You had your apartment then. Do you remember when I broke my collarbone?"

"Vaguely."

You couldn't be bothered with me. You and your best friend were having too much fun.

"We'd been out to the Coronado Islands. Mom and BJ let me go overnight because Shawn's folks were there and some other people." Simone shook her head. "Mom was so naïve. Anyway, we were coming back and I was up toward the bow, standing up...."

She stopped, remembering moments of distilled joy on the *Oriole*. The pinprick of spray striking her face, her stinging eyes, the taste of salt on her chapped lips and the hot, sticky feel of her skin.

"I know exactly what I was thinking when the accident happened. The night before Shawn and I had had this conversation, sitting up on deck under the stars. We decided that after high school we'd hire on as crew on a sailboat. We didn't care where we went but we needed the practice so that someday we could buy our own boat and go live in the South Pacific. I knew there would never be anything I liked better than flying over water, like at any minute I could take off and soar."

"Sailing and sex and a broken collarbone." Roxanne's expression had gone from amazed to puzzled to almost upset.

With herself, Simone thought. *She doesn't like to think there's anything about me that gets past her.*

"I was standing there, thinking how happy I was, and then someone yelled my name and the next thing I knew the boom slammed into me and I was in the water. And it was cold, really cold." The *Oriole* flew by, her sails fat. "I couldn't breathe or see anything. I suppose I would have drowned if it weren't for Mr. Hutton and that life jacket."

"You were rescued."

"Well, obviously."

Looking back, Simone knew that she should have gone out again immediately, the next weekend. Even with a broken collarbone she could have worked in the galley or polished the brightwork. Instead she had stayed home, nursing her pain, feeling sorry for herself and thinking about icy water and sharks and the *Oriole* flying past. If she closed her eyes now she could see the way the name of the boat was written across the stern.

After her shoulder healed she wanted to sail again but by then it was too late.

"Mom went berserk when I mentioned it. She said I was almost killed. BJ went along with her, of course."

And I didn't fight for it. I didn't rebel. They were afraid for me and pretty soon I was afraid too.

Time went by and after she and Johnny were married they leased a condo right on Mission Beach. The beach was gray and empty and beautiful in the winter after the tourists retreated and the broad strand belonged to the seagulls and pelicans and people bundled in parkas. Sometimes as she walked along the water's edge, long walks from the estuary almost to Bird Rock, schools of dolphins arced through the surf running parallel to shore as if they wanted to keep her company. In the beginning she had watched the sailboats on the horizon but they made her sad so she stopped looking out to sea and focused instead on the million-trillion grains of sand at her feet, feeling small and insignificant and safe.

Simone became pregnant and Johnny was ecstatic, even more so when the obstetrician and his nurse technician read the ultrasound images and assured them that a boy was on the way. Merell's birth shocked Simone into the deepest depression of her life. Watching television one afternoon she saw something that convinced her a mistake had been made in the hospital nursery: a distracted nurse had exchanged her baby boy for someone's girl. Johnny, her mother, and Roxanne dismissed her concern and blamed her mood on the blues, promising her she would feel more like herself in a week or two. Her obstetrician, Dr. Wayne, told her it wasn't unusual to have such thoughts. He called it postpartum depression.

Merell left the Frisbee-throwing, and after grabbing two cookies and shoving them in the pocket of her shirt, she swung herself up onto the first branch of the pepper tree, about five feet off the ground. She grabbed the branch above and hauled herself higher.

Watching Merell climb, Simone's breath caught in her throat. "Be careful," she cried.

"Daddy says this is the best climbing tree in San Diego."

"But if you break, I can't put you back together."

"I won't break, Mommy. Promise."

Merell was the kind of child who could do whatever she wanted. Climb trees, swim, ride a bike: it was all easy for her. Simone tried to believe that she had given birth to such a strong and competent child, but in nine years she'd never been convinced.

She watched her daughter make her way up into the heart of the tree and thought of all the things she'd never done because she was afraid of the risk or couldn't figure them out or had no aptitude at all.

"D'you know, I've never even climbed a tree?"

Roxanne jumped to her feet. "Come on, then, there's no time like the present."

"Now? I'm pregnant."

"Listen, if you could sail a boat, you can climb a tree. There's nothing to be scared of. You'll do great." She held out her hand. "I won't let you fall. Never, Simone."

"You promise?"

"I'll hoist you up to the first branch. You can stay there, or go higher. Whatever you want."

The branch was between five and six feet off the ground. Merell had been able to jump and swing herself onto it but Simone could never manage that, so to give her a boost Roxanne made a stirrup of her laced fingers and, as Merell clapped and cheered and the twins and Franny came running, Simone put her foot into her sister's hands.

"Up you go!" Roxanne said. "Now swing your leg over. . . . That's my girl."

And there she was, astride the branch, stunned and shaking, looking down on the tops of the twins' heads.

Merell called down from her perch eight feet above. "Grab hold and stand up. It's easy, Mommy."

Easy.

As much as she wanted to try, she wanted to be back on the ground; and while she thought about how it would feel to grab the branch and stand, she was thinking at the same time of what it would be like to fall, no water to soften the landing. She reached overhead. The rough pepper bark scratched her palms.

Just take a breath and pull yourself. Just do it, don't think and whatever happens—

Valli clapped her hands.

"Higher and higher and higher," Victoria demanded.

Merell cried, "Come up to me, Mommy."

"Mommy can't talk," Valli said.

"Mommy's crying."

Chapter 5

When Roxanne got home Ty was on the deck staring out over the canyon. Down in Mission Valley there was gridlock on Interstate 8, an emergency vehicle and two cop cars on the shoulder, their lights flashing. The air was still and hot and smelled of eucalyptus.

"I'd about given up on you."

"We have to talk."

He looked at his watch. "We can talk on the plane."

"There's time."

"Not if you want to get a hamburger."

"I'm not hungry, Ty. Can we sit down?"

He paused for a long moment, not taking his eyes off her; and though she wanted to hold his gaze, she couldn't. Across the canyon someone was playing a complicated set of piano scales, the pattern of notes repeating again and again in endless variation. She looked down at the litter of bougainvillea bracts scattered across the deck like faded gold coins.

"I should sweep these up before we go," she said.

"Just tell me what happened at Simone's. That's why you went over there. What did she say?"

"Same as the radio but I don't believe her."

She thought of Shawn Hutton and the other boys in Simone's life and remembered what Simone had said about Johnny. *It's not that hard to fool a man who wants to be fooled.* The same could be said of an older sister.

She forced herself to look at Ty, owing him that much at least. "I can't just fly away as if it doesn't matter."

She saw his expression harden like a flexed muscle.

"I want you there with me, Roxanne."

"And I want to go. But the state I'm in? I'd be no good to you." Drops of sweat popped out across the back of her neck. "I'd be a distraction. You're better—"

"Bullshit."

"Don't walk away from me, Ty." She followed him into the house. "Look at this from my point of view."

"Oh, I have. Believe me, I've examined your point of view from all angles."

"You can't expect me to ignore Simone. She's vulnerable—"

"When I get the job—*if* I get it—what'll you do then? Chicago's two thousand miles from your vulnerable little sister."

"Tyrone, I will move with you to Chicago." She spoke to him as if he were a student who needed a lesson repeated one time too many. "I told you I would and I meant it."

"Thanks for the sacrifice, Roxanne."

She heard the sarcasm that was so unlike him and the vibrations of a long, minor chord echoed through her like a warning. She dropped onto the couch.

"I love you, I love her." Ty could take care of himself but Simone could not. "I thought you understood."

"Haven't you heard, Roxy? Understanding's the booby prize." He sat on the hassock opposite her. "I knew when we married that this thing with Simone would be a struggle, but I underestimated how it would make me feel." He stared down at the square of carpet defined by his athletic shoes. "And I thought, I believed, we could work it out because we felt the same about marriage and making a commitment to each other. I mean, otherwise we could have gone on as we were, just living together. Isn't that right?" He stopped. "Why did you marry me, Roxanne?"

"I love you." His question, so simple, was really a trap; and she knew that however she replied, she'd never get it right. "I want to spend my life with you."

"What about kids?"

"We've had this conversation, Ty. You know I want us to have children."

"And if we do, who'll come first? Our kid or your sister?"

"Well, our child, of course. How can you even ask?"

He nodded as if his hypothesis had been confirmed. "That puts me third in line, doesn't it?"

Panic fluttered in her throat. "This is a stupid conversation. These numbers don't mean anything."

"But they do, they do. Listen to me." He took her hands in his. "All that old-fashioned stuff in the marriage ceremony? I believe it. Sickness and health, rich and poor, forsaking all others. Those words mean a lot to me. Before we got married, I read the ceremony a dozen times, Roxanne. I wanted to make sure I meant it when I promised to be faithful to you for as long as I live."

"And you're saying I didn't?"

"I'm saying when you made that vow you were already pledged to be faithful to Simone. You just tacked me on after her."

"That's so unfair."

He seemed not to have heard her. "Your happiness, your health and well-being and all, it comes first with me. I don't even have to stop and think about it. If we have kids you'll still be number one with me."

Did he expect her praise because his priorities were simple? Did that make him a better person or just one who'd never been tested?

He said, "If you really, powerfully, do not want me to go to Chicago, I won't go. I'll call them up right now and say I've reconsidered and decided to stay at the Salk."

This *was* what she wanted but admitting it would be the same as saying that she *couldn't* leave Simone, that she was bound heart to heart to her sister in a way that she was not to him. Even if that were true—which, of course, it wasn't—she wouldn't have given him the satisfaction of hearing her say it.

"Just tell me," he said. "Do I make the call or not?"

"Ty, it's just not that easy. You come from a Norman Rockwell family. No big neuroses, no hidden agendas. You and your siblings are all grown up and independent and happy."

She knew she was exaggerating. Among Ty's siblings there were disagreements, private grudges were held, emotional brokering went on as it did in any family.

"I am the only person Simone completely trusts. If I let her down, she has nothing. Forget our mother, she'll always put her own life first. And Johnny loves an image of Simone. When she gets on his nerves or disappoints him, he leaves for the office or goes fishing with the mayor. Or he hires another babysitter or cook or whatever. I'm the one who stands beside her no matter how awful she is. I'm the one who always picks up the phone."

"Well, you've got to stop doing that."

Maybe. Yes. But not this weekend, not today.

Ty said, "I watch the struggle that goes on in you every time she calls. And when you talk about her—listen to your voice sometime, Roxy—it's like there's this subsonic scream under your words. It's tearing you apart, but you've been caretaking Simone for so long, you don't feel anything. You don't know what this relationship is doing to you, but I do. And I hate it, and sometimes I hate her."

He dragged his hand down his face. "I know you had a weird childhood and I know you can't get yourself untangled overnight. But it's gotta happen, Rox, or you and I aren't going to make it. Even if I could accept that I'll never be the most important person in your life, I can't see you suffer like this. I'd rather let Simone win."

She heard his words, the ultimatum, but they were spoken in a language she barely understood.

"I can't fight anymore," she said.

"We're not fighting."

"This isn't a fight?" She tried to laugh. "What is it then?"

"Sorting stuff out, I guess."

Her brain wasn't fit to sort out anything. It moved in slow motion like an ancient computer the size of a battleship.

"I just know I love you." The words weren't enough. He wanted a pledge of some kind, a scientific proof that he could see. "And if you truly want this job then I want it too. Go to Chicago. I know my relationship with Simone isn't good the way it is. Elizabeth has been harping on it since the day we met, but..."

She closed her eyes, seeing constellations.

"I've tried to get free of her so many times, Ty. But it never lasts. I'm like one of those game fish who's bitten on the hook and can't get free. It fights and fights, but eventually it just can't struggle anymore."

"It's going to work this time, Roxanne, because you don't have to do it alone."

"I fear for her."

"I fear for you. And us."

"I'll try," she whispered. "I swear I'll try."

Because our life depends on it, because I love you.

Constellations, galaxies, universes beyond number: time and gravity and energies as yet unknown tore at them; and yet, wondrously, the stars and planets survived and the center held. Maybe love did that. Maybe love explained it all. Who knew?

Roxanne and Chowder drove Ty to the airport, and afterward she was afraid to return to the empty house on Little Goldfinch. She'd left her phone there; in the car she was cut off from all demands and responsibilities. She had made a promise, one she meant to keep. But how was she to begin to do what had always before been impossible?

Go home, she told herself.

Keep busy, she thought.

She sat in the car at Mission Bay, watching children in bathing suits with sand stuck to their bottoms as they played in the last light, pushing and shoving and crying while the adults around them packed up blankets and towels and chairs and coolers. In the backseat of the car Chowder whimpered and squeaked, making sure that

Roxanne knew Mission Bay was a great dog-walking place. She fastened his leash and they set off north in the direction of the Hilton Hotel. After half a mile she wanted to turn around, but Chowder was enjoying himself so she kept going until they reached the turnaround in front of the Visitors' Center. Back in the car, Chowder licked her ear and lay down on the backseat, happy and contented.

It takes so little to keep a dog happy.

On Sunday she had breakfast with Elizabeth, waiting in line thirty minutes for bacon and eggs at a joint in North Park that served the best hash browns in the city and made creamery-style milkshakes. The long narrow space smelled of coffee and hot grease, and the fry cook—a stocky woman known in the neighborhood as the shit lady—muttered the same expletive over and over as she tended the sizzling grill.

"Remind me why we come here," Roxanne said, scooting into a booth, avoiding a torn strip in the leatherette.

"The classy atmo? The irresistible lure of bad cholesterol?"

Roxanne thought about what Ty teasingly called her addiction to fast food, and suddenly she was mad at him, resentful of his ultimatum and eager to enlist Elizabeth on her side. She told her about their fight, or conversation, whatever it was. Where details had begun to fade, she filled in the spaces with indignation, the sense of having been wronged growing in her as she recalled the way he went on about vows and forsaking and fidelity. She told Elizabeth about her promise to stop being Simone's caretaker.

"Good luck, huh?" She ate a bite of bacon. "I am so screwed up."

"I'd have to agree with that."

No one, not even Ty, knew Roxanne better than Elizabeth.

On the first day of student orientation at San Diego State University, a searing hot Friday blowing up a Santa Ana wind, Roxanne met Elizabeth Banks: best friends forever, soul mates, the daring duo. If they had met a few years earlier Roxanne would have been distracted by Simone's demands; a few years later and their lives would have veered off in different directions. Instead they stood next to each other in line on a day when each was carbonated with excitement, full of hope and a little scared but eager too for new experiences and someone to share them with.

They were as different as two eighteen-year-old girls from the poles of California could be. Roxanne tall and thin, buttoned-down and orderly, Elizabeth a blue-eyed blonde, pretty in a preppy way, but with a flamboyantly slapdash personality that completely contradicted her appearance. She lived by a collection of New Age beliefs she seemed to make up as she went along. Her parents, Santa Cruz academics, and her two ungoverned younger brothers took Roxanne in like a stray and found in her orderly ways much to amaze and amuse them.

Elizabeth persuaded Roxanne to ditch orientation. They bought sodas and sprawled on a patch of yellowing lawn outside the Aztec Center.

"Tell me everything about your life," Elizabeth said.

No one had ever made such a request of Roxanne. She started talking and couldn't stop. At one point she surprised herself, saying, "If Mom had her way, I'd stay home and babysit Simone for the rest of my life."

"Omigod! I'd die. I'd slit my wrists." Elizabeth fell back on the grass, arms spread wide like a sacrifice, then sat up. "What do you do for a life?"

For a long time that question had been living in the suburbs of Roxanne's mind, but she had only surveyed it from a distance, never let herself visit the possibility that life might hold more than caretaking her sister. The mantra that had calmed her down and restored her patience when it flagged was all about the future. There would be time for that when she was out of high school, was out of college, had a job and could support herself. On that hot day Elizabeth invigorated her like a breath of Arctic air, announcing with the one hundred percent confidence that seemed to characterize her, "Your future begins today!"

Riding the energy of her new friend's outrage, Roxanne went that same night to her stepfather, BJ, and asked him to intervene for her with Ellen and persuade her to let

Roxanne live in a dorm on campus instead of at home as originally planned. He agreed, and following several noisy discussions with Ellen behind closed doors, he prevailed. As if Roxanne were moving to South America and not just across town, Simone wept and screamed; and from then on she nagged Roxanne to come home, calling at all hours of the day and night. She was relentless. Ellen offered money and a new car if she came back. In retrospect, Roxanne was surprised she hadn't succumbed and knew she had Elizabeth to thank.

A sluggish waitress in a hairnet and a ruffled white apron over a uniform the color of dried blood paused to refill their coffee mugs.

When she had moved on, Elizabeth said, "You should have gone to Chicago. If Eddie were here I wouldn't let him out of my sight."

Elizabeth's husband was a Marine in Afghanistan and had been gone for seven months. Early in his deployment Elizabeth had gone through a time when she was fragile and couldn't speak of Eddie without tearing up; now, after months apart, she had learned a stoic resignation unimaginable in the vibrantly impatient girl Roxanne had met the first day of orientation.

"I'm such a jackass, Liz, going on and on when you've got real things to worry about."

"This morning I thought I heard him say my name. It was a dream, of course, but you've got to pay attention to dreams. You never know what they might mean. I keep thinking maybe his spirit might be trying to get through to me." Under the fluorescent light her eyes shimmered. "What if he's dead and I don't know it? No, I'm sure I'd know. We're too connected. I'd know, I'd have to know."

Roxanne didn't know what to say to this. Her own concerns seemed trivial compared to her friend's.

Elizabeth said, "There are a lot of hard things about military life, but the one you don't hear so much about is the way it stalls your life. Couples like Eddie and me who don't have kids or a lot of years together, we have a hard time believing in our marriages sometimes. I mean, how long did we have together, just normal married life? Not even four months. And now we've been apart twice that long. We're missing out on all the little things that build a marriage. . . ." She stared down at her plate. "Sometimes it makes me so sad, thinking about the years we're wasting."

"I don't know what that means. Build a marriage?"

"Sure you do. It means going to Chicago or wherever. If you had a great job offer in Fargo, he'd go with you. That's right, isn't it?"

Now she was cross with Elizabeth. At this rate she'd end up with no friends and no family except Simone.

"I love my sister."

Elizabeth groaned. "I am so sick of hearing you say that, Roxanne. The loving thing to do would be to let that girl go."

Roxanne saw Simone overboard, the *Oriole* flying past. Even Elizabeth could not understand how she was her sister's life jacket.

"You're on his side."

"Side, shmide. Listen to me, Roxanne. It's time for you to take care of yourself."

Conversations going on in other booths were a low, congenial hum occasionally syncopated by laughter. It seemed that only Roxanne had brought her troubles to breakfast.

"Angels are real," Elizabeth was saying. "I'm convinced of it, only they don't have wings and halos and all. They take the form of the people who come into our lives. Like I was an angel for you when we first met because if that hadn't happened, you'd probably still be living at home."

They had talked about this before. Roxanne liked the idea of Elizabeth as a pretty blond angel flying into her life, tucking her wings and robe away, putting on jeans and a glittery T-shirt.

"And then Ty came and he was the angel who told you it was okay to get married and have a family of your own." She laughed. "An angel named Tyrone. But I think you've had your share of heavenly assistance. Now it's up to you, Roxanne. You have to be your own angel."

Chapter 6

During the rest of July and most of August Roxanne often paused to be thankful that Merell's 911 call and Ty's Chicago trip had occurred in the same week, forcing a crisis that, however difficult, seemed to have given new and stronger life to her marriage. When Simone whined that Roxanne hadn't been to see her, when she nagged Roxanne to shop for her, read to her, play rummy, or wash her hair, Roxanne could say aloud that breaking free of Simone was the most difficult thing she'd ever done, but it was happening.

There were times that August when Roxanne was aware of the slow unfolding, untwisting of herself. She slept late and read on the deck while she drank her morning coffee and worked in the garden, up to her elbows in compost and mulch. She'd read somewhere that gardeners were by nature optimistic because they believed in the future. That described Roxanne that summer. On weekends she and Ty hiked all their favorite trails in the Cuayamaca and Laguna Mountains, explored shops and restaurants in beachfront towns from San Diego to Dana Point. They laughed, made love, and were happier together than they had ever been. They talked about having a baby. No longer yoked to Simone, no longer the always-responsible sister-caretaker, Roxanne would be a wife and mother, as ordinary and wonderful as that.

They did not say much about Chicago as they waited for the formal job offer they were sure would come. But as days became weeks and no word arrived, the subject became a tender spot, a pinched nerve they favored by avoidance. When the call finally came from a biologist who would have been Ty's colleague and who had been particularly supportive of his candidacy, it took less than three minutes to lift up their life and drop it down in a new direction.

Ty put down the phone, went into the kitchen, and poured himself a tall glass of ice water from the refrigerator. Roxanne stayed where she was in the living room, folding laundry, biting the inside of her lip.

"They gave it to a guy from Harvard." He stood in the arch between the two rooms, his expression unreadable. "Edgar Lessing."

"Ty, I'm so sorry." She had never wanted to go to Chicago, but equally as much she wanted Ty to be valued by the world as he deserved to be.

"I know him. He's a good man. Probably a smart choice."

"They should have given it to you." She threw a T-shirt into the basket unfolded. "Were there any reasons?"

"They didn't think my heart was in it."

"Your heart?"

"Yeah."

"What does that mean?"

"I think it's a way of saying something and nothing at the same time."

A look of puzzled disappointment flickered across his expression and was gone, like the shadow of a moth by candlelight. Then, as she watched, his expression reshaped itself into a mask of neutrality. She understood and didn't blame him for not wanting to deconstruct his time in Chicago, for not wanting to analyze the interviews or parse the conversations. Roxanne knew the kind of thing that might have been said in public twenty years ago: *If a man's heart was in the job, where was the wife? Why wasn't she there to support him?* Probably the same thing was said now in private and unofficially.

Days passed and Ty had almost nothing to say beyond the smallest of small talk, which was somehow worse than if he had not spoken at all. It seemed to Roxanne that either the house had shrunk around them, or they had grown large and clumsy as they hadn't been before. They stepped around each other carefully, were excessively polite, and apologized for things that didn't matter—mail left in the box out front, a single unwashed glass abandoned on the kitchen counter. She had no idea if this was how Ty normally processed disappointment or if he was angry with her or, as she thought more likely, a combination of the two ate at him. His thoughts had voices. She heard him accusing and regretting her. Finally she could stand it no longer.

"You're disappointed, Ty. I know. I feel like it's my fault. If I had gone with you..."

"It's over, Roxanne. Let it go."

"Please, talk to me."

"There's no point, Roxanne."

His curt responses infuriated her and she began to harden against him. Conversations were like rooms, she realized. She had opened the door but it was up to him to walk through, and when he wouldn't she felt as insulted as if he'd looked in, seen nothing of interest or importance, and walked away.

Roxanne began spending more time with Simone just to get out of the house, and although she knew she was moving backward, that the distance between her and Ty grew in relation to the hours she spent with Simone, she did it anyway.

She wasn't going to beg.

One day at the end of August Roxanne was getting ready to go home after spending the afternoon with her sister while Nanny Franny took the children to SeaWorld. As she was leaving she met Johnny coming into the kitchen from the garage. He opened his arms wide, enveloping her.

"Rox, what're you doing here?"

"I took the twins to the dentist. Nanny Franny took them to SeaWorld for a reward. No cavities."

"That girl makes them brush morning and night."

"I made an appointment for Simone. I don't think she's had her teeth cleaned in years. You can see the tartar."

"You're a good sister, Roxanne. I really appreciate all the stuff you do. Come on in to the study and have a drink with me."

"I'm on my way home."

"Gin and tonic, right?"

He was a big, handsome, smiling bulldozer with a nearly irresistible flash, an incandescence that stopped conversations when he walked into a room. In the beginning it had been hard for Roxanne to trust a man so charming, so good-looking; but over the years her doubts had been vanquished by his obvious devotion to Simone and his family. He had a temper, of course, a streak of meanness that could cut; but Roxanne had learned to avoid that.

In his study the desk was littered with building plans and specifications, envelopes, files, and stuffed manila envelopes. Roxanne hoped he never had to find anything fast. Pictures of Johnny with the governor, the mayor, and both California senators hung on the wall beside photos of Simone and the girls, Johnny's sisters and parents.

Roxanne let herself be guided to a comfortably worn leather chair.

"Put your feet up," Johnny said, shoving the hassock toward her. "You're a schoolteacher. Schoolteachers have tired feet."

It was a very Johnny thing to say. He wanted her to feel welcome and appreciated, but Roxanne doubted if he knew when school started or if he'd ever given teachers and tired feet a moment's consideration before the thought came conveniently, charmingly, to his mind.

He spoke from behind the wet bar. "How was Merell today?"

"Every time I looked for her, she had her nose in a book."

He handed her a crystal highball glass bubbling with tonic water. "That stuff last month, I knew it'd blow over, although I still don't know quite what happened. You and me both know Merell's too smart to call 911 for no reason."

What Roxanne knew was that smart children could do crazy things in a family where there wasn't enough grown-up attention to go around. The best nanny in the world could not take the place of a loving parent.

She said, "I think... It's possible that maybe she's feeling a little lost. All the babies... and Simone. She probably wanted attention."

Johnny frowned and stared into his drink.

"I see it all the time, Johnny." Roxanne wanted to take

away any hint of blame. "It's so easy to overlook smart, capable kids. We tend to forget they're still children."

She told Johnny about a harried single mother she'd met at a parent-teacher conference. Though her boy had just turned thirteen, he was already taller than six feet, pushing two hundred pounds, and shaving twice a week. But he was a good kid, academically and socially one of the best.

"I asked his mom what her secret was. She said, 'Just because he's big doesn't mean he don't need hugs.'"

As she spoke she thought of Ty, of the unresponsive mask he had worn since the call from Chicago. It was hard to believe in love when it was hidden.

Johnny said, sounding miffed, "Merell knows I love her."

"It wouldn't hurt to remind her."

Not for weeks had Roxanne and Ty looked at each other in the way that said *I see you, I know you, I love you.*

Johnny said, "You know, I can almost tell you the exact moment when I fell in love with your sister." His smile was neon, melting worries about the 911 call and little girls in need. "The parking lot at Mesa was completely empty except for this little yellow BMW convertible sitting by its lonesome under one of those sulfur-colored parking lot lights, and this incredible girl was standing next to it looking so vulnerable. She'd locked herself out and her cell phone in. I woulda helped her no matter who she was, but you can't imagine how beautiful and helpless she looked. I fell in love right then."

Roxanne thought, *You wanted a helpless wife and that's what you got.* Ty wanted just the opposite, an independent woman who loved her work. At least that was what he said. Now it seemed he would prefer a wife willing to drop everything and follow him like a pet dog. Oh, it wasn't so, he didn't want that, and she hated thinking this way.

Johnny didn't notice her distraction.

"After I got the door open, I asked her to have coffee with me. I didn't think she'd say yes. I mean I was a total stranger to her and she was so young. Eighteen, yeah, but a young eighteen. I was what? Twenty-nine? I'd been dating a long time, and I'd never met any woman so feminine but what got me was her innocence. It was like someone clobbered me."

For the first time in days Roxanne wanted to laugh out loud. What would Johnny do if someone told him he'd been duped, that Simone's innocence was an act? Right away she knew the answer. He wouldn't believe it. Roxanne barely did herself.

On the night Simone and Johnny met in the parking lot and after they'd spent an hour at Starbucks, Roxanne was in the apartment she shared with Elizabeth. It was close to midnight and she hadn't finished grading a pile of essays. Elizabeth was in her room, surfing the Web, visiting the various reincarnation and angel visitation sites she favored.

Someone pounded on the front door, Roxanne dropped her red pencil, and Elizabeth came out of her bedroom followed by her barking miniature schnauzer.

Roxanne looked through the peephole, opened the door, and stepped back as Simone ran into the room.

"Roxy, I'm in love. I met the most wonderful man."

Elizabeth laughed, picked up the dog, and went back into her room.

"He's twenty-nine years old and he has his own business and he's the most handsome and so polite. He's a gentleman like BJ, you know. He opens the door and that kinda stuff. He made me feel like a doll, like I could break." She wrapped her arms around Roxanne, squeezing hard enough to bruise. "I'm going to marry him. He wants to take care of me."

"He said that?"

"No. But I can tell."

She danced around the small apartment, spinning and dipping and pirouetting, singing his name over and over. "Johnny Duran, Johnny Duran, he's the sexiest man, Johnny Duran."

Somewhere in the house Celia was running the vacuum cleaner and the television was on in the family room though no one was watching it. Roxanne started to say it was time for her to go home but Johnny interrupted her, switching back to Merell.

"After that 911 shit I talked to the chief and God

almighty we're lucky he's a good friend. He said if Merell was his he'd get her a shrink. You think that's a good idea?" Before she answered, he went on. "I don't like the idea of psychiatrists, bringing a stranger into the family doesn't sit right, you know? It's like when you're measuring and by accident you add an extra inch. It throws everything out of whack."

"Merell would love to spend more time with you."

"Yeah, yeah, it'd be nice. I'd like it too, only I'm going flat out right now. We're building a hotel in Vegas and it's taking all my time." He gestured toward his untidy desk. "I'm not sure I woulda gone for the contract if I'd known how demanding it was gonna be. These clients, these Chinese guys—fucking billionaires, let me tell you—they wanted me to work over Labor Day weekend but I told them I was going to the lake with my family. No argument, no negotiation." He grinned suddenly. "You should come with us, Rox."

Johnny dropped into the leather chair behind his desk and finished his drink in a long swallow. "How's Ty?'

Roxanne would do almost anything before she let Johnny Duran in on her personal problems. "We'll celebrate a year in October."

"Wedded bliss, huh?"

"Pretty much." Her smile, the tone of her voice: it was all phony but she wasn't worried that Johnny Duran would notice. He saw and heard only what suited him.

"Hey, let's have an anniversary party here. This house

hasn't seen a real shindig since your wedding." He sat forward. "I'll swing for the catering and we'll get a little band. Nothing would give me greater pleasure, Roxanne."

His eagerness engulfed her and in a corner of her heart she wanted to say yes just to give him pleasure.

"I think we'll probably sneak away somewhere, but thank you for the offer."

"You change your mind, just say so." He sat back again. "What's he working on now?"

"Same as a year ago, some kind of super antibiotic. He says the flu bugs'll never know what hit them."

"You understand that shit?"

She laughed. "Only enough to ask halfway intelligent questions."

"Got him fooled, huh?" Johnny poured himself a second shot. "You females. We don't stand a chance around you."

Johnny was never insulting to women, the opposite. But under his chivalry, his flattery and affectionate teasing, she sensed a profound condescension, as if he wanted her to know he didn't respect her at the same time he coerced her into going along with the pretense that he did.

It was time to go, but before she did there was something she had to say and if it made him angry to hear it...

"Simone is skin and bones, Johnny. She shouldn't be pregnant so soon after Olivia." She might also have added that Simone was depressed, disoriented, and unable to parent the children she had. "I think it confuses the girls to see their mother doing nothing, handing them off to Nanny Franny."

A fraction of a second passed. "You know about these things, do you? Had a lot of experience?"

Before she could think how to respond, he went on talking. "You think of all the stuff Simone's been through and you can appreciate...She's tough. Those miscarriages? Most women would have quit a long time back."

"She did it for you, Johnny. If it were up to Simone I don't think she'd have *any* kids."

"She knows how much I want a son, Rox. Men need sons. It's how we're made."

That afternoon Simone had told Roxanne she was sure that this new baby was a boy. In another week she would be far enough along for ultrasound to confirm her conviction.

"A woman's happy when her husband's happy. That's the way marriage works, Roxanne."

His comment stung with what appeared at first glance to be the truth. If she had gone to Chicago, if she had made a stellar impression on the gathered scientific dignitaries: she didn't want to think that in the end this described a happy marriage, a woman keeping a man happy by being agreeable. She was not so angry with Ty that she would accuse him of believing this.

Johnny was saying, "Simone's young and it looks like

we got years ahead and maybe we do. But maybe not. No one can say, right? She might carry this new baby to term or she might not. There's just no guarantee. Olivia might be our last. That's why we have to keep trying.

"You met my dad. When he came to this country he was just a boy, never even drove a car until he was almost seventeen. Went from carrying concrete blocks on his back to owning his own business. He was my hero, you know? Sure you know, Roxanne. You've heard this before."

And you're going to tell me again. And she was going to be agreeable and listen.

"Dad always wanted a son, to carry on for him, and my mom made sure he got one."

Seven girls and at last a boy.

He seemed to sink into himself. "Dad told me how he felt on the day I was born, the first time he held me. He said he finally understood why he'd been born." His voice trembled with emotion.

She watched him blink back tears and drag his hand across his eyes. She saw the color of embarrassment rise in his cheeks, and realized that her feelings for her brother-in-law didn't swing between love and dislike. She felt both at the same time. This capacity of the human heart to hold such opposite emotions simultaneously perplexed and troubled her, offending as it did her need for order in the world.

"I should go."

"No. Wait." He grinned, and with the flash of his

smile the mood in the room changed, and Johnny was the charming bulldozer again. "We go to the lake on Friday and I want you to come with us. No argument. It's the last long weekend of the summer and you and Ty need a vacation."

He was doing more than simply offering a holiday. After revealing himself to her, this was another way of asking for approval. If she accepted the invitation she would be telling him she didn't think he was weak for speaking candidly and that she understood his love for his father and need for a son.

"We'll come home Monday morning early. You'll have all day to get ready for school on Tuesday. Please, Rox. It would mean a lot to me. To all of us."

"Chowder—"

"The dog. No problem. We're taking the plane and he can come with us."

"You own a plane now?"

"The company leases it. I spend so much time in Vegas, it makes sense."

"And you fly it?"

"Jesus, no, when would I have time to learn? We hire a guy."

The granite-boned Sierras, the forest, and a quiet lake.

"Actually, it'd be just me," she said. "Ty's supervising an experiment all weekend."

This experiment marked the end of a second stage

series, and he had told her he would be sleeping in his office for a couple of nights. He'd never done this before and at the time she had thought that he was making an excuse to be away from her, but now she thought the separation would be a relief for both of them. If he could get away, why couldn't she? A lake weekend would give her extra time with Merell. Simone would be happy and Chowder would be delirious.

Johnny said, "This'll make Simone so happy, having you right in the house. It'll be just like the old days."

The old days...

Roxanne stayed at her grandmother's ranch in Daneville until she was nine, and in that time all that had been strange came to feel comfortable and homey. During those years, her mother never paid a visit; but sunny-faced greeting cards signed *Be good. Love, Mom* appeared in the mailbox once or twice a month. Sometimes there was a note about what she was doing, but more often there were the same four words: *Be good. Love, Mom.* Saturday night phone calls from San Diego became shorter and more awkward as the weeks and months passed. No matter how eagerly Roxanne anticipated these calls, she could never share her thoughts and feelings with her mother. Ellen would say something like, "How're you doing up there, Roxanne? Is she keeping you busy? I'll bet she is." And Roxanne rarely knew how to respond or if a reply was even called for. During the long wordless stretches she heard her mother's breath singing on the phone line, a note of melancholy and discontent that lodged in Roxanne's heart and ached there for days after.

And then, when Roxanne was nine years old, like a freak tornado blowing up out of the south, Ellen called on a Thursday to say she would arrive on Saturday and take her daughter back to San Diego. She had no time to hang around the ranch. She had to be in class on Monday morning.

That same day Gran drove into Daneville and came back with a red canvas suitcase to carry all that Roxanne had accumulated during her years at the ranch—the blue jeans and school clothes, a pair of patent leather shoes for best, a book of dog stories, and a box of small treasures and souvenirs. On Saturday morning the suitcase lay open on Roxanne's bed, a gaping mouth waiting to swallow her life in Daneville and spit it out in San Diego. Gran's warm, rough hand pushed gently on the small of her back, urging her to hurry up.

"She'll be here before dinner." Gran's voice was brusque. She cleared her throat. "I'll make a supper you can eat in the car. Your mother will want to get back on the road right away."

"But I don't want to go." Roxanne wrapped her arms around Gran's solid body, pressing her face against her grandmother's flannel shirt. "I want to stay here with you."

Roxanne knew that argument would be a waste of breath. Not because Gran was stubborn (which she was), and not because she wanted to get rid of Roxanne (which they both knew she didn't). Gran had come right out and said she wished Roxanne could stay on the ranch. But her mother was in charge of her because that was the law. Gran said your heart could break and the law didn't care.

After the years in Gran's big house, the apartment in San Diego felt cramped and smelled dirty no matter how much Roxanne scrubbed it. And scrub she did, the way Gran had taught her, getting into the corners and up under things where the spiders went to die. She tried to be happy and she became so good at pretending that she could even fool herself. But when she went to bed at night, or in the morning if she woke up early, the thoughts that came to her were of Gran, who called her *my girl*.

It meant everything to be someone's girl the way she said it.

Once, when she had been back in San Diego about a week, Roxanne asked where Simone's father was. Ellen's reply put an end to that conversation and any in the future. "I don't know and I don't care and neither should you if you know what's good for you."

The old days.

Roxanne had quickly learned how to care for her sister. At dinnertime Ellen came home from real estate school and changed into the clothes she wore to tend bar at

Captain Jack's in Mission Beach. Simone was often irritable at night and to settle her down Roxanne took her into bed with her. Simone's skin was soft and as warm as if a bonfire burned within her.

She was a tiny nervous creature who smiled all the time but couldn't do anything but lie on her back and jerk her limbs like a turtle overturned. Her eyes were large and of a darker, deeper brown than Roxanne's. In certain lights Roxanne couldn't tell where her pupils ended and the irises began. When she was asleep, her lashes lay like tiny brushes on her cheekbones.

Sleeping was one of the ways in which Simone was different from the babies Roxanne read about in the book Ellen gave her about infant and child care. She didn't roll over or sit up according to the schedule in the book. Ellen said not to worry about it. "She's lazy, that's all. Not everyone's a whiz-bang like you."

For most of that first autumn, Ellen had kept Roxanne out of school.

"What if someone sees me? I'll get in trouble for ditching."

"Stay inside." Ellen had an answer for everything. "No one'll know you're here."

"I might forget how to divide." And there were interesting things called fractions that Gran had just started to explain. Finally and worst, "What if I get held back?"

Ellen laughed. "When pigs fly."

But as if she had taken some of Roxanne's fears to

heart, Ellen bought her a stack of math practice books with pages and pages of arithmetic problems printed on soft gray paper with the answers at the back so she could check herself, books of crossword puzzles for kids, big drawing tablets made of the same gray paper that was almost like cloth, and a giant box of Crayola crayons. She pleaded poor to the woman at the thrift store next to the real estate school and got a carton of old *National Geographic* magazines for free.

"These'll keep you busy," Ellen said, dropping the box on Roxanne's bed.

Roxanne had kept track of Simone's development on the pages of a calendar; and she decided that while lazy was an accurate description of Simone, it still did not explain what was odd about her. At an age when the books said she should be walking, running, and exploring the world, Simone was happy to sit and play alone, taking toys out of their plastic bin and putting them back in, over and over. She whined when Roxanne wouldn't carry her, threw tantrums when she was taken from the stroller and told to walk: Ellen couldn't study with all the noise! She told Roxanne to pick her up or push her or find her pacifier.

Ellen promised Roxanne, "This is worth it, believe me. Someday I'm gonna make big commissions. We'll be rich."

Roxanne had learned not to trust most of what her

mother said, but this promise did come true. Ellen could read home buyers; and it was like a game to her, connecting people to the properties that suited them. Five months after she went to work for the Vadis Group, they moved to a town house in Point Loma that had two bedrooms and a balcony from which a tiny triangle of blue bay was visible.

Roxanne attended school in Point Loma, and after a couple of weeks she caught up to the rest of the boys and girls in her class. She was surprised to discover that most of them had never heard of fractions, and when the subject finally came up, she soared ahead. She wrote long letters to Gran about what she was learning; and until she died, her grandmother wrote back every week.

A babysitter was found for Simone, a woman who tried to drive Ellen into the poorhouse. Every day after school Roxanne walked three blocks to the babysitter's house, where Simone waited for her. From the end of the path Roxanne saw her little sister teetering behind the screen door and heard the bang of her small hands against the aluminum frame. Simone cried out, not quite Roxanne's name but something close, and banged harder. Roxanne had never felt so loved by anyone as she did when she heard that wordless celebration of reunion.

Thinking back on those days as she waited for the electronic gate across the Durans' driveway to swing back, Roxanne could admit that the relationship between herself and her sister had been too close to allow either of them to develop fully independent lives. At the same time, she resented Ty's insistence that she turn her back on Simone's love so generously given, especially now when he was brooding and uncommunicative.

Chapter 7

Huntington Lake, August 2009

On the flight up to the lake house Merell was so excited, she couldn't stop talking even though she knew she sounded like an encyclopedia. As the plane flew above the road that wound up from the San Joaquin Valley through the foothills and into the gray stone coolness of the rocks and pines, she told Aunt Roxanne that Huntington was the oldest of the Edison Power lakes, a man-made oblong of icy cobalt-blue water built in the 1930s to capture the runoff from the snows in the Sierras. She was explaining how the water was piped from Lake Edison to Huntington to Shaver Lake when Daddy told her to give it a rest, put a plug in it. But not in a mean way. Merell knew that he loved the lake too.

Chowder was first out of the plane when it landed, making clear his preference for solid ground. He eyed with suspicion the white Range Rover driven by Aldo, the lake house caretaker, and was reluctant to get in until Aunt Roxanne told him he could ride on her lap, all eighty pounds of him.

Besides the mountains and the lake and the house, Merell liked the road around the lake. That's all there was, just that one road and a lot of private driveways—most of them not even paved. Through the woods she pointed out the stilted mountain cabins built hard against the steep mountainsides, many of them already boarded up as if expecting an early winter.

The road seemed old-fashioned—she liked that too—narrow and twisty with mostly deep forest on either side. There were a few hotels but Mommy said she'd rather sleep outside than in one of them. No fast food anywhere. Daddy said that to find a Jack in the Box they would have to drive all the way to Fresno, over a hundred miles away. There wasn't any downtown at the lake, no Costco or drugstore or supermarket; but near the airstrip there was a marina with a hundred boats and a place to buy sailing, fishing, and camping gear. Aldo told Daddy that the gas station across from the marina got rich off motorists who didn't have the sense to fill up down in the valley. In one hotel a ranger gave wildlife talks in the evening for the people who put up their tents in the campground that was only half-full even though Labor Day was the last big weekend of the summer.

"It hardly ever gets full," she told Aunt Roxanne, "'cuz

big boats don't work really good up here. They can't go fast because it's too high."

"Keeps development down," Johnny said. "Kinda quiet."

"We like it that way," Merell said.

* * *

Johnny called the lake house a cottage and Roxanne had expected something rustic with a porch where mice danced across the backs of shrouded furniture in the off-season. In fact it was a graceful two-story residence shingled in dark brown with a steep roof and rows of windows with Mediterranean-blue shutters.

"Johnny never should have spent so much money," Simone said as they drove through the gated entrance. "But I'm so glad we have it. Nobody ever sells their property up here, especially not a big spread like this. Johnny says it's more valuable than gold."

Leaving the men to unload the car, the sisters and children walked around the side of the house toward the water. They could hear Baby Olivia behind them, crying.

"Franny'll take care of her," Simone said, and grabbed her sister's hand. "I'm on vacation, I don't want to talk about Olivia."

Ahead of them Valli and Victoria tried to imitate Merell's perfect cartwheels in the grass. In their red and blue shorts and bright T-shirts they looked like three flowers tossed about in a hurly-burly wind.

"Sometimes I think it would be nice to live here all the time. Everyone seems happier, you know? But the road gets closed in wintertime. We couldn't even hire a plow." Simone watched her daughters, smiling. "He thinks the kids'll want to bring their friends here in the summertime, have dances and sailboat races. He's even got plans for a couple of tennis courts off to the side. He calls tennis and sailing 'elite' sports." She giggled, hugged Roxanne, and whispered, "You know those Ralph Lauren ads? That's how Johnny wants to live."

Arm in arm they swung down the lawn to a shoulder-high stone wall that bordered the cliff thirty feet above the lake. Leaning on the wall, they looked over. Below, at the foot of steps cut into the granite, there was a floating dock with a small sailboat and dinghy tied to it.

"You have a boat, Simone. Why don't you sail here?"

"I don't like it."

"Why not? Sailing's just sailing, isn't it? Wind, water. What's missing?"

"I don't like fresh water," Simone said. "Salt water kind of lifts you up and it slips on your skin, feels kind of thicker. I feel safe around salt water."

"So why have a sailboat up here?"

"Merell's going to sailing camp next summer and whatever she does, the twins'll copy."

"That's your opportunity, isn't it? The two of you could go together."

"Yeah, but the camp's up here."

"It doesn't have to be. You could do it together down at Shelter Island."

"Stop organizing me, Rox!" Simone punched her sister in the shoulder hard enough to hurt. "What I told you about sailing? I never would have mentioned it if I knew you'd harp on it. That time is past for me now."

"Simone, you're not even thirty years old. You can do anything you want." Roxanne rubbed her shoulder. "You should take kickboxing."

"It's not just the water. It's what's down there. Underneath."

The lake was too choppy to see anything below the surface.

"You know what Merell was telling you, about how the lake got built? Well, before the engineers came, there used to be a steep valley here with a river at the bottom and a little town and when they made the dam the water just covered it all over but it's still down there." She shuddered. "Creeps me out."

Valli ran up to them. She had thrown off her shoes. Grabbing Simone's hand, she cried, "Twirl, Mommy, twirl."

Simone stepped out of her sandals. "Remember how we used to do this? Come on, Rox, it's fun."

On hot days after Roxanne picked Simone up from the babysitter after school, they walked up the hill to the neighborhood park to play in the sprinklers, wearing shorts and rubber thong sandals that kids in Roxanne's school called *go-aheads*. As they did now, they had held hands and turned in circles, leaning out with their heads tilted back so all they could see was the spinning sky. Now the ground tipped and turned beneath them, and overhead the clouds and sun circled in dizzy pursuit. They twirled until they fell on their backs, groaning. Overhead the clouds chased across the enamel-blue sky, plump as gilded dumplings. Under the sun's yellow eye the earth rose to meet the sky and the sky filled the lake with blue and gold.

Lying on the grass, Roxanne felt ill but happy, laughing, thinking, *This is why I have a sister, with a sister I never have to stop being a kid.*

Valli sat up. "Let's do it again."

Simone moaned. "I forgot I'm pregnant. I never should have...I think I'm going to barf." She lay back again, laughing. "Did you make a wish? You gotta close your eyes when you fall and make a wish before you open them."

"You always make up new rules," Roxanne said.

Simone sat up and pulled a twin into her lap. "What did you wish for, Victoria?"

"Ice cream for dinner."

"Me too," cried Valli. "I wished first."

"And I wished the same thing!" Simone cried and got to her feet. She pulled Victoria up after her and pointed her in the direction of the house. "I declare this the Ice Cream Vacation. We'll have ice cream with every meal."

"And snacks!" Valli cried.

Simone yelled, "Ice cream vitamins!" and shoved Victoria up the lawn. "Tell Nanny Franny I said we're having ice cream before dinner. Two scoops each."

Victoria ran up the grass with Valli after her.

The wind rose, playing the pines like oboes; and the dumpling clouds became pillows and featherbeds bolstered by the mountaintops. Sun and wind chopped the water into a million bits and pieces of gold. Below the cliff, the dinghy banged the hull of the sailboat.

Merell had disappeared.

"She's got all these hiding places. Everywhere we go, she finds a hideout, but especially up here. She's never satisfied unless someone's looking for her."

* * *

Merell had decided that having an aunt was one of the best things ever. Especially an aunt with a big rompy dog who liked to chase after balls and sniff around the wildest parts of the compound. After several hours outside he came into the cottage and flopped down in front of the fireplace. Two minutes later he was snoring and twitching in his dreams.

Aunt Roxanne played Monopoly and really tried to win, and she listened and asked questions when Merell talked about all the stuff she was going to do when she grew up. Like go to China and sail a boat to Hawaii by herself. Aunt Roxanne's questions made Merell think about details, like *why* did she want to go to China and *when* was she going to learn how to sail.

Her mother was livelier when Aunt Roxanne was around. She talked more and laughed, and there wasn't a meany-man anywhere.

Aunt Roxanne and Nanny Franny laughed as they made lunch and Mommy did a jigsaw puzzle with the twins and for once there wasn't any yelling or hitting. Lunch was Merell's favorite: tuna with mayonnaise and lettuce and French fries cooked in the oven. And sodas, which they never had at home. While Franny got the lunch set up, Aunt Roxanne changed Baby Olivia's diapers and talked to her in a silly squeaky voice that made Olivia laugh and Merell's stomach feel warm. After lunch Aunt Roxanne asked Merell to give her a tour of the compound. The twins wanted to come along but Franny said they were too rambunctious and if they didn't settle down she was going to tie them to a post.

On the west side of the house there was a play yard and in it was the playhouse Merell shared with the twins. It had a pointed roof and a chimney and a pretend fireplace. Sometimes they imagined it was a school and Merell was the teacher.

"The twins can't even count."

They walked beyond the playhouse to the big piece of land where Daddy was going to build the tennis courts next summer. Chowder raced among the trees, and Merell talked and Aunt Roxanne didn't tell her to be quiet.

Merell asked, "Do you have a best friend?"

"Sure. You know Elizabeth."

She would have liked it if Aunt Roxanne said that she, Merell, was her best friend; but she knew this was a silly wish.

"Does she sleep over sometimes?"

"Not anymore, but we used to share an apartment."

This sounded wonderful to Merell. "Do you tell her secrets?"

"Sometimes."

"What kind of secrets?"

"I don't remember any of them so they must not have been very important."

They leaned against the wall at the edge of the cliff, their arms folded on the cold stone.

"Our house was in a magazine," Merell said. "Daddy has a copy of it in his study." She laughed, thinking how silly one of the skinny models looked standing on the roof in a long purple dress. "Daddy says we're not to call it a house. It's a cottage and all the land around it? That's the compound."

The sky was dark with clouds now and the wind blew hard. In the middle of the lake a pair of kayaks fought their way against the wind.

"If they sink they'll go down to Vermillion. That's the town under the water. Daddy says there was this old man who lived there and when the engineers came and told him he had to go or he'd be drowned, he said he didn't care. So they just left him. With his dog and a mule.

Their bones are all down at the bottom." Merell stared at the water. "I don't like to think about him. About drowning."

Roxanne took her hand.

Merell said, "If I tell you a secret, will you promise not to tell anyone? Cross your heart?"

All day long she had been thinking about the promise she had made to Gramma Ellen, feeling it in her head like one of Mommy's meany-men. She had not wanted to promise in the first place, and wished that instead she'd been brave enough to walk away, out of the room to one of her hiding places until everyone forgot about what happened at the pool, although she was afraid that wouldn't be for years and years. It was a weary thing to carry an important secret alone.

"Merell, the thing about a secret is, once you share it with someone, it's not really a secret anymore."

Merell scuffed the toe of her sneaker into the lawn so hard she dug up a divot of grass. She held her breath and wished hard that Aunt Roxanne would change her mind and promise not to tell. But a teacher hardly ever changed her mind about anything, even if she was an aunt.

"There are caves down by the dock. Wanna go see 'em?"

"I'm not crazy about caves, Merell. They make me nervous." Aunt Roxanne looked up at the sky. "Besides, I think we're going to get some rain."

Merell took her hand and gently squeezed it. "It's safe."

She explained that in the spring when the snow at higher elevations melted, the creeks overflowed and runoff dug rivulets down the hillsides and the level of the lake rose. In the summertime it retreated as water was regularly released to irrigate the farms in the San Joaquin Valley. By Labor Day the water line was several feet below where it had been in the spring.

"Last time we came up here the cave was almost out of the water but I still couldn't climb in. Now I bet I can. Want to?"

"We should go inside, Merell."

Merell knew that she would be a grown-up someday, but she understood it the same way she understood that a man had once stood on the moon. It was both true and impossible at the same time. To be a grown-up she would have to get bigger and learn things and that would be good, but she would also have to give things up. She never wanted to become a person who was afraid to explore.

To the southwest, needles of lightning threaded the storm clouds and the growl of thunder reverberated off the mountain peaks.

Nor did she want to grow up if it meant being worried about getting wet in the rain. Daddy called mountain rainstorms *gully washers*, and Merell knew they could come on fast. Even so, she wanted to stay where she was in the whip of the wind, lightning dancing about her, daring her to be afraid. The air was electric with possibilities. At any second something thrilling might happen.

She couldn't see the kayakers anymore, but near the far shore a sailboat struggled to reach land. There might be children aboard. They'd be scared and Merell knew what it was to be frightened. Not the fun kind of scared like storms and caves; the deep-down scared that made her feel like her legs wouldn't hold her up anymore.

It was good she hadn't told her secret. Bad things would happen if she did.

* * *

By nightfall the lake was socked in under a low ceiling of blue-black clouds, and a cold wind ripped at the trees and rattled the shingles and shutters. Aldo brought in candles and hurricane lamps and laid wood in the two fireplaces in the great room and the one in the big bedroom upstairs. Johnny still wasn't home when the downpour began.

At dinner Simone picked at the plate of lasagna and salad Franny set before her. Afterward, the twins begged her to play Monopoly and dragged her to a chair. Each time the play came around to her she seemed surprised and stared at the dice as if she didn't know what to do with them.

Roxanne guessed she'd taken a pill of some kind.

Simone went upstairs and an hour later Johnny came through the door dripping rain and tracking mud. The twins squealed when they heard him in the mudroom. He had brought with him a gallon of rocky road ice cream and served the Monopoly athletes huge, bone-chilling portions, their third or fourth of the day but Simone had declared it an ice cream weekend and so it was. Johnny entertained with details of the horseback ride he'd taken to somewhere called Goose Lake, about the ducklings he'd seen and the bear scat and getting caught in the rain and how the lightning was so close it singed his eyeballs.

Johnny's love for his daughters was like an adjustment to the thermostat they all felt and responded to. He sat at the table with Baby Olivia squirming in his arms and his three older girls arranged around him, each starry-eyed with adoration. He smiled and teased, and when Olivia began to cry, instead of handing her off to Franny he hoisted her onto his shoulders and told the girls to form a line behind him. They played follow the leader around the downstairs: kick to the right, kick to the left, jump, tag the sideboard, and turn around. With squeals and laughter and shenanigans they traipsed from room to room, Franny and Roxanne bringing up the rear, Olivia wailing.

Late that night, like a well-loved child tucked up in a warm bed under the eaves, safe from the elements and content to drift in a half sleep, Roxanne wished Ty were there with her and then remembered they weren't getting along and for a while she worried that she should have stayed in San Diego that weekend, in case he needed her. Her thoughts wandered while the rain drowned out other sounds in the house. She thought about the scene in the great room and about her stepfather, BJ Vadis, a large, burly man with a thick shock of silver-gray hair and piercing blue eyes under bushy brows that moved up and down to punctuate his sentences. A sober Scandinavian without much humor in him but loving and generous in his fashion, he had adored Ellen and been kind to Roxanne and Simone.

Roxanne didn't think he'd ever cavorted like Johnny. Cavorting just wasn't in his nature.

Roxanne had no particular memories of BJ before she was ten or eleven, when he began to distinguish himself as someone important to her mother. With one memorable exception, they never ate a meal alone together. Shortly after the party to announce Simone's and Johnny's engagement, BJ invited Roxanne to dine with him at Rainwater's, an expensive steak house favored by conservatives in the business community. At the time Roxanne shared an apartment with Elizabeth and was paying off school loans and credit card debt, trying to save for the down payment on a house. Filet mignon was a rare treat.

"Glad you could come, Roxy," he said, sounding like he meant it. He pulled out her chair. "I thought maybe those students of yours mighta wore you out."

The students at Balboa Middle School did wear her out, but they entertained and stimulated her too. It had been her good fortune to find the work she loved early in life. That night she had talked for a while about the challenges posed by a classroom crowded with more than thirty boys and girls deep in puberty.

"You deserve hazard pay for that job. And a martini? One's not gonna make you tipsy."

They talked about Simone and Johnny.

Roxanne said, "I like him."

"Do you suppose there was ever anyone who did not like Johnny Duran?" BJ pulled the olive off the toothpick with his teeth. "Your mom's happy, although between you and me and Old Blue Eyes, I think she was hoping for someone with a title."

Roxanne laughed, though it seemed a little dangerous to be out in public with BJ making fun of Ellen.

"He's going to be a very rich man someday. I talked to a couple fellas I know, builders like Johnny, and they say he's a man to watch."

Roxanne had only one reservation. "It'll be a big life. I wonder how she'll manage." It wasn't necessary to explain what she meant.

"We talked about that. I told him the same thing you would. You'll always be there to help her out, make sure she doesn't get overwhelmed."

Roxanne remembered her reaction to his words, the impulse that rushed into her making her want to stand up and walk out of Rainwater's. She'd never do it but the urge was there and powerful enough to make her hands shake. When had she become a tool to be handed around as needed?

"Johnny knows she's young and got a delicate disposition. He promises he'll take it easy, bring her along slow."

BJ leaned back, resting his forearms comfortably along the arms of the chair. "And what's gonna be so hard for her anyway? It doesn't take many brains to give a party. All she'll have to do is hire the right people, and you and Ellen can help her do that. And what pretty girl doesn't like to buy a new party dress?"

Roxanne had wondered how much BJ actually knew about Simone, what he guessed or had been told. Her mother had insulated him from the worst of her moods; and if he noticed that she often missed school and stayed in her room for days at a time, he never commented to Roxanne.

BJ pulled an envelope out of his lapel. He laid it on the white tablecloth beside her wineglass. "You can open this now or later. Your choice."

"What is it?"

"Take a look if you're curious."

She slit the envelope with her knife and drew out a check written on BJ's private account.

"This is our little secret, okay?" He reached across the table and took her hand. "You're a good girl, Roxy."

She looked at the check, counted the zeros.

"I don't understand."

BJ beamed, enjoying her confusion.

"Why're you giving me this?"

"Let me ask you something, honey. Your mother and me have gotten along pretty good over these years, wouldn't you say? Not too many fights, not a lot of noise? But just so you know, I didn't always agree with her." He toyed with the stem of his glass. "But when we met, she'd been through some rough times so I was inclined to cut her some slack. I was right out of the military and back then I had a pretty rigid view of married life. I just figured if I brought home the paycheck it was Ellen's job to manage the house and you kids. I didn't object to women's lib, I just didn't think it'd ever apply on my watch." He snorted softly and shook his head. "Well, I sure was wrong about that. Your mom's a crackerjack, was from the git-go." He grinned at Roxanne. "That woman could sell the Brooklyn Bridge.

"And it made her happy to work. I saw that the more money she made, the prettier and happier she got. I wasn't going to fight success like that. Only one thing we disagreed on and that was the way she made you look after Simone. I didn't think it was fair to you, and I never thought it was very good for your sister either."

Roxanne folded her check in half, lining up the edges precisely.

"But the more I pushed one way, the harder your mom pushed the other. She said you were the only one who could handle her. Made a list to show why." He counted off, using his fingers. "She had slow motor skills, of course. She was moody and hated water and threw a fit when she had to have a bath. And she had that thing with her feet. Remember? She wouldn't go barefoot or wear sandals. Refused to take off her shoes unless you promised not to look at that funny little toe of hers."

A broken toe had healed crookedly and for a couple of years afterward, Simone had sworn it wasn't her toe at all. She swore someone in the ER had pulled off the old one and given her a new one that never fit right.

BJ drained his glass, and without being asked the waiter brought him another. "I told Johnny you'd be around to help out, but I don't think that'll happen much. Basically, I think their wedding is going to be the Fourth of July for you. Independence Day. And to celebrate and say thank you..." He tapped the check with his index finger. "I know you want to buy one of those houses on Little Goldfinch. They're a good investment. This oughta help you make the down."

Roxanne unfolded the check and smoothed it out on the white linen cloth. She stared at the figure written in BJ's almost illegible hand. The number five with four zeroes after it.

It rained most of Friday and all day Saturday at the lake. Occasionally there was a break in the weather and a flash of sunlight when the clouds opened up, but these lasted just long enough for the family to look up from their books and jigsaw puzzle and board games with quickly swamped hope. The only one whose good humor did not seem dampened was Franny. Her stores of creativity and energy were apparently unlimited. She made bowls of popcorn and pots of hot chocolate with an inch of melted marshmallow on top. She produced long forked sticks for roasting hot dogs in the fireplace, and graham crackers, Hershey chocolate bars, and a fresh bag of marshmallows for s'mores. There were extended games of Chutes and Ladders and Monopoly. When the charms of these faded, she set up a crafts table and brought out several new boxes of brightly colored clay that excited the twins.

In the great room Roxanne lay under a comforter reading a mystery that didn't require much concentration, and Johnny, stretched in a recliner in a far corner, played a game on his phone with Merell hanging over his shoulder, watching. Restless, Simone moved from chair to couch to another chair, stared out the window, and thumbed through celebrity magazines. She wasn't interested in clay, she said, the smell turned her stomach; but Roxanne joined the girls and Franny and altogether there were four of them at the table, modeling monster faces meant to terrify. The twins poked their scary creatures at Simone, making her fake-scream and pretend to faint; but in the way of small children they didn't know when the joke went stale. They giggled and danced until Roxanne, who could see her sister's cheer unraveling, got them back to the table. Franny produced yarn for hair and buttons for eyes and they were all having a good time when Olivia, who had been asleep upstairs, began to cry.

Throwing her monster head on the floor, Victoria announced, "I hate that baby!"

A short, hard laugh and then a sigh escaped Simone's lips. Olivia's cries rose to the octave of screams. Johnny's fingers froze on the keys of his phone and Merell stepped away from him to a place in the shadows. The screams changed again, becoming sharper and shorter as if Olivia were being repeatedly stabbed. Roxanne met Franny's gaze. Victoria hummed as she retrieved the head of her monster and began to reshape it.

Finally, Simone put down her magazine and left the room.

Franny called after her, "I'll make a bottle. I'll put some of her medicine in it."

Simone returned with Olivia, red-faced and sweaty, crying in her arms. She took the milk from Franny without thanks and settled on the couch. For a few minutes the only sounds in the room were the baby's gentle slurping and the rain hitting the awning over the terrace. Valli and Victoria made lips for their monster heads, fat kissy lips prompting sound effects and fall-off-the-chair hilarity. Franny shushed them gently; simultaneously they looked over their shoulders at their mother.

Olivia shoved the bottle away and it fell to the carpet and rolled under the couch. She stretched, arching her spine like a gymnast doing a back bend, widening her eyes as she twisted and squirmed and began to scream again.

Roxanne said, "I'll take her for a while."

"No."

"Simone, I'm stiff from sitting. Let me walk—"

"I'll do it."

Franny said, "I'd be happy, Simone—"

"Are you both deaf? I said no."

The house throbbed with rain, a toneless roar beneath the baby's cries.

Simone walked to Johnny and stood in front of him. "Why doesn't it stop?" she asked, raising her voice to be heard.

"You know she can't help—"

"Not Olivia." She spoke as if Johnny were stupid for misunderstanding. "I mean the fucking rain."

Olivia burped loudly. There was a second of silence, followed by laughter. Valli and Victoria began a burping contest.

Simone said, "You told me it would be beautiful up here, Johnny. You promised me."

He put his phone aside. "What do you want me to do? Do you expect me to control the weather?"

"It's global warming, isn't it?"

Johnny said, "You don't have to worry about global warming."

"Of course I do. We all do. Do you think I'm stupid?"

The room shrank with tension.

"Simone—"

"I know that by the time our babies grow up the world won't be worth living in." She spoke to Johnny as if he personally were to blame for the catastrophe. "Why don't we all just kill ourselves and get it over with?"

Merell said, "Mommy, I can help."

"Omigod, Merell, will you stop trying so hard? It's not your job—"

"That's enough, Simone." Johnny put his hand on the small of her back. "Let's go upstairs. Franny'll take Olivia." His voice had the kind of false calm Roxanne associated with police dramas, the officer on the street trying to talk a jumper off the roof.

"I want to go home."

"We don't have a plane here and even if we did—"

"We're trapped."

Franny tried to take the baby.

"No!"

Simone jerked away and as she did, Olivia slipped from her arms and fell. The twins screamed and Roxanne dropped to her knees beside Olivia, who lay on the floor on her back, stunned into silence.

"Shit," Johnny said.

"Bad Daddy!" Victoria began to cry.

Roxanne did a quick examination. "She's okay. Just surprised." Franny took the baby.

Johnny said, "Go upstairs, Simone. Now."

From Franny's shoulder Olivia, temporarily more curious than unhappy, looked at her family with wide, wet eyes.

"She hates me."

Johnny reached for Simone, but she jerked back as if his hand carried an electric current.

"You all hate me."

She began to wail, a half-human sound that rose and grew thin and splintered into racking sobs. Roxanne knew she should do something to help her sister but like the rest of the family she was spellbound by the scene playing out before her and waiting to see what would happen next.

"Well, go ahead and hate me." Simone's eyes were huge and black. "The more the fucking merrier! You can't hate me more than I hate myself."

* * *

Late Sunday afternoon the mountains of cloud cover began to break apart, revealing ponds and lakes and eventually oceans of blue sky and finally the sun.

Daddy said, "Come for a walk with me, Roxanne. I want to go to the general store down the road. Bring Chowder. Do us good to get the kinks out."

"Can I come too?" Merell asked. "I could ride my bike." The mountain bike was black with a silver stripe and the lake was the best place to ride it.

"Let her," Roxanne said, laying her hand on Johnny's arm. "She needs a break too."

In the sunlight the forest seemed enchanted, like in a book. Every leaf and needle, the trees and shrubs and even the surface of the mulch that lay deep on the ground, sparkled as if, just seconds before Merell rode by on her bike, a wizard had passed among the trees and sprinkled everything with gold dust and diamond bits. She liked that idea and wished there were such things as wizards who could cast spells and grant wishes.

Chowder gamboled ahead of her, ranging into the woods and back to the road, checking on his humans every few minutes, his tail whacking with joy. Merell enjoyed the wet dirt smell of the woods and the quiet broken only by Chowder's thrashing and the sound of water rushing down every gully, dip, and furrow of land. Water after a storm was like laughter. Merell squinted and imagined the forest populated by gleeful elves and fairies no bigger than her hand. She wished for a wizard to make Mommy happy, then whooped and sped through a deep puddle, throwing up a rooster tail of water that drenched Chowder from head to tail. He stood where he was, barking rapturously.

She biked on the road most of the time, ahead of her father and aunt, occasionally falling behind when she detoured up a private road to one of the houses already boarded up for the winter. None of these houses was as handsome as the cottage and some looked shabby and neglected. Chowder went crazy, smelling mice under every porch and deck. A red plastic toy in the weeds, forgotten, no longer favored at the summer season's end, meant kids had once spent their holidays there. The fishing pole against a shed wall was probably a man's. Merell got off her bike and spied through a window into a roomful of boxes and furniture covered in sheets. She pretended the window gave her a view into the future and it was the cottage at the compound that was closed up, its toys and fishing gear abandoned.

She wondered if other people could feel two things at the same time the way she did: happy to be out in the enchanted woods, but at the same time melancholy. *Melancholy* was one of her favorite words. She'd found it in a book and looked it up, and immediately she'd understood exactly what it meant. Sad in the head and in the heart and in the bones.

* * *

Johnny walked with his head down, and so fast that Roxanne barely kept up with him. His stride was half again as long as hers and he seemed determined to reach the general store as fast as he could; but once it was in sight he slowed down and stopped. He stood a moment, staring at the CLOSED sign in the front window.

"The twins are going to be disappointed." He'd promised to bring them a special candy only sold in this store. He shrugged and confessed to Roxanne that the walk to the store had been an excuse to get out of the house. They watched Merell turn down a side road that led to the water, one of the lake's few stretches of beach. They followed her for a few steps and then Johnny stopped again. In the fading light he looked like two men, their faces superimposed on each other, one young and handsome, the other haggard and old.

"What am I going to do? Tell me, Rox. Help me." He sank back against a tree and covered his face. "I don't know how much more of this I can take."

He wanted her to sympathize, but she couldn't although she knew exactly what he meant. Trapped in the house, Simone's tormented spirit was contagious. But how could she feel sorry for Johnny when it was he who insisted on more and more children in pursuit of the ideal, a son?

He said, "She wasn't always like this. Remember? At first she was perfect. I was the happiest man on the planet."

They watched Merell bounce along the potholed road with Chowder loping close by, the first child of a perfect wife and the happiest man on the planet.

He said, "I know a side of Simone that no one else does. Even you, Rox. She and I, we had so much fun together. She made me laugh. . . ."

He walked back to the main road, where they waited for Merell to catch up.

"You've got to get her help, Johnny."

"Help? She's got a housekeeper and I pay Nanny Franny more than I pay my secretary."

"I mean she needs to be in therapy. Someone good."

He shook his head. "No, that's out of the question. I told you, when we were talking about Merell, I said—"

"I know what you said, but that doesn't change the facts."

"I am an old-fashioned man, Roxanne." She could tell from the way he said this that he thought *old-fashioned* and *superior* were synonyms. "I don't want to fight and I don't want to be the bad guy and I am so fucking tired of worrying about Simone. I could send her to all the therapists in the world and they wouldn't do her any good. Psychology isn't a science. Mostly it's just professional nosiness."

She might as well run head-on into the Great Wall of China as hope to change his point of view.

"Listen," she said, going at the wall from a different direction. "Here's something I've been thinking about. Did you know that Simone used to sail?"

"There was some kid who chased her all over the boat until she had to give it up just to get rid of him."

Shawn Hutton's history rewritten.

"I think if you told her she could—"

"Sail? Her?"

"She and Merell could take lessons together."

"Merell, sure. But Simone, no way."

"Why not?"

"I love my kids, Rox, but I don't want to raise them alone. Besides, I've taken her out on the boat up here, and she sits in a corner like a scrunched bug."

"She doesn't like fresh water."

"Water's water. If she really liked sailing, if she wasn't just talking, she'd do it anywhere."

Off in the woods Chowder barked at something. Johnny looked toward the sound, suddenly irritable.

"You better call that dog. Get him on a leash before someone complains."

"Sailing would empower her."

"She doesn't need power, she needs you. You keep her level, Roxanne, you're the balance she needs."

"Johnny, that's not fair!"

He said, "If you didn't work, or maybe if you worked part-time..."

She walked back toward the compound, using all her self-control to keep from running. Chowder tumbled out of the woods and ran circles around her, wet from scrambling through the undergrowth. Ahead, Merell was trying to ride with no hands. Roxanne couldn't drag enough oxygen into her lungs. After a moment she stopped in the road and bent over double. Johnny's hand touched her shoulder.

"Don't do this to me," she said. "Don't make this about me."

"I don't know what it's about anymore," he said, embracing her. Though she wanted to tear away from him, though she despised him at that moment, she was grateful for his arms around her, holding her up. "I just know what I can't do. And this therapy stuff—"

"It's not magic or witchcraft. A therapist is just someone to talk to, a neutral third party."

"You're someone, Rox. Why not you?"

"I have a life, Johnny. I have a husband and we want to have a family before I get too old. I have a job I love. I can't be Simone's caretaker for the rest of my life."

"But it wouldn't be the rest of your life. Just for a while, until she gets through this rough patch."

"How long do you think it'll last? Until you have your son? It might take years, it might never happen. Meantime my clock is ticking. Hear it, Johnny? Tick-tock, tick-tock:

it's telling me I'll be forty before long. I don't have much time."

He interrupted. "You're wrong about a therapist being neutral. Whoever she is—and they're mostly all female, I know that, it's a female kind of business—she'll take Simone's side and she'll shove a wedge between us. You know what they'll talk about? Me."

A therapist might give Simone the courage to stand up to him and refuse to have more children. Of course, he feared that.

"Simone and I talk about you, Johnny. What's the difference?"

"You don't want to turn her against me."

"Honest to God, Johnny, I'm not that neutral. If I could teach Simone to stand up to you, I would."

It might be too late for that.

Chapter 8

The family returned to San Diego on Monday. The next day Simone got out of bed at nine a.m., drank six glasses of water, put on a loose blouse and a skirt with an elastic waistband, and took a taxi to her obstetrician's office, leaving Merell, Olivia, and the twins with Franny.

After sitting in the waiting room for twenty minutes trying not to think about her full bladder, she was shown to an examination room and directed to lie down. A nurse wearing scrubs patterned with Disney characters asked her to pull down her skirt and on Simone's exposed stomach she applied a clear gel, warning her first that it might be chilly. The woman spoke as if by rote and Simone knew what she was going to say before the words were out of her mouth. She warmed the transducer between the palms of her hands before she laid it on Simone's abdomen. Again she warned of chilliness. After listening a moment she grinned and said, "That's a good strong heartbeat. I'll call the doctor."

Simone had been with the same obstetrician since

her first pregnancy. Dr. Wayne was in his early sixties, a white-haired man with warm pink hands and a daunting confidence that Simone assumed came from having brought so much life into the world. He treated her with a proprietary manner she found reassuring at the same time she was certain he knew virtually nothing about her apart from her medical history.

"Let's see what you've got in here," he said, as if he thought she'd swallowed something plastic from the twins' toy box. He hummed, repeating the first bars of "White Rabbit" as he moved the transducer over her belly, watching the image on the video until he saw what he wanted. Simone tried to imagine him as a young man of the Woodstock generation smoking weed and making medical student hooch with pure alcohol.

"Here we go, here we go." His grin was very wide and toothy. "Wow, what a great picture. Simone, you are a pro and this one's a real movie star." He turned the monitor so Simone could see the screen.

She closed her eyes. "Just tell me."

"Looks healthy," he said. "Strong heart, fingers and toes where they're s'posed to be."

"Tell me."

Dr. Wayne sighed and patted her hand. "You've got another girl, Simone."

At home she reset the bedroom air conditioner to sixty-five degrees Fahrenheit, drew the blinds, took off her shoes, and got into bed fully clothed. It was a little after eleven on the first blue-and-gold Tuesday in September, and she wanted to sleep for the rest of her life, which she hoped wouldn't be too long. Her eyelids trembled and wouldn't close completely. She put on a sleep mask but they still quivered. Blindly, she reached for the Xanax vial. It wasn't where she'd left it. She shoved up her mask and rummaged through the drawer in the bedside table. Johnny had hidden it from her. Or possibly Franny had sneaked into the bedroom while she was at the doctor's. She grabbed the water glass beside her bed and heaved it across the room where it hit the deep pile carpet with an unsatisfying thunk.

Somewhere in the house Olivia was screaming.

If that girl would just do her job . . .

The nanny's faults lined up in Simone's mind: her incompetence, her air of superiority, her ingratitude.

She got out of bed, shoved her feet into slippers, and went downstairs to the family room, where Franny was walking back and forth before the French doors, holding the glassy-eyed, red-faced baby. In the midst of the screaming din, Franny looked offensively cool and tidy in her T-shirt and shorts.

"Give her the medicine."

"She's already had the max. Poor little pumpkin must think there's nothing in life but misery."

"Put her in the car and drive around until she falls asleep."

Franny stopped pacing and looked at Simone with what felt like a challenge. "Are you going to watch the twins?"

"Where's my mother?"

"She left about an hour ago."

"It's not even noon! Where did she go?"

"You know I can't ask her that, Simone."

Franny's tone said, *She's your mother, you ask her.*

It seemed to Simone that Franny never said just one thing straight-out; a second meaning always swam beneath her words.

She added *sneaky* to the list of Frances Biddle's faults.

Franny blew back a lock of straw-blond hair that had fallen across her cheek. Her strong arms and legs, tanned and freckled after a summer lolling beside the Durans' swimming pool, were an affront to Simone.

Franny shifted Olivia to her other shoulder. "I called the pediatrician and told his nurse she has to have something stronger. I wanted to give her a double dose but the nurse gave me a mini-lecture about how the crying's worse for us than for Olivia. Don't you think that's insensitive? I mean, being miserable all the time? It *can't* be good. I practically had to bribe her, but she finally said she'd make room for you at three-thirty."

"Me? Today?" Simone wished she had stayed in her room, her sanctuary.

"We were lucky," Franny said. "He had a cancellation."

"I've already been out today."

Franny opened her mouth and then shut it. "Omigod, I forgot. What did the OB say?"

Simone stared at Franny as if she were speaking Martian.

"The baby's okay?"

From the tot lot beside the house the twins' squeals scraped Simone's eardrums like the tines of a fork. She dropped onto the hassock near the sectional and let her head fall forward between her knees.

"Oh. Another girl? I'm so sorry, Simone. Really. I know you wanted—"

"I am not going into another doctor's office today. You'll have to do it."

"He won't see me."

Dr. Omar had a waiting list of young families, all of them apparently willing and grateful to drop everything for an appointment. He would not deal with nannies under any circumstances.

"You saw my mother leave? What was she wearing? Was she dressed up?"

"She looked fantastic."

"Call her cell, tell her there's an emergency and she has to come home."

Olivia's sweat and tears had left a damp spot on Franny's white T-shirt. "It's not my place."

"Your place, my place, whatever." Lazy and insubordinate: the tally of Franny's faults had grown so long

Simone would have to write it down or she'd forget. Simone wanted to confront her; but the way she felt now, she couldn't pull it off. If she wasn't lying down in the next five minutes, she was going to fold in the middle.

"I have a headache, Franny."

"You're probably dehydrated." Franny leaped on the idea. "That makes for a wicked bad headache. Get a glass of water and go on upstairs. I'll bring you some lunch when I feed the girls. That'll give you time for a nap after and I'll wake you at two."

Bossy as a cattle prod.

"We can load everyone into the Cayenne and all go to Mission Bay when you're done at Dr. Omar's."

"I told you I'm not going to the damn pediatrician. And don't look at me like that. You're the nanny. You're supposed to take care of these things. Make a pest of yourself and she'll give you what you want just to shut you up."

They both knew this would not work.

"Tell the nurse you're me. She's so busy she won't know the difference. It's not a crime. I'm giving you my per—"

Simone heard a scream, the sound of running feet on gravel, and she turned toward the stairs. She didn't want to know what had happened outdoors; she couldn't stand to be in the room and listen to the twins and Merell pick at each other. But before she could get across the family room, Merell hurtled through the French doors and announced that whatever had happened, it wasn't her fault.

"Victoria fell off the merry-go-round, but I didn't do anything. She wouldn't hang on."

"You lie!" Valli shoved Merell. "She did it, Franny. It was her. I hate Merell." She kicked her sister's shin.

"Stop it, you two!" Franny transferred Olivia from her shoulder to her hip. "No kicking, Valli."

Simone stared at her daughters, frantic little banshees always running and yelling and crying and complaining. The sight and sound of them disgusted her in a way that went deeper than simple dislike. Her whole body needed to reject them, almost as if its survival depended on escaping the contagion they carried. At that moment Victoria wailed in from outdoors and threw herself against Simone's legs, almost knocking her over.

Merell said, "I didn't do anything wrong, Mommy."

"She pushes too fast," Valli said.

Their voices had fingers, fingers with claws prying up Simone's skull section by section as if it were an orange.

Merell said, "If I go slow on the merry-go-round they yell, so I said I'd push fast one time and they had to hold on but Victoria didn't."

"I hate you, Merell."

"Yeah, me too."

"Shut up!" Simone covered her ears with her hands. "Right now, all of you!" Her hand shook as she pointed in the direction of the stairs. "You, Merell, get up there and close your door. Don't come down until your father gets home."

"But I didn't do anything wrong. What about lunch? Don't I get any lunch? I'm starving."

Franny said. "It's no trouble for me to take something up to her."

"Why do you undercut everything I try to do?"

"I'm sorry, Simone." Franny stepped back, obviously surprised by Simone's response. "I just don't think—"

"I don't care what you think."

Franny shut her lips tight and followed Merell toward the stairs. "Olivia's wet. I need to change her diaper."

"You think I'm a bad mother."

"It doesn't matter what I think."

"It sure as hell doesn't!"

Merell and the twins watched, their eyes glistening with curiosity. Even the baby had stopped crying and was attentive to the argument. For several breaths no one said anything. Simone could see that Franny was trying to control her temper, and it pleased her to get a reaction from the normally unflappable paragon.

"I don't think you're being fair, Simone."

The girl measured each word as if she were speaking with a child prone to tantrums. Her condescension made Simone feel small and stupid.

Franny said, "You ask me to lie to the doctor's nurse and in almost the same breath you punish Merell because you think she's lying."

"Since when did you get so honest?"

The girl's round face went red. "Simone, I love your children and I'm glad for this job—"

"I guess you better be. We pay you a lot of money—not to mention certain *bonuses*—and from where I'm standing I don't see you doing much to earn it."

"You've had bad news this morning. I'd be upset too. Can we talk about this later, when you're feeling better?"

Simone held her breath and shut her eyes. For a moment she felt as if she were still upstairs, fast asleep and dreaming. A nightmare had chased her into a cul-de-sac at the top of a mountain, and now there was nowhere to go but back or over the edge of a cliff. Fly: the word sang in her thoughts and suddenly she was wide awake and alert. Strange how that happened, how in the space of a breath she went from confusion to a wonderful clarity. One moment before she'd been blind and now she could see.

"Frances, get out. You're fired."

Chapter 9

Huntington Lake had been a disaster, Roxanne could think of it in no other way; and capping the weekend in a glorious disregard for any needs and desires she might have, there was Johnny's request that she sacrifice her career on the altar of Simone. She didn't know what was worse, the request itself or his obvious sense of entitlement when he made it.

But if Huntington had been terrible, her homecoming had been even worse. Needing a hug and a sympathetic shoulder on which to unload the details of the miserable weekend, she found Ty asleep on the couch, unappealingly grungy in sweats and two days' beard. The kitchen was a mess of unwashed dishes, and four messages blinked red on the answering machine. Roused, he was in a foul mood with smiles and hugs only for Chowder. The weekend's experiment had gone poorly—don't ask him why because he didn't fucking know—and been terminated late Saturday night.

"Lately, I can't seem to pick a winner."

He'd come home to an empty house, not even Chowder to commiserate with. Obviously, he had wanted her to say she was sorry for not being there when he needed her; but her heart was heavy with her own problems so, though she made the effort, it was unenthusiastic. When he seemed somewhat mollified, she told him about her own weekend, not bothering to be either funny or philosophical as she related the weekend's many low points, at the same time dumping her laundry and cleaning the kitchen.

He wasn't listening to her.

"What's the matter?"

"Go on, I'm all ears." He was at the kitchen counter, sorting through a pile of catalogs, most of them addressed to her.

"What was the last thing I said?"

"Let me make a wild-ass guess. You were talking about your sister?"

"Well, I'm sorry if I'm boring you." The plastic bottle of dishwashing liquid slipped from her hands and bounced on the kitchen floor, spreading a pool of gooey green. "Fuck!"

"Yeah, right."

He grabbed his keys off the hook by the door.

"Where are you going?"

"Lab."

"But you said there's nothing—"

"Don't wait up, Roxy. I'm not gonna want to talk."

The next morning he was up early and out before her alarm went off at six, taking Chowder with him. She banged around the house feeling sorry for herself—no dog, no husband, a quarter inch of milk in the bottom of the carton. On the way to school she stopped for coffee and succumbed to the temptation of a doughnut and now, the roof of her mouth furred with sugar, baking soda, and powder, and her stomach glurking, she wished she hadn't and blamed Ty for ruining what should have been a great morning.

Balboa Middle School occupied the oldest school complex in San Diego. In Roxanne's wing there was no air-conditioning, but the wall of windows in Room 110 could be cranked open using a long pole with a hook on the end. Four ceiling fans with ten-inch paddles moved the air. Circulating air and a wall of natural light were advantages Roxanne appreciated every day. She believed she was a better, more patient teacher because she could see the sky and trees from wherever she stood in the room.

But it was going to take more than air and light to make her a good teacher today. On a typical first morning it wasn't hard to be enthusiastic and positive; but this time all she thought about was the negatives. She had thirty-five names to learn, a new aide to train, mandated diagnostic tests, small uprisings to quell, and technology to contend with. Cell phones of all descriptions: OFF.

BlackBerries and Apples and any other fruit: OFF. No e-mail. No texting. No surfing. No Twittering. There was no end to the possible mischief.

She checked her phone to see if there was a message from Ty. Nothing.

When all the days of the school year were considered, minus Mondays and Fridays and holidays and the days leading up to them and immediately following, she had decided that real learning took place on Tuesdays, Wednesdays, and Thursdays between Christmas and spring break. The first day of the year was mostly housekeeping and Roxanne had learned to set reasonable goals for herself and to be sustained by small victories. Her ambition on this day, if she could summon the energy and manage to do it with a smile on her face, was to speak privately to each student. The boy slouched on the chair beside her desk was number eleven. Great. Only twenty-four to go.

She had known countless surly adolescents like this one, a rangy black kid with a good start on a mustache. He would be handsome in a few years, but at the moment none of his parts and features matched. The note on his record said he was *morose* and *uncommunicative*, which was about normal for a thirteen-year-old male. She only wanted eye contact with this boy. A smile wasn't even on her wish list.

"You look sleepy, Ryan. Are you tired?"

He shrugged. They all shrugged. In every teenage

demographic it was the same: body odor, bad skin, and the shrug.

And none of them slept enough. Roxanne's kids shared their bedrooms with siblings, pets, telephones, and televisions and computers. She was afraid to ask what else. Many, perhaps most, had *never* had regular bedtimes and probably hadn't been well rested since they learned to climb out of the crib.

"If you talk to me it'll be easier for both of us. We don't know each other—"

He looked up. "I know you."

Roxanne often taught siblings and cousins. The unfamiliarity of Ryan's last name, Moline, meant nothing. Over the years there were divorces and adoptions, foster homes, stepfamilies; and sometimes boys and girls just arbitrarily changed their names.

"My cousin was in your class. Taryn." His jaw squared. "She got shot."

At orientation, the guidance counselor had told the faculty about a teenage girl, once a student of Roxanne's, shot in her own living room where no one had noticed she was watching television.

Ryan shifted his buttocks and slid down on the chair, curving his back like a tortoise shell. "My uncle and this dude Chauncy, they was talkin' how my uncle owed him money. Chauncy, he pulled out a big ol' forty-five."

She imagined a pistol's reverberant roar in the living

room of a small house and the smell of cordite that would never come out of the drapes and upholstery.

In some situations there was no right thing to say. Whatever collection of nouns and verbs Roxanne could put together would just sound fatuous to Ryan. She remembered Taryn's eyes.

"Her eyes were beautiful."

"Green," he said. "Like them grapes."

After he took his seat, she didn't call another student. Leaving the classroom aide to distribute a personal questionnaire Roxanne kept for her private files, she went into the hall and called Ty's cell phone. The image of Taryn watching television and unnoticed by either her father or Chauncy, the sound of a .45 pistol ricocheting off the walls of the living room, a door opening, and a mother's screams were the sound track for a movie running through her imagination. Ty didn't answer and she was too disheartened to leave a message.

Later, as she was eating lunch with Elizabeth in her classroom, the powerful image of the girl's death had not diminished.

"She was right there in the room and no one paid any attention to her. She might as well have been invisible until then." She dumped her lunch in the trash; the smell of ham turned her stomach.

Elizabeth fished a tissue from her purse and handed it across the desk.

Roxanne had planned to start the year with a young

adult novel based on the story of Cyrano de Bergerac. For enrichment and entertainment she had ordered a movie, Steve Martin's comic retelling of Cyrano's story. Later in the term a pair of actors from San Diego State would visit Room 110 and enact several scenes from the classic play. There would be a fencing demonstration.

"But why should a boy like Ryan give a shit about Cyrano? Maybe I should find something grittier, more—"

"What? Relevant? Just in case Ryan forgets his cousin got shot in the head? That's not going to happen. And poor old Cyrano's so far from his experience, it could be what the kid needs right now. Steve Martin might make him laugh."

Elizabeth was a wise and experienced teacher who, despite her diminutive size, could manage a classroom full of hard cases, and her opinions mattered to Roxanne. It was such a relief to be talking about Ryan, not holding his story inside where there was already so much piled up, unresolved.

"Rox, when you strip away all the fancy language, isn't Cyrano just a play about low self-esteem and learning to speak up for yourself?"

"You're saying it's perfect for eighth graders."

"My own brilliance blinds me."

They listened to the noise of kids at the outdoor lunch tables where they ate on all but rainy days. Elizabeth asked about the weekend at Huntington Lake, and Roxanne shared the grisly details until her cell phone rang from the depths of her purse. Hoping it was Ty, she checked it fast, but when she saw the caller ID she let it ring through and listened to the message.

"That was Merell. She wants me to ask the principal if I can leave work early. Simone's fired the nanny." Roxanne laid her forehead on the desktop. "I can't do this anymore."

Even if she wanted to be responsible for the Duran family—which she didn't—there was no way she could do it without risking her marriage.

Despite Elizabeth's often repeated conviction that they happened every day, Roxanne was skeptical about miracles. Elizabeth believed in so many things that made no sense. Auras and directed dreaming, angels and spirit guides, and extraordinary and unlikely events brought about by planetary alignment or the hand of an unseen god. Roxanne could laugh at most of these, but miraculous was the only way she could explain Ty and the great good luck of their meeting: two very different people who somehow, against all odds, met and discovered they were perfectly suited. An everyday miracle. Forced to choose between her sister and a miracle, she had to choose Ty. To do otherwise would be to turn her back on the future, on hope and laughter and all good things. But at the lake she had seen how stretched thin and perilous Simone's family situation was, and it was unthinkable that she would abandon her sister and nieces when their need was so great. She would have to find a way to satisfy everyone.

She remembered Merell's excited conversation on the plane, her breathless tour of the compound and the way she stood up on her bike pedals and bounced along the swamped road.

"She's such a needy kid."

"Heads up, Rox, they're all needy." Elizabeth stood, brushing crumbs off the front of her denim skirt. "But it's your life. You can decide if you want to jump into that suck hole or stay away. Whatever you decide, I've got your six."

Your six. The one who watches your back. The military figure of speech reminded Roxanne that Elizabeth had troubles of her own. Her husband, Eddie, had been in Afghanistan for months. "I must be the worst friend in the world, Lizzie."

"Nah. I think Dick Cheney's got that honor. You never tried to shoot me."

"What do you hear?"

"Same as ever. Nothing. I got a call from his friend Calvin last night. He said Eddie wanted me to know he was safe but he couldn't get to a phone or a computer." She stared down at Roxanne's desktop. "I just realized. Eddie's the opposite of these kids, Merell and all. They all need to be noticed and Eddie's life depends on staying out of sight."

Roxanne left school soon after the closing bell, parked her car at the side of Simone's house, and walked around back, where she was surprised to see Johnny down at the pool with the twins. She waved to him and walked into the house, where she came upon Simone standing in the center of the family room.

She said, "I knew you'd come."

"You fired Franny and then you called Johnny away from work? You're out of your mind, Simone. I swear to God. Bonkers."

"He'll call the agency and find someone else."

"Save him the trouble. You call Franny right now, I'll dial the number. Apologize and give her a bonus."

"Why should I? I didn't do anything wrong." Simone hurried Roxanne out of the family room and across the entry to her study adjoining Johnny's. "I need to talk to you about something else right now."

"Why are you whispering?"

Simone's study was a suffocatingly feminine room, a flurry of florals and stripes in pastel blues and pinks in which Roxanne would have found it difficult to accomplish anything constructive. Simone closed and locked the door, took a deep, audible breath and stepped behind her ladylike desk—too small to be useful to anyone who really had work to do. She began sorting absently through a pile of unopened mail.

"Look at me, Simone. What's going on? Why did you fire her?"

"I got sick of the way she acted like she knew my own family better than I did. And she treated me like I'm an invalid. And an idiot." Simone looked up from the mail and her sudden grin swept years from her face. "I climbed a tree last week so don't fuck with me."

"You could climb a mountain and you still wouldn't have that girl's talent for kids." Roxanne recognized the grandiosity that often accompanied Simone's bursts of mania. There was no telling where her mood would go next. She could swing from helpless to unrealistically confident to abysmally miserable in a matter of minutes. Under such circumstances Roxanne would normally tread carefully, but on this day she couldn't be bothered. "You can't get along without her."

"When was the last time anyone gave me a chance?"

"She was the best nanny in the world. She was golden. Who'll take care of your kids?"

And who will take care of you? Roxanne was afraid she knew the answer to that question.

Simone reached into her purse and handed Roxanne a photograph, an ultrasound image, speckled and blurred as if taken through a windshield on a snowy day. Roxanne isolated the bud of a retroussé nose, a prominent forehead, an arm.

"If you're looking for the ding-dong," Simone said, "don't waste your time. It's another girl and you know what that means. Once she's born, I have to go through the whole fucking thing again."

Simone's moods were mercurial; she could be cunning and she was often secretive, but in some ways she was predictable. Swearing was always a bad sign.

"Quit complaining and have your tubes tied, use birth control."

"I have another plan." Simone grabbed the photo and dropped it in the wastepaper basket beside the desk. "That's why I told Merell to call you. You've been so snotty lately—"

"I just spent the whole weekend with you!"

"—I didn't think you'd come if I called."

"What kind of a plan?"

"Today, when I was having it out with Franny, I got this feeling. I can't explain how it works, but it's like knowing something without having to think about it. The feeling just comes into me and I know what I have to do. *I know.*"

This isn't good.

"What does this have to do with Franny?"

"You don't get it, Rox, because everything works for you. You've got the world all figured out, lined up and alphabetized. You always have." Simone's mouth tightened into a line. "Just imagine what it's like for someone like me who doesn't have *anything* figured out. Then all of a sudden I get this click in my head and I understand something perfectly. I *know.*"

After a weekend swinging between extremes of mania and depression, Simone had settled in a position of unassailable certainty it was pointless to argue with.

"Starting today, everything changes." Spots of red bloomed in her cheeks. "The first thing I'm going to do is tell Johnny that I am not having another damn baby. I didn't want to do it until you got here. Just in case he decides to kill me." She laughed.

Nervously, Roxanne thought.

"The second thing is, I called a clinic and made an appointment. For an abortion." She looked as pleased as a child displaying an A exam after weeks of failing grades. "I have to talk to a counselor first so tomorrow morning I need you to drive me there and then bring me home. I can't take a taxi. I need your moral support. Then after it's all over I'll tell Johnny I miscarried again, and he'll never know."

She looked at Roxanne expectantly.

"And I'm going on the pill." She laughed again. Electric, dangerous. "I'll say they're vitamins. For my hair." More laughter.

"How far along are you?"

"I don't know. The picture came out so good, the doctor says he thinks we might have miscalculated."

"Five months?"

"Something like that."

"Did you tell them that on the phone?"

"Who?"

"The clinic."

Simone pouted. "You don't want me to do it."

"I'm saying, Simone, you're pretty far along." Outside the study window Roxanne saw the sparkle of sunlight on water drops as sprinklers rainbowed the lawn, flashing like the aura of a migraine. "It's going to make a difference."

"Five months is nothing."

"It's fingers and toes, Simone."

"You believe in the right to choose. I know you, Rox, you give money to Planned Parenthood."

"That's true, but you're not eighteen years old and unmarried." And Johnny wasn't an abuser, a cheater, or a deadbeat. He loved his wife, and his four little girls were precious to him. "He has to be part of this decision. And the counselor's going to say the same thing."

"I told her I was single. Divorced."

"He has a right—"

"What about me? Why don't you talk about *my* rights? Roxanne, he'll never let me do it." Her voice rose, shattering between them like glass. "Abortion's murder to him."

"That may be so but you still can't ignore—"

The doorknob rattled. "Simone? What's going on in there?"

"I'm your sister," Simone hissed as she went to the door and unlocked it. "You owe me this."

Simone's study wasn't large and Johnny was a big man. Three long strides took him into the middle of the room. "You ought to be getting dressed, Simone. Have you forgotten we're going out tonight?" His eyebrows dug a crevasse between his eyes. "You chose a great day to fire Franny. I bet you didn't even think about getting a babysitter."

Simone blinked, looked at Roxanne and back at Johnny. "You can go without me."

"Jesus, Simone, it's the Judge Roy Price Dinner. We're at the mayor's table."

"He'll never miss me," she said, her hands fluttering up. "It's you they all like so much."

"That may be true but after what Merell did I want you beside me so the gossip machine doesn't start."

"I don't feel good."

"So what? You never feel good."

Roxanne grabbed her purse and headed for the door. Johnny put his hand on her shoulder to stop her.

"Could you help us out here, Rox? We'll be home by eleven, tops."

"Ask Mom."

"It'd be a real treat for the kids. Get Ty over here too. There's great steaks in the freezer. You want me to pay you? Hey, you're a professional, I get it."

"Don't insult me, Johnny."

Stunned by her tone, then hurt, he looked down. Roxanne saw the exact moment when his eyes focused on the ultrasound image in the basket near his feet.

He picked it out and squinted at the image. As if he couldn't believe the evidence before him, he brought it closer to his face. "You went to the doctor? Without telling me?"

Simone clutched her hands behind her back and stood straighter, holding her shoulders so high they almost touched her ears.

"It's a girl, isn't it?" For a fraction of a second Johnny

looked disappointed and then he laughed. "I don't think you know how to make a boy, Simone."

"Sperm determine the sex of the child," Roxanne said. "She has nothing to do with it."

"No kidding. Really?"

"It's been that way for some time."

"So I'm like my dad, right?" He appeared pleased by this news. "It took him seven girls to get me. We've already got four so after this one"—he flapped the ultrasound picture—"there's only a couple more to go. Right? Eight's the magic number."

Roxanne's throat tightened like the first day of the worst cold she would ever have.

Simone rushed into the silence, her words tumbling over each other in a dash to have them said. "I don't want another baby right now. I've decided to have an abortion."

The word sat in the middle of the room.

Roxanne watched Johnny, saw the word register, and waited. Her neck tightened in anticipation of his explosion. The sprinkler clicked from side to side.

He put his hands on Simone's shoulders and turned her so she faced the silver-framed mirror between the bookcases. She winced under the pressure of his fingers.

"What do you see?" he asked.

Roxanne's neck ached with the strain.

"Answer me."

"I see me, Johnny." Simone spoke in her little girl's

voice, the one that wheedled and begged and cajoled so well. "And I see you too. I see us."

"What d'you see, Rox?"

"Let it be, Johnny."

"You know what I see? I see a murderer."

Simone's face spasmed. Roxanne moved closer to Johnny.

"Leave her alone."

"I see a baby-killer."

"You son of a bitch." Roxanne slapped him so hard that she felt the blow vibrate up through her arm and into her shoulder. For the thinnest, razor-cut sliver of a fraction of a second, she thought he would slap her back.

Simone rushed between them.

"He was just talking. He says things but he doesn't really mean them. You're sorry, Rox. I know you are. You didn't mean to hurt him."

"Are you deaf, Simone? Did you hear what he called you?" *Did his tone of voice even register?*

"It's only words, that's all. I don't care about words." Simone waved her hand between them as if she could that easily erase the scene. "But I love you both so much, I can't stand it if you fight." She spoke rapidly in her sweetest voice, the voice Roxanne remembered hearing all her life when things went wrong. "I need you. Both."

Light-headed, Roxanne moved toward the door.

Simone grabbed her arm. "Everything's fine. Honest to God, none of this matters. Really. Don't leave me again."

Sometimes, just when Roxanne thought she had seen every one of Simone's performances, the curtain went up on something outrageously new. First: Simone strong and determined, taking charge of her life. *Knowing.* Independence. Abortion. The pill. And now: mewling and needy. *Everything's fine. Don't leave me again.*

Again? *When have I ever really left you, Simone?*

"You said you'd take care of the girls."

"What are you talking about? I didn't promise anything."

"We're counting on you," Johnny said, and slipped his arm around his wife's waist.

Roxanne was living in a movie where reality shifted from frame to frame.

"Just answer me, Simone. Did you hear what Johnny said to you?"

"Oh, of course I heard him." She dipped her head with what Roxanne knew some might see as a beguiling femininity. "He didn't mean it, Rox. You know Johnny. He gets upset, that's all." She elbowed him gently in the ribs. "Isn't that right? Say you're sorry for being so mean."

"I was way out of line, Roxanne. I get mad, I say things...." He rubbed his cheek. "You've got a hell of a right cross there. Married people have these... flare-ups. You're practically a newlywed. You'll know what I mean in a few years."

"Are you telling me you don't want to terminate this pregnancy, Simone?"

"The ultrasound was a shock, that's all. I just got a little loopy." Simone made a corkscrew gesture beside her head and leaned into the protection of Johnny's arm, a posture that seemed both voluptuous and childlike at the same time.

It came to Roxanne how little she actually knew about her sister's marriage. Maybe Simone's plan to end her pregnancy had been a hormonal outburst or an excuse to make a scene. That business about *knowing* something was just more talk. All she really wanted was a bit of drama to punish Johnny for giving her another daughter or to provide him with a reason to rant at her for firing Franny and get it out of his system. Maybe he was hiding his anger now or maybe Simone's two-step and sashay had worked, he'd lost his temper and that was that. Behind closed doors his name-calling might be nothing out of the ordinary. All Roxanne knew was that in some way to which she was not privy, a bargain had been struck between husband and wife. Theirs was a marriage that permitted scenes like the one she'd just witnessed. Perhaps required them.

Chapter 10

Ellen Vadis's earliest memory was of the sweaty summer afternoon she was attacked by yellow jackets.

It was too hot for a nap. Wearing seersucker shorts with a torn pocket and a cut-off, no-sleeve white T-shirt inherited from her father, she crept barefoot down the narrow back stairs for a drink of cold water and a sugar cookie; but when she heard them arguing she changed her mind, her stomach suddenly heavy. Sometimes she threw up when her mother and grandmother had fights.

Instead of going into the kitchen she tiptoed along the back hall, through the laundry room, and out the screen door, into the ripe summer heat. Wet sheets hung on the carousel clothesline, and from across the grass she smelled the bleach her mother used to make them white. She thought she might find her father in the shed where he sometimes fixed things like the rusty plow he told her was a beautiful antique. It looked plain old to Ellen, but she believed what her father said because he was a soldier.

In the hot, murky shed, spiderwebs drooped across the corners from the rafters and the air smelled of oil and sawdust. She imagined a black widow spider crawling up between her bare toes and ran out the door, back onto the grass. She didn't want to look behind her because she was afraid of what might happen. The world was strange and mysterious and maybe black widows could swell up to the size of her whole body and they had all those legs to chase her. She sat on the back steps, breathing hard but safe. A drop of sweat rolled into her eye, stinging.

Ellen wished she lived at the beach.

She heard a buzzing sound like Daddy's electric hair clippers coming from a blue wheelbarrow tipped on its side under the pink crape myrtle. She walked across the yard and smelled rotting nectarines. Looking down, she saw a pile of squashed fruit crawling with yellow jackets, the black-and-gold wasps that buzzed against the kitchen window screens when Ellen's grandmother made fig jam. They piled over each other, fighting their way to the sticky sweetness.

The tangy fruit smell made the inside of her nose feel like the sound the yellow jackets made. As she lifted her hand to wipe her sweaty forehead, some of the striped buzzers boiled up off the fruit and orbited her head. In an instant they were in her ears and on her eyelids, at the corners of her mouth. Their tiny feet walked on her skin. Screaming, she ran for the clothesline and twisted herself in the wet, bleachy sheets.

* * *

She remembered another day, this one a few years later, a winter day after a week of slow, cold rain. A thick tule fog blanketed the Central Valley and radio newscasters reported multicar pileups on Highway 99. She stood between her mother and grandmother on the porch of the big house, looking down at her father where he stood beside Grandpa's Hudson in the driveway, a duffel bag over his shoulder. Ellen wore woolen pants and a blue sweater and a pair of Buster Brown shoes scuffed to a dull orange at the toes.

Daddy looked serious, but his eyes were jiggery: she could tell he was excited and trying not to show it. He had orders he told her came from Washington. Dressed in his army uniform, as handsome as Dana Andrews in the movies, he was shipping out to Japan, and then he was going to Korea to shoot some Reds. He had shown Ellen where these places were in the big map book.

A disembodied voice in the fog said, "Wayne." Sitting in the Hudson, Ellen's grandfather flashed the headlights on and off.

Ellen's grandmother said not to drive too fast and watch out for black ice on the roads. Daddy nodded, but he didn't look at her because his eyes were on Mommy like if eyes could eat they would swallow her up. He came up the stairs two at a time and held her in his arms for such a long moment that Ellen became impatient. Mommy started crying and he turned away and went back down the stairs. Ellen's grandmother told Mommy to get hold of herself. *Don't make things worse!*

At the bottom of the stairs Daddy turned and held out his arms and Ellen jumped into them. He said she was his crackerjack and swung her up and then gave her a bear hug so tight his medals dug into her skin. She liked medals and it was a good hurt.

Ellen had a lot of memories of the time after her father went to Korea, some of them bad, a few really good; but mostly they were no more than glimpses of people and events and places that mattered so little, she wondered now why they took up space in her mind: lines from songs, snapshot memories of her mother crying and staying up all night putting together jigsaw puzzles, of school and friends and Jimmy Nissen teaching her to smoke in the seventh grade, chugging Olympia beer under the bleachers at football games and in cars parked by the reservoir. She remembered driving the Hudson into a ditch in the fog; and the old man, mad as a yellow jacket, saying in his quivery voice that he didn't know where on God's green earth Ellen had come from. *Sure as holy hell not my family.*

Her father went to live in Texas and got a new wife and other children; and after a long time, Ellen's mother stopped crying. From then on all she thought about was ranching and stretching pennies and organizing the breath of life out of Ellen. The fights they had were worse than the ones Ellen grew up hearing between her mother and grandmother.

One Sunday morning Ellen stood in the kitchen and screamed, "I hate you! When I grow up I'm leaving this dump and I'll never come back."

The day after high school graduation, Ellen boarded the Greyhound to Los Angeles. In school she'd been a mediocre student except in the business courses, where she won the Future Executive Secretary Award three years running. By the time she went looking for a job in LA she typed almost ninety words a minute on an IBM Selectric and took shorthand fast enough to get hired at a Pontiac dealership on Pico Boulevard even though she was only eighteen. There were boulevards all over Los Angeles, streets lined with skinny palms like giant swizzle sticks, stoplights at every intersection, department stores and movie theaters with towering neon marquees. *Boulevard.* Sometimes Ellen repeated the word aloud, loving the luxurious, Southern California sound of it.

Being around a car dealership was a great way to meet men. But she never lost her preference for a uniform.

Years later, when Ellen was a grandmother and twice a widow, she started meeting men online and hoped for a retired officer, a colonel maybe, a commander or a captain. San Diego was full of retired military, and it seemed a reasonable expectation. Instead she had met a chief and a couple of master sergeants and each with the disheartening look of years and hard work on them. She knew BJ would tell her that the world needed machinists and plumbers, but she didn't.

She had been about to give up on the whole enterprise when Dennis Dwight responded to her online message. He said he was fifty-two which probably meant he was close to sixty. (No matter how fit and good-looking, sixty was the border no one crossed in the online dating world.) Ellen had told Dennis she was forty-eight, an age she thought she could pull off when she made an effort.

Though not a military man, Dennis had much to recommend him. He knew the Central Valley and had grown up in Modesto, which was bigger than Daneville but just as much a dead end. Like her, he couldn't leave home fast enough. He spoke in a vague way of having worked overseas and mentioned Kuwait, Istanbul, and Saigon. She interpreted his cryptic answers as meaning he did government work he wasn't at liberty to talk about. After a few weeks of e-mailing, they had begun to speak on the phone, often late at night in the hours when Ellen would otherwise be lying awake, missing BJ. On the phone Dennis had a deep and reassuring radio voice, and a wonderfully quick and easy laugh. He told her jokes that were just a little bit dirty, but never offensive. He asked her what she was wearing when they talked, and she began to dress for their calls. She bought a white silk nightgown at Neiman's, backless and sheer.

She thought BJ looking down from heaven would

understand if she lied about her age. And he would forgive the nightgown and the things she said things to Dennis on the phone that made her blush when she remembered them the next morning.

They had made plans to meet this evening for the first time. Tuesday was a strange night for a date, but never mind. If things worked out, they would have all the Saturday nights in the world. With other men she had insisted on a quick coffee first, what she thought of as a tryout date. It didn't seem necessary with Dennis. They had talked so much and about so many things that she knew they'd be compatible.

Even so, she was nervous and had gone to some lengths to make the right impression. That morning she'd had her hair cut and colored, a manicure and pedicure. She held up her hands and admired the new polish the color of raspberries. In the salon that morning, the Vietnamese woman who did her nails had told her it was a very nice color, very pretty. The women in the salon talked constantly in their complicated language as their thin white hands filed Ellen's nails and massaged her feet in a way she wasn't sure she really liked. She tried to ignore them, but she suspected they were gossiping about her. When she tried to imagine their San Diego lives away from the salon, ordinary lives with husbands and children, what came to mind was the stretched and puckered scar where BJ had been shot in the shoulder.

* * *

Sometimes Roxanne forgot that there was a time before everything about Simone became so fraught. She made an effort to remember the endearing tyke who collected round white stones for a snow garden and, when she couldn't find enough of them, painted any round stone she could find with white-out from BJ's desk, the three-year-old who wouldn't eat her ice cream until it "got warm," who climbed into Roxanne's bed in the morning and whistled in her ear to wake her up.

In college, she and Elizabeth once snatched Simone out of school—where she never seemed to learn much anyway—and took her up into the Laguna Mountains, where five inches of snow had fallen, the local equivalent of a blizzard, closing roads to all but vehicles like Elizabeth's truck. Simone had never seen snow and bounced on the bench seat between them, excited as a five-year-old though she must have been eleven or twelve at the time. For a sled they used a hubcap Elizabeth had found somewhere. On the downhill Simone squealed so long and loud, that whole winter they'd called her Piglet.

For her fourteenth birthday they took her to LA to see a production of *The King and I,* and afterward she made them buy her a DVD of the movie. And because she wanted to watch it all the time, she was motivated to finally learn how to use the DVD player BJ and Ellen had bought her the year before. After *The King and I* she begged to see any play that had words and music and learned the scores to all of them. She couldn't memorize the times tables but she could sing every song from *Phantom of the Opera.*

She was ten and Roxanne was in college when Ellen could no longer ignore Simone's mental impairment. For a while she dragged Simone to doctors and specialists of all kinds who said variations on the same thing. Simone had neurologically impaired balance and coordination and a borderline mental disability. In other words, her intelligence was subnormal. Later they added manic-depressive to their diagnoses.

School had been a challenge requiring special classes and tutors in most subjects, but in due course Simone learned to read and write and add a column of figures. Teachers passed her from grade to grade despite the gaps in her learning. Ellen and BJ wouldn't have it any other way. As far as Roxanne knew, her sister had never read a book from beginning to end, although she devoured style and entertainment magazines and had subscriptions to eight or ten of them. Recipes, directions of any kind, confused her. If she couldn't do something right away, she didn't want to take the time to learn. No one had any idea what she would do with her life until she met Johnny Duran.

Behind Roxanne the screen door slammed shut, and Ty called out from the tiny bedroom they had made into a joint office.

"Hey," he said, and taking hold of her hands, he pulled

her down onto his lap for a kiss, surprising her. He was using the computer; pictures of windows were on the screen.

"What are you working on?"

"Fenestration," he said.

"Fena-what?"

"Windows for the addition."

This, like the surprising kiss, was a good sign. Since Chicago they had stopped talking about the remodeling project.

"See these?" He indicated the windows on the computer screen. "They open out, they're vinyl, double-paned with blinds between the panes. Expensive as hell but I think we ought to go for broke on this addition. If we don't we'll regret it."

"You're not mad at me anymore?"

"I've been a bastard, Rox, and I'm sorry, I really am. The last month's been a bitch, and then the weekend... I gave you a hard time, didn't I?"

"You've hardly even spoken to me. For weeks." *And when you did you were barely civil or alert.* "You were mad because I didn't go to Chicago. If I'd been there you would have gotten the job."

"That might be true, but it doesn't really matter because, bottom line, they were right, I didn't want it that much. I've been going over the whole business ever since I got the call and then this weekend, it was like the last puzzle piece fell into place."

She realized that he was going to tell her something important, something wonderful that would make her happy, make them both happy; and then she would have to ruin a perfect night of reconciliation, a night they both needed, by running back to Simone's.

She needed to say it and get the worst over with. "I've been at Simone's and I've got to go back and babysit. She fired the nanny."

She waited for him to be angry. Instead he reached his arms around her waist and pulled her close. Against her body his heart beat and his chest rose and fell. They breathed the same air and she could not distinguish the beat of his heart from her own. In that moment she understood that she had already made the break with Simone. It would take time to convince her sister of this, but the hardest part was over. She wanted to tell him this but stopped herself, aware that there had already been too much talk of Simone in their house. He was a scientist and wanted proof of change. Well, she would give it to him.

"You don't mind that I'm going?" She pulled back and looked into his eyes.

"Of course I mind."

"Then what...?"

"You have to do it your way, Rox. I've been trying to force you to make this break with Simone for me. Because it's what I want. And I finally figured out that you've got to want independence for *yourself* as much as I want it for you."

Now was not the time to applaud his insight.

He said, "After the call came from Chicago, I couldn't understand why I basically didn't care."

"You barely spoke to me. You were furious."

"I thought that too but this weekend I realized I never really wanted to leave Salk."

"The experiment—"

"It was a mess, but it'll work next time. I've got a great team and the science is good. The main thing is, I realized that Chicago would have been a big mistake."

"Then why did we go through all this?"

"That's what I kept asking myself last night. And then—bam!—it hit me. I wanted Chicago because I thought it would get you away from Simone."

"Oh, Ty, I'll do it on my own. We don't have to leave our home."

"But you have to go away tonight."

She nodded. "I do."

"Call them up. She fired the nanny and forgot to hire a babysitter. So? Let her figure out how to solve the problem. It's not exactly Schrödinger's Cat. I think even your sister's got the brain power to figure it out."

"I've got to do this my way, Ty."

"I guess I just said that, didn't I."

"Stay awake for me, okay?"

"Don't take too long. We don't have forever, Roxanne."

At bedtime Valli and Victoria demanded a story but were asleep before Hansel and Gretel discovered the witch's cottage. Olivia fussed and cried, twisting her small body left to right, arching her back like a gymnast. Roxanne walked the floor with her until her digestion settled down, and she could lie back, propped on a pillow sucking her binky until she fell asleep. Merell was still awake when Roxanne closed the nursery door. She popped up out of bed, talking nonstop.

"Just let me show you this one thing, okay? It's really special. Okay? I promise I'll go to bed after." She crossed her heart. "Anyway it doesn't matter when I go to bed. It's Tuesday and there's no school until next week and besides sometimes I stay up until midnight."

"Not when I'm here you don't."

"Just fifteen minutes?"

Roxanne pointed to the face of her watch, trying not to smile. "Fifteen minutes and that's the limit."

Merell ran through the house and into the garage. Johnny had driven his Porsche to the dinner that night, and the two cars remaining were both Simone's, a black Cayenne van parked beside a big Mercedes sedan, also black, with darkly tinted windows. They looked like mob transportation.

As if she were conducting a tour for visitors, Merell

said, "Daddy bought the Cayenne so Mommy could take us to the beach and the zoo and stuff, but she's too nervous." She ran across the garage to a far door with a window in it. "I bet you didn't even know we have two garages. It only got finished three weeks ago. We aren't supposed to go in so Daddy keeps it locked."

A set of keys hung on a hook by the door, just beyond Merell's reach when she stood on tiptoe. "We can look through the window, though. It's okay to do that." She clicked a light switch, illuminating the second garage. "But we gotta remember to turn the lights off when we go back because did you know lights make heat? This garage has a controlled temperature so it never gets really hot or really cold. The air-conditioning makes it always exactly sixty-five degrees."

The first thing Roxanne noticed, looking through the twelve-inch square of window, was how clean the new garage was. There were no stacks of plastic bins full of old clothes and Christmas ornaments. No skis or surfboards bridged the rafters; no open shelves cluttered with tools lined the garage perimeter. Near the back wall the garage floor was carpeted—pale blue—but most of the expanse appeared to be polished hardwood on which five vintage automobiles were parked, lined up with their headlights facing the back wall, the overhead lights blindingly reflected in their mirror-finished bodies.

Merell went on, telling Roxanne some things she knew but some that she didn't. "Before he got the new garage,

Daddy kept his cars in a warehouse. I bet you never saw them, did you? Daddy said it wasn't any fun when they were across town, and besides he didn't trust the man who owned the warehouse. He left the doors open. There's gonna be a special air filter so the air'll be really pure and if any dust gets in on accident, there's special, super-soft rags to clean them with." Merell waited a second for her words to sink in. "Mommy likes the yellow one best. Daddy let her drive it once when he first got it. He calls it the Yellow Bird. Mommy says she'd be the happiest woman in the world if he'd give it to her but he says it's too valuable and she'd probably wreck it."

A V8 yellow Camaro from the sixties and beside it a bullet-shaped, cherry-red Studebaker, probably ten or fifteen years older.

"The red one's my favorite 'cuz it looks like a rocket ship. Daddy says it's almost as old as Gramma Ellen and it still has the paint it got from the factory."

Next to the Studebaker was a silver-blue cloth-top roadster from the twenties: long and low, its fenders like breaking waves. Parked beside it, looking humble, a woody station wagon, and against the far wall a black sedan.

"It used to belong to a really bad criminal," Merell said, lowering her voice. "There's bullet holes in the side of it, and Daddy says that makes it more valuable. Vintage cars are an investment." She looked up at Roxanne through her shaggy bangs. "Do you know what 'investment' is?"

"You tell me."

"It's kind of like a savings account that gets bigger even though you don't put any more money in it. Daddy says you should have a lot of different investments in case something happens to one of them."

Roxanne thought about the Johnny Duran who took the time to teach his nine-year-old daughter about investment strategy. She thought about the Johnny who led his children on a follow-the-leader conga line. And she thought of that afternoon's Johnny, the contemptuous man she'd slapped because her sister wouldn't or couldn't or didn't know she had the option.

"Which is your favorite car, Merell?"

Merell looked at her strangely. Roxanne realized her mistake.

"Silly me. You told me that, didn't you. It's the Studebaker." She mussed Merell's hair. "You have to forgive me, Sugar Pie. It's been a long day."

Merell nodded sagely. "You're worried because Mommy and Daddy had a fight, but it's okay. They always make up when Mommy says she's sorry. Sometimes Daddy says she's crazy and before the police came, Gramma Ellen said she ought to be in a hospital. If she goes to the hospital who will take care of us? Mommy fired Franny and Daddy has to work and Gramma doesn't like us very much."

"She likes you fine. But she's not very good at showing it."

Merell tugged on her bangs, staring down at her feet.

"I saw on TV about these kids who had to go to a foster home. What if that happens to us?"

"It won't happen, Merell. I promise it won't."

Roxanne held her niece close, feeling under her hands the girl's vulnerable framework. As often happened when she worked with children, Roxanne experienced a painful empathy, a sense of what it meant to be a child in the modern world. Though childhood had been brutal and dangerous at the dawn of human life, at least back then most threats were simple and easily understood: starvation, injury, disease. A child like Merell was threatened by these but more powerfully by a vast menu of horrific possibilities: drugs, gangs, murder, rape, pandemics, nuclear annihilation, and climate change, details of which were readily and luridly available on the Internet and television. Children had always been powerless, but never more than now when, despite Merell's intelligence, she possessed nothing with which to defend herself.

"You'll never be sent to a foster home, Merell, I promise you that. You're surrounded by people who love you. Nothing bad will happen to you or your sisters."

Chapter 11

Ellen had arranged to meet Dennis Dwight at the bar in the Mariposa Hotel in downtown La Jolla. She wanted to get there early and have a drink to settle her schoolgirl nerves.

Before she knew BJ, Ellen had been more of a drinker than she was now. BJ had been abstemious by nature. A man who liked a martini or two before dinner and wine and beer in moderate amounts, he made it clear that drunken women disgusted him. Eager to please, Ellen had fitted herself into his way of living as she had once fit into Dale's. It was hard now to recall that earlier incarnation of herself, the woman who had drunk enough to black out and done something so terrible she could never forgive herself.

But tonight she needed a drink to settle her nerves. She imagined that BJ would tell her there was nothing wrong with her nerves, but it was easy for a good-looking, successful man like him to say that. A sixty-year-old woman on a first date: she needed her head examined. Or a Valium. Short of those options, a martini would do the job. Dating had been much simpler when she was a kid and knew the rules. Or thought she did. But in the world of cyberdating—*senior* cyberdating—she didn't know if there was a timetable of appropriate behavior and expectations, a list of things one must not say or assume. She had actually made a special trip to the bookstore in search of such a guide; and when she couldn't find one she was too embarrassed to ask a salesperson for assistance.

"How'll I recognize you?" Dennis asked on the phone the night before, a languid drawl in his beautiful, deep voice. "You gonna wear a red rose?"

"I'll hold it between my teeth." Late at night, on the telephone, she felt brave and flirtatious and hummed a few sexy bars from *Carmen*.

She compared the sick nervousness she felt now—like four black coffees on an empty stomach—with the scary excitement of stepping off the Greyhound in LA with no job, nowhere to live, and not a single friend. Back then she thought she knew about the world because she'd groped around with boys in the senior class, thought she knew men because her best friend's father had made a pass at her. She trusted that life would give her what she wanted if she made herself available, and some of the time it had. Eventually she'd even found BJ, but on the way to him there had been so many mistakes in judgment. The memory of every one of them was in the car with her, driving into La Jolla to meet Dennis Dwight.

Ellen was lucky to find a parking place on Herschel, not far from the Mariposa Hotel. She pulled down the visor mirror and looked at herself. Was her hair too blond? Was the cut good? If it were shorter would her jaw look firmer? She picked up the red rose she'd cut from a bush at the house. It was a day or two beyond its glory, but would have to do. In the Mariposa's lobby, logic told her that the desk clerk and concierge didn't care if she was there to meet a man she'd only spoken to on the telephone. But she felt conspicuous anyway and slightly ridiculous holding a red rose, teetering in shoes designed by Torquemada.

A blue-tiled arch led into the narrow bar, where there was subdued lighting and heavy carpet, small tables and deep-cushioned, suede-upholstered easy chairs. No mirrors or booths, no vulgar display of bottles. At the Mariposa the alcohol was discreetly concealed below the granite bar. A trio of enlarged photos of butterflies hung on the bar-back wall.

Ellen ordered a vodka martini, and when the hostess brought it, she told herself to drink slowly. She deliberately did not look down at the glass for several minutes. She wished she had never quit smoking, thought about BJ, imagined what Dennis Dwight would look like, checked to see if she had lipstick on her teeth. Just one swallow and then she could sit back and relax. Business in the bar grew brisk and several men and women in suits and stylish sportswear entered from the lobby. She felt ridiculously overdressed in four hundred dollars' worth of tucked silk from Neiman Marcus.

"I'm meeting someone," she explained to the hostess and immediately wished she hadn't.

The girl asked, "Can I get you an appetizer while you wait?"

"No, thank you. We'll be dining later."

It seemed as if she'd just taken the first sip and her glass was empty. She couldn't remember if it was her second or third. Her rose lay on the table, its petals limp. For a few moments that felt like forever, she fiddled with the stem of her glass, thin as a drinking straw, and then ordered another. She couldn't just sit there with nothing in front of her.

More people came into the bar and now the tables and barstools were full. Across from Ellen the place where Dennis Dwight was meant to sit confronted her like a toothless grin. She didn't wear a watch but she sensed that she'd been sitting in the bar at least forty-five minutes. Meetings at Starbucks were better. In a coffee shop she could read a newspaper as she waited. If she finished her coffee and left, no one had to know that she'd been stood up.

A tall man in a gray suit—expensive though a little snug and a few years out of style—stood at the entrance to the Mariposa Bar. He saw her; she was sure he saw her. He was the right age and his comb-over was presentable. He was definitely closer to seventy than fifty but she forgave him his lie and hoped he wouldn't find hers out quite so readily.

She didn't know if she should look at him again or pretend to be fascinated by something. The butterflies on the bar-back—brilliant turquoise and black with flecks of gold in their hugely magnified wings—were like the ones she and BJ had seen in the rain forest in Costa Rica. He called them flowers with wings.

She looked up, holding the rose, trying to smile, but the man was gone.

* * *

The night sky over San Diego was starless, the light of a million suns blotted out by the gray urban glow. To the east a cantaloupe-colored moon rose from behind a scrim of lemon-scented eucalyptus trees. Stretched out on a chaise on the terrace, thinking about that evening's conversation with Ty, Roxanne found her mind resting easier than it had in many weeks. She dozed until jolted awake by the slam of a car door. Glancing at her watch, she saw that it was too early for Johnny and Simone. A moment later her mother hobbled around the side of the house, one shoe on, one off, muttering under her breath.

A gust of warm, citrus-scented wind lifted the hair at the back of Roxanne's neck.

"Mom, are you okay?"

"This dress cost four hundred dollars and I spilled red wine on it. I don't even know why I was drinking wine. And these shoes!" She threw them over the edge of the terrace into the yellow lantana and walked on. She stopped and held up the skirt of her dress, which was discolored by a dark stain. "Maybe it was Scotch." She looked at Roxanne. "Does Scotch wash out?"

Seeing her mother intoxicated brought to Roxanne a flood of emotions so old they were barely more than shadows cast by the memory of shadows.

"Did you drive yourself home?" Her mother nodded. "Mom, you shouldn't have."

"Stop managing me."

"Where'd you go?"

"Why are you here anyway? Where's Franny?"

"Simone fired her."

"And you're babysitting?" Ellen looked suddenly stricken. "No, no, no." A moment ago she had been rigid with fury over a broken heel and stained dress; now she was close to tears, broken, a house of cards collapsing. "You should be at home with your husband. You don't know how quickly, how suddenly..."

"Mommy, what happened?"

"When?"

"Tonight, of course."

"Oh. I don't remember." She sat on the edge of a chaise. "I'm telling you, Roxanne, you can't waste this time. You're young and you love each other, I know you do, but you take him for granted and one day you'll be sorry. You'll think of all the meetings and open houses and signing conferences you just had to attend and then he'll die ahead of you because they always do, and you'll regret it all...."

In Roxanne's eyes, Ellen had always moved through the world unhampered by self-doubt and regret; but tonight it was achingly clear that her confidence was a thin shell mapped with cracks. Roxanne didn't want to know this. She didn't want to feel sorry for the mother who had abandoned her.

"You should go up to bed."

"Don't dismiss me! Just hear what I'm saying. I never gave you much advice, did I? So when I do, you should listen. You're so judgmental, like your grandmother."

Don't you dare criticize Gran. Roxanne wanted to walk away and leave her mother alone, feeling sorry for herself. *She saved me. You abandoned me.* The hurt was as fresh as if it had only recently happened....

It was dark when they arrived at Gran's. Roxanne remembered getting out of the Buick and standing at the foot of the verandah steps. As she looked up, the woman on the porch with her large, muscular arms folded across her chest had seemed by the light of a single yellow bulb to be an enormous creature, a colossus. "What are you doing here, Ellen Rae? You should have called ahead. You can't barge—"

"Take her, Mom." Ellen thrust Roxanne forward so she stumbled against the first step and sat down, whimpering as she rubbed her shin. "I can't deal with her."

"You should have thought of that before you had her."

"Don't lecture me, don't say I told you so. Just for once, say nothing. I'm begging you, Mother. You have to do this."

The memory of that day filled Roxanne's mind, expanding to include the huge, empty house, the thousand rows of fruit trees standing witness, a harvest moon.... She remembered the bright light of it, Ellen's fearful and exhausted expression, the tremble of a nerve at the corner of Gran's pursed lips. That night, this night: there was something about the oversize moon, the warm night air...

Ellen talked on, half to herself. "You want to be smart for your kids and do all the right things, but if you did the right thing you never would have had them. In the first place." She looked at Roxanne, light glittering in her narrowed eyes, and poked a manicured finger in her direction. "You're not a kid anymore, Roxanne, so pay attention. I know what I'm talking about.... There isn't time.... You gotta let your sister... I know I shouldn't have made you take care of her... all the time. BJ said it wasn't fair...."

To Roxanne's knowledge her mother had never admitted to any flaw or apologized to anyone for anything. Now this remorse: was it real or alcohol talking? She could be in a blackout right now and remember nothing in the morning. Was there any point in listening?

Elizabeth had a theory that before birth, souls choose

their families, specifically their mothers and fathers, for what they can learn from them. So what karmic lesson was Roxanne learning from Ellen? Don't drink, don't abandon your kid. Lead an orderly life because if you don't, everything will fall apart around and over you.

"Come on, Mom. It's getting cool out here. Let's get you up to bed. You'll feel better in the morning."

Ellen looked at her, blinking. "Why are you here? You're always here. Someday...Did I say this? They always die, Roxanne. They die and they're gone and you're alone." She pulled up her skirt and sobbed into the stained silk.

"That's enough now, you'll ruin your dress."

"Don't take that tone with me." Ellen shoved past Roxanne. "I'm not a child, I was never a child."

That makes two of us.

As Roxanne watched her stagger up the stairs to her apartment over the garage, she remembered that there had been a time before Gran and Simone when her mother was drunk every night. She had put her mother to bed, cleaned up her messes.

From the top of the stairs Ellen called out loud enough to wake the neighborhood. "There's something wrong with this damn key."

A sheet of pale gold moonlight fell across the carpet in Ellen's bedroom. Roxanne pulled back the bedspread and helped her mother lie down. There was something about this night and the moon's calm expression observing through the window beside the bed. Roxanne shook her head to clear it, and the mist shimmered and swirled and parted and came together again.

A night for remembering.

Ellen and Dale liked parties, poker parties, mostly. Roxanne remembered the arguments and laughter and the LP records stacked on the spindle of the stereo, the clink of red, white, and blue poker chips as her father spilled them back and forth between his hands. In the morning the house smelled sticky-sweet and smoky as she washed the glasses and emptied the ashtrays. By contrast Gran had been a teetotaler except for one glass of red wine at dinner on Sunday night and another when she worked on her jigsaw puzzle. Roxanne thought of the parties in Logan Hills and she recalled Gran and the ranch; and when she did, the old, never-completely-asked, never-honestly-answered question rose from the calm surface of her thoughts.

"Tell me, Mom." If she'd had enough to drink, she might actually tell the truth. "Why did you take me up to Gran's and leave me there?"

"You ought to thank me for that. I did the right thing."

You broke my heart, you marked me forever, how could that have been the right thing?

"I can't get it out of my mind, Mom. I've tried, all my life I've tried, but I can't." She touched her mother's wrist, put her lips on the pulse she felt there. "You didn't visit me once. Not once."

"You don't understand."

"Help me understand, Mom. Just tell me why."

From the peak of the roof came the song of a mockingbird, a serenade.

"I never wanted you children. Not your sister, not you. It wasn't personal. I just wasn't cut out for it: motherhood. When I got pregnant with you, I wanted an abortion, but we didn't have the money. Back then it was either pay some old woman with a crochet hook or a decent doctor over the border, and one of those cost five hundred dollars. I thought I'd do it myself, but I just couldn't."

Roxanne had read of the women who tried to end their pregnancies with bent wires and plumbers' snakes, even long-handled soda spoons. Over the centuries, millions of women and girls and their unborns had bled to death in bathtubs and basements and out-of-doors behind garden sheds. She and her mother might easily have been two of them.

"I was a little off my rocker. I thought if I ignored you, you'd go away. I threw up all the time and I told them at the dealership that I had flu, and they believed me, but your dad knew better and what a rampage he went on. I thought I couldn't live without him. I thought I'd die if he left me."

"You loved him."

"I was a fool."

In the night garden, by the glow of an orange moon,

crickets sang songs of love and black moths sacrificed themselves to the light.

"He was the sexiest man I'd ever met. Not a high school boy or a car salesman trying to make his quota in a cheap suit. Your father was the kind of man who came into a room and everything stopped. The women all wanted him and the men envied him and looked up to him and did what he wanted. When I was with him I felt hypnotized." Ellen looked at her. "You have no idea." Her eyes were glassy with drink and tears.

"I know what love is now, but back then . . . Lust. Love. I got them confused. I thought love was doing whatever I wanted and not making excuses to anyone. And lots of sex. I loved him that way."

Roxanne did not think she had ever been as young as the girl her mother was describing. She knew she'd never been in blinding love that way and never wanted to be.

The majolica clock on Ellen's dresser chimed the half hour. Roxanne rested her head on the edge of the bed. Simone and Johnny would be home soon. She should go back to the main house. Ellen's hand touched her head and stroked her hair. Memory had long nails that caught and held.

Sometimes there was still music and gambling in the house when the sun came up. After a long night and if he'd won enough, Roxanne's father was in a jokey mood and made his special huevos rancheros and foamy, fruity vodka drinks in the blender. Sometimes the guests stayed to watch football. Whenever they left, Dale and Ellen went to bed and slept the rest of the day.

Many nights her mother and father crossed the busy street to a bar called the Royal Flush. They left Roxanne alone in the house because they didn't have money for a babysitter; and besides, her mother said, what could happen when they were right across the street?

One night she begged them not to leave her alone. She had an earache and the whole left side of her head hurt, from her jaw way up under her hair. Her father told her to stop making a racket and get the heating pad from under the sink in the bathroom.

Everyone gets earaches.

You'll survive.

Standing on a chair at the front window she watched them run across the busy street and walk in under the bar's neon sign, a splayed hand of face cards. She went looking for the heating pad, but it was useless to her because the cord wouldn't stretch from the enclosed porch where she slept to the outlet in the living room. In the garage she used a yardstick to turn on the light switch and eventually found an old extension cord on a hook over the workbench her father never used. In the living room she plugged it in and connected it to the heating pad and put the pad on her pillow. She lay on her side and set the regulator to a cautious low. It didn't warm so she turned it to high and scorched her ear. She got out of bed and found a clean dish towel in the plastic laundry basket. She folded it into fourths and laid it over the heating pad. At its highest setting, the pad soothed her throbbing ear and soon she fell asleep.

She woke to the smell of burning. She thought about getting up to check but she was very sleepy. When she opened her eyes again the smell was stronger. She got up and in the living room she saw smoke coming from the wall socket. She stood with her hand over her ear and watched and waited to see what would happen next. She tried to pull the plug from the outlet, but it burned her fingers; and now she was frightened. Roxanne had seen a movie on television about a fire that burned down a house and all the kids inside were killed and the dog too.

At the Royal Flush her mother and father were with their friends, drinking and playing pool. She knew her father made money playing pool and tonight when they left the house they had been talking about scoring big. He would get mad if she interrupted him. The lights at Mrs. Edison's house were all out and there was no car in the driveway.

A serpent of smoke arose from the electric outlet, and the room smelled bad.

Roxanne dug around under her bed and found her yellow plastic flip-flops. She ran down the front path to the sidewalk. In the street, cars and trucks and motorcycles sped by in three lanes, honking their horns and playing their car stereos with all the windows open. Her ear ached with reverberation. To the right and left the pedestrian crosswalks looked far away; and even if she ran to the end of the block, there wasn't time to wait for a light. In half a minute there might be flames. Fire trucks would come but too late to save the house from burning to the ground.

She saw a break in the traffic and dashed, getting only as far as the middle lane, where she stood in her yellow flip-flops and shorty pajamas while cars sped by and drivers yelled at her and hooted and blasted her with their horns. A car full of jeering boys in a sharky sedan veered into the middle lane as if they meant to run her down. She turned and looked back at the house. She couldn't remember if she'd turned a light on in the living room. The window glowed yellow.

At the next traffic break she ran, her sandals slapping her heels with a sound like applause.

At the entrance to the bar she pushed the door open with her shoulder. Inside it was dark and it smelled of beer and cigarettes like her parents' bedroom. No one noticed her standing near the door, her eyes searching for a familiar face. She moved a little further into the long, narrow bar, taking short careful steps. From the back she heard the clack of a cue stick hitting a ball and her mother's laugh. Roxanne screamed their names. Not *Mommy* or *Daddy* but *Dale, Ellen.*

Fire!

* * *

Ellen held to a precarious equilibrium, neither asleep nor awake: aware, but disconnected, and unable to wrap her concentration around anything for long. She opened her eyes enough to see through the fringe of her eyelashes and there beside the bed was Roxanne—her difficult, grown-up daughter. And then she saw the other Roxanne, scarecrow-thin with ragged hair, wearing pink-and-yellow-striped shorty pajamas.

All Ellen had wanted was to have a good time, and for this to happen Dale had to be happy and eager to come home to her. A baby she never wanted to begin with, a full-time job, a husband who demanded attention: she couldn't manage it all.

Memory came at her through the moonlight, a streak of bullet light she could not duck.

Someone from the Royal Flush had brought Roxanne back across the street to the house. It wasn't much of a fire, a few sizzled wires and a section of smoldering carpet, but the fire truck came down the street with its sirens wailing; and while their friends from the bar gawked, Ellen and Dale were questioned by the police. They were made to feel like bad children and told not to leave Roxanne alone again. Eventually they drove off, and the fire truck did a U-turn in front of the house; Ellen's and Dale's friends returned to the bar, but because of Roxanne, they had to stay home. They drank beer while they watched *The Tonight Show* with Johnny Carson.

Roxanne complained about her ear and whimpered in bed and they yelled at her.

Shut up or I'll give you something to cry about.

Back then Ellen would do anything Dale wanted if it made him happy to be with her.

Goddamn you, Roxanne.

She wanted her heart to beat in time to his. If she could have synchronized her breath with his, she would have done it.

I've had about enough of you.

Who moved first? Ellen had never been sure. One of them turned the volume on the television up as high as it would go. Maybe he walked ahead or she went first onto the porch. Ellen only had to look at Dale to know what he was thinking and wanting. She got down on her knees and reached under the chaise for one of Roxanne's flip-flops.

Now I'll give you a real earache.

The roots of Ellen's hair were on fire.

Roxanne said, "You're going to be thirsty in the morning, Mom. I'll get you some water so you'll have it when you wake up."

"Stay— About your question..."

"You didn't want me. I get it."

"No—yes, but..." Ellen shook her head and her stomach lurched. "I was alone then too. And afraid." She wanted to fall through cold forever until her memories were iced out. "...I was afraid...if you stayed...I'd... hurt you."

* * *

Ty had fallen asleep reading. Roxanne stood a moment looking down at him, loving him. Her mother was right, time with this man was too precious to waste.

Simone and Johnny had gotten home by ten-thirty. Simone went up to bed immediately, saying nothing to Roxanne; but words weren't necessary when she carried her mood around her like an enveloping black cape. Johnny asked how the children had been and thanked her perfunctorily. Roxanne watched him stand in the kitchen and pour a jigger of vodka from a freezer bottle.

"Is she all right?"

"No. She's pretty low. Which makes two of us." He threw back a second jigger of icy vodka. "You said it this afternoon, Roxanne. You've got a life of your own. Go on home."

She stood on tiptoe and kissed his cheek. "I'll call."

Chowder, curled at Ty's feet, lifted his head and thumped his tail. Gently, she walked over to Ty, removed his glasses, and closed his book, marking his place with a Post-it.

"You!" He pulled her down on top of him. He kissed her, a peck that became slow and warm and deep. "You came back."

"I couldn't wait to get away."

"That bad, huh?"

"Merell's got the idea they might all get sent into foster care. Where do you suppose that came from?"

"Who knows? Harry Potter?" He slipped his hand up under her shirt. "Are you planning to come to bed or are we going to talk about the Durans all night?"

She held his wrist. "I have to tell you something first." She described Ellen's appearance, drunk; what she confessed, and what she, Roxanne, had remembered.

"I always thought she sent me to Gran to get rid of me, because she couldn't be bothered anymore. What I know now... She wanted to protect me." She lay beside him, too tired to undress. "And I think that's why she brought me back from Gran's and put me in charge of Simone. She was at her wit's end with her just like she must have been with me. She wanted me to protect Simone from her."

"That woman's a regular ad for Mother's Day."

"She was just a kid. She didn't really know what was going on herself. And she had the good sense to get rid of me." She touched her ear. "There are worse things than being sent to live with your grandmother."

"And does this change the way things are now?"

She sat up, letting Ty pull her shirt off over her head. "Wherever I was, whatever my life was, I always thought the good stuff was contingent. I don't think I ever stopped believing that if I wasn't a really good sister, Mom could *still* haul me off and dump me somewhere."

"Chow and I will protect you."

She pressed closer to him.

"Aren't you ever going to take your jeans off?" he asked, sounding plaintive.

"If I was orderly, if I organized everything and knew where things were and got A's in school..." *And if Ellen never had to worry or be disturbed*... "So long as I wasn't any trouble to her, I was safe."

"Not quite. You've still got one really big problem and it's getting bigger."

What had she done? What had she left unexplained?

"You think too much." Laughing, he pulled her into his arms.

Sensing a new mood in the room, Chowder jumped off the bed, padded into the living room, and lay down, resting his head on his neatly crossed paws. Outside the moon was a small, white ball tossed too high to chase. On and off through the night he rose from his bed and walked softly from room to room, once or twice standing beside the bed, watching Ty and Roxanne as they slept. He stood guard at the windows in the living room, keeping an eye on the canyon, watching the moon, protecting those he loved.

Chapter 12

The next morning Johnny left for work without waking Simone; and in the middle of the morning his secretary called to say he was in Las Vegas and would be late getting home, she shouldn't wait up. That night she lay in bed watching Conan, but his jokes and interviews couldn't make her smile. Normally Johnny called her several times from work, but on this day, when she most yearned for the reassuring sound of his voice, the phone had been ominously silent. Even Roxanne hadn't called and Ellen stayed in her apartment, no more company than a hermit.

In the empty hours Simone had lined up in her mind all the things she'd said and done wrong over the past weeks and especially last night: her omissions and errors of judgment, all the multiple ways in which she had disappointed Johnny. The list was virtually endless and it wrapped around her like a shroud. She knew that if she died in their bed, if he came home and found her body, he would grieve; but in the secret corners of his heart he would be relieved to be rid of a burden and a worry, a great irritation.

It was almost midnight when she heard the groan of the garage door rising. She switched off the television and burrowed under the bedcovers, pretending to sleep. If he was really angry he would probably wake her, but perhaps his day had been exhausting and he would choose sleep instead. Whichever, she must make sure she did the right thing and pleased him. She held her breath as he came into the bedroom and went directly to his dressing room and shut the door. The shower ran a long time and she fell into a light sleep from which she was awakened by his hand gripping her shoulder.

"I want to talk to you. Sit up."

She rolled over, pushing the hair out of her eyes, and all at once the words and tears rushed out. "I'm so, so sorry, Johnny. Please say you forgive me."

"Don't cry, Simone. I'm over it."

It wasn't hard to say she was sorry. She knew she had behaved very badly at the Judge Roy Price Dinner. Leaving the table during dessert just as the interminable speeches were beginning, she had spent the rest of the evening in a stall in the ladies' room. Johnny had to get her out when it was time to leave.

"Nobody cared I was gone. Hardly anyone spoke to me all night."

"Why should they, Simone? You never have anything to say."

"I would if you'd help me like you used to."

In the early years of their marriage Johnny had prepared her for events like last night's dinner by giving her magazines to read about current affairs and quizzing her on the stories. He talked to her about city and state politics so she would understand the conversations of his friends. She had never found any of this remotely interesting and formed no particular opinions on the subjects others found endlessly engaging: the location of a new airport, negotiations with the pension fund, the ins and outs of city politics. Johnny said it didn't matter if she was interested so long as she pretended to be. With his help she had become expert at pretense.

In those early days Simone had friends, other young women married to rich and prominent men. One had studied marketing in college and another had a degree in music, but none cared to work when they didn't need the money. They were creatively idle and engaged in good works. Simone tagged along frequently enough to be considered one of the group and became the queen of envelope-stuffing. On Tuesdays and Thursdays these women played tennis and she met them for lunch afterward on the terrace at the club. If someone asked her to make up a doubles team, she laughed and said she was a klutz, born to watch sports but never play them. That had been a happy time as Simone remembered it. The women didn't seem to mind that she was quiet during their conversations, a lot of which went right over her head. She knew these expensive and intelligent women included her in their group because Johnny was her husband, that otherwise they would not be interested in her. But sometimes she was funny and they laughed at her jokes and she thought that in a small way they liked her.

After Merell was born she had been too depressed to go out. Occasionally she was invited to lunch or a movie but not often and after a while not at all. When they met at dinners and benefits the women drew Simone aside to ask, their voices just above a whisper and so sympathetic, if it was true she'd had another miscarriage. She sensed how the misses one after another embarrassed and fascinated them. There was a kind of thrill in their horrified sympathy.

Roxanne was the only real friend Simone had ever had unless she counted Shawn Hutton. When Billy Winston called Simone a dummy, Roxanne chased him, caught him, and thumped him until he begged for mercy. In first grade a girl with corn-colored hair called her a retard, but she took it back when Roxanne twisted her arm. And yesterday she had slapped Johnny, defending her. Recalling the shock on his face would make Simone smile for the rest of her life.

"What I said about getting an abortion, you know I didn't mean it. I'd been upset all day."

"You're upset *every* day."

He sat on the edge of the bed, his shoulders bent, reminding Simone of his father, who had risen every morning before sunrise and carried bricks on his back for eight or ten hours. A wash of love and regret overcame her, and she laid her head against Johnny's shoulder, feeling the damp warmth of his freshly washed skin on her cheek, the citrus fragrance of his cologne. She didn't have fingers and toes to list all the times and ways she had let Johnny down. "You'd be happier with someone else."

"Leave it, Simone. I'm too tired to talk about this."

"I'll try harder." To be estranged from him in any way was unbearable. "I promise I will, Johnny."

"Let's just get you into the third trimester. You'll feel better then."

The late months of pregnancy were her reward, a time when she fell under the enchantment of her body's astounding ability to stretch and shift and make room, always more room. At night the baby kicked or rolled or jabbed her with its bony elbows and her bladder was under constant pressure, but she didn't mind being kept awake because after a day when her hips and knees and back—even her feet and toes!—ached as if the bones would shatter under the strain, lying down was a blessing for a few moments, until even being stretched out flat became uncomfortable. Mostly, during the last trimester she lived in a kind of daze, her mind clouded by the miracle that she who was unable to serve a tennis ball or properly pronounce the governor's name could create a human life and hold it inside her for nine months, until it was more perfectly accomplished than anything Johnny built or Roxanne crossed off her endless lists. She liked that her belly grew huge and cumbersome and seemed to roll out ahead of her so that people in stores and on the street smiled when they saw her coming and moved aside to make room. Anyone looking at her could see that she wasn't just a pretty, slow-witted girl pointlessly taking up space in the world, that she had importance, a purpose, a reason for breathing and being.

She ran her hand down the swale of Johnny's backbone. "Did you have a bad day?"

"Long," he said, stretching. "These Chinese guys are really perfectionists and working with an interpreter slows everything down. It bugs me I never know what the dudes are really saying to each other."

He talked, and she let her thoughts drift away and back again. Eventually, talked out, he pulled the sheet over them. "How'd you manage without Franny?"

"I called Roxanne three times, but she didn't answer. I left messages."

"She's got her own life, Simone. You forget that sometimes."

"Merell was good."

Morning and afternoon, while Simone dozed intermittently on the sectional in the family room, Merell had kept Valli and Victoria occupied. At lunchtime she found a chicken-and-rice casserole in the freezer, and Simone put it in the microwave. They had eaten the leftovers for dinner.

"Olivia?" Johnny asked, his voice drowsy.

Simone had put the baby in her crib and closed the door. She and Merell and the twins went into the tot lot and she pushed them in the swings and on the merry-go-round. It was quiet in the house when they went back inside and watched a video.

"I think maybe she's getting better."

"We can all hope for a miracle." He yawned again. "I'm going to call Alicia, get her over here to help out for a few days. She might be better than someone from the agency."

An arrow of alarm shot through Simone. Mention of Johnny's oldest sister confirmed her fear that his forgiveness was conditional. Simone had to remodel herself or Alicia would come in and take over everything. Childless Alicia had been divorced for decades and had run the accounting office of Duran Construction like a totalitarian state before she retired. If she walked into the house carrying a suitcase, she'd never leave.

"You know she doesn't like me." Simone pressed herself against him, whispering. "Be patient with me, Johnny."

"I've been patient since the day we got married. It gets old, Simone. If there was just something you knew how to do, that you liked to do, you'd have a reason to get up in the morning. If you weren't so fucking helpless."

He threw his forearm up over his eyes. "I can't come home to disaster every day. And forget about me, it's not good for the girls either. Firing Franny was the last straw,

Simone. You've done a lot of stupid things but that was the worst. We needed her to make this work."

"You wouldn't divorce me, would you?" She blurted the horrible question without thinking, followed by a short, squealing giggle unlike any sound she'd ever made.

"No, honey, not divorce, never divorce. I'll always take care of you. I promised that. But maybe we could make some kind of arrangement. Alicia could live here. She could manage the kids and the house."

"She's too bossy, Johnny, and the girls don't like her."

"You could have your own little house."

"I don't want my own house, I want you."

"The girls and I would live with Alicia and you'd see them, of course."

She was terrified into silence.

"And then if you got better..."

"I'm not sick!"

"You're miserable all the time, Simone."

"I can be happy."

"And you lie in bed like an invalid. If you'd just *do* something."

I am doing something, she thought. *I'm having another baby. For you.*

"You knew what I was like when you married me. Why did you marry me?"

Convulsively, he grabbed her, pulling her close. "Because you were beautiful and I could see our children in you. My son."

He pushed her away, making a sound—a sigh mixed up with a laugh or a sob. She didn't know what a sound like that meant, and she was afraid to ask.

*   *   *

Ellen spent Wednesday mousing around her apartment in her dressing gown, eating nothing but aspirin and a few saltines, and drinking flat ginger ale to settle her stomach. Her phone rang and she didn't answer it. She left her computer unopened. She did not fully remember Tuesday night after she left the Mariposa but she must have gone somewhere else; there was Scotch all over her dress. The blackout had brought back too vividly the memory of her years with Dale, and if she could have crawled under the house to hide from herself she would have done it. Later in the day, when her brain had stopped banging against her skull, her mind cleared enough for her to remember what BJ used to say, that no experience was so terrible it couldn't be learned from: no more drinking and no more online and telephone love affairs.

By Wednesday she felt herself to be back on track.

During her twenty-four-hour recuperation she did a lot of hard thinking and admitted to herself that she was never going to be happy while she lived over Johnny's vintage-car garage. Ellen wasn't cut out to be a boarder; and nice as it was, this apartment would never be home. But she could not just leave with the home situation so precarious. First something would have to be done about Simone for the sake of the children. Ellen and Johnny were going to have a good talk and she would share some down-home truth about his wife. If she had to tell him what really happened at the swimming pool that made Merell call 911, she would even do that.

But by the time she got down to the house on Thursday morning Johnny had already left for work. Upstairs she found Simone dressing for the day and abuzz with determined energy. There had been a girl in one of BJ's offices years ago who chewed amphetamines like breath mints.

"Have you taken something?"

"What?" Simone asked. "You mean Xanax? Hardly!"

"Where did all this energy come from?" Simone had showered, and the door to her steamy bathroom was open, filling the bedroom with the fragrance of lemon leaves. "Are you sure you're not taking diet pills or something?"

"The kids and I are going to make cupcakes." Simone's beauty had a fire in it when she was manic. "Want to help us?"

On Ellen's list of one hundred possibilities for the day, baking with her daughter and granddaughters had its own special place at the very bottom. Still, she wondered if it was safe to leave Simone alone, and did her resolve to be the new and improved Ellen require that she make cupcakes?

"Where's Merell? Will she be here?"

"Of course. School doesn't start until next week."

"Let her help you, Simone. Don't try to do too much."

"I'm fine, Mom. Really. You don't have to hang around. You have plans?" She cocked an eyebrow. "Coffee date?"

Ellen felt her cheeks flush. Matter-of-factly, she said, "I'm having breakfast at the Hob Nob. Alone. After that, I have some appointments."

She would order poached eggs and bacon and read the real estate listings while she ate. Since early that morning her mind had been occupied with plans.

Though Ellen had been half out of her mind for several months after BJ died, she was not so far gone that she let any of her licenses lapse. She had sold the Vadis Group and the new owners had kept the name to capitalize on the reputation of the firm. They would hire her back but she didn't want to work for anyone.

She liked the highbrow ring of *Ellen Vadis Properties*.

* * *

In the kitchen Valli announced, "The milk's got chunks."

"I'll take care of it," Simone said. "Merell, go around the house and check the windows, make sure they're closed."

The air conditioner whirred noisily as it struggled to cool the big house.

Merell said, "Daddy says it's broken." She pointed to a printed sheet of numbers tacked to the wall next to the phone. "You can call the repairman."

"Just close the windows like I told you to. We'll keep the cool air inside."

In the pantry there was a big box of powdered milk she would mix with cold water and whirl in the blender. If she rinsed out the carton of sour milk and poured in the reconstituted, the twins wouldn't know the difference, and Merell could do without if she didn't like it.

The pantry smelled of onions and old apples, of a life far away from the one she was living. Simone wished she could pull the door shut and just sit in that place for a while, breathing in the comforting, rural smell; but she had a full day ahead of her, and it was going to be a wonderful day. It had to be. What was the saying? *Today is the first day of the rest of your life.*

For now she would pretend that everything Johnny had said last night was a nasty dream; and if his words came into her mind, she drove them away by singing the alphabet song. The twins thought this was hilarious and joined in at the top of their lungs; and then they all got silly, mixing up the letters on purpose, and Simone forgot what she didn't want to remember.

She found the dry milk, and while she was about it she grabbed up the flour and sugar and chocolate she knew she'd need for cupcakes.

In the kitchen she sang out, "Countdown to cupcakes! Ready-set-go in a few minutes." She set the canisters of flour and sugar on the counter.

"Mrs. Duran." Celia, the housekeeper, stood between the kitchen and the family room with a dust rag in her hand. Though she had been with the Durans since Merell was an only child, Simone had never warmed to her. "Upstairs already it's hot."

"Well, I can't help that. The air conditioner's on as high as it'll go. Complain to Mr. Duran if you're unhappy. Did you check Olivia?"

"Is not my job to babysit."

"I know that, but it wouldn't kill you to look at her."

"She not crying."

"Never mind then, just do your work."

Simone stared at the directions on the side of the powdered milk box until they made sense, dug around in drawers and cupboards for the measuring cups, and poured dry milk into one of them. There was probably an expiration date printed somewhere on the box but she didn't want to know it. Watching every move she made, the twins pressed against her until they made her skin itch and she pushed them away. The reconstituted milk roared in the blender.

"Are we having a milkshake?" Valli asked.

"I want chocolate."

Well, why not? Simone thought with a bounce of happiness. It was already hot and ice cream was a dairy product. Calcium for the bones.

The twins cheered as she dropped enormous scoops of chocolate ice cream into the blender, whirled it again, and poured it into tall plastic glasses. "Drink fast," she said.

When Merell returned to the kitchen the twins were

outside in their play yard, and Simone was putting their drinking glasses into the dishwasher.

"What's for breakfast?"

"Toast." Something wormy and resentful in Simone wouldn't let her make a milkshake for this daughter. "And peanut butter."

"We ate all the peanut butter yesterday. For snack."

"Have jam then, or cheese. Don't say it. There's no cheese."

"Do you want me to write a list for Celia?"

"I don't want you to do anything except eat if you're hungry and then watch your sisters."

Merell got a box of crackers from the cupboard and smeared several with strawberry jam.

"You know what, Mommy? I saw on TV, you can order groceries by computer and they get delivered in a van." She shoved a cracker in her mouth and wiped her sticky fingers on her shorts. "You don't even have to leave the house. And the man'll bring the bags in too, so you don't have to carry anything."

"What makes you think I don't want to shop?"

"You could tell me what to get and I could order for you."

Johnny had bought Merell a computer when she turned seven. Simone had no idea how it worked and was afraid to ask, dreading the humiliation, already knowing it would be too complicated for her.

"I can live without you managing my life, Merell. You're as bad as Roxanne." *And Alicia.*

She felt the first pinch of a headache, the kind that began between her shoulder blades and groped its claws up the back of her neck, dug under her skull. Aspirin couldn't touch it but she swallowed four anyway.

Merell sat on the counter and watched her. "Mommy, are you going to have another baby?"

Simone opened a cupboard and took down a blue-and-white-striped coffee mug and then put it back. It was too hot for coffee. A shadow of profound, bone-melting lassitude fell over her.

God, no, not today. Please, not today.

"I like babies, Mommy."

"Well, that's lucky because you're going to be helping me take care of this one. And Olivia. And the twins." And after this one, another and another until Johnny got his boy.

She poured a glass of ice water from the spigot on the front of the refrigerator and drank it down without breathing. A fist of numbing cold slugged the back of her throat.

"Mommy, I bet if you called up Nanny Franny she'd come back. She likes us."

"I don't want her back, Merell. And I wish to God you'd quit telling me what to do." The muscles in her neck weren't strong enough to hold up her head.

"Is anyone coming to help us? Can I call Aunt Roxanne?"

"Use the brains God gave you, Merell. Your aunt's got a job, she's a teacher. It's Thursday and school is in session."

Merell tugged hard on her bangs.

"You'll go bald if you keep doing that. Make yourself even uglier."

Merell's expression pinched; and Simone wished she could take the spiteful and unkind words back. Merell couldn't help being someone else's baby, it wasn't her fault that she'd been switched in the hospital nursery, exchanged for Simone's real child, a baby boy. Voices in Simone's head—a chorus of Johnny and Ellen and Roxanne—told her that never happened, that it was a crazy thought; but Simone didn't know if it was or not. There were times when she just couldn't tell where the truth stopped and imagination began.

If you weren't so helpless . . .

She hummed the alphabet song and focused on gathering the necessary ingredients and equipment for making cupcakes. One afternoon, watching the cooking channel from her bed, she had seen a stout, dark-haired woman make chocolate cupcakes in about five minutes. Measure the dry ingredients, then the wet. Mix and put in the oven. What could be simpler?

She opened several cupboard doors before she found

the mixing bowls and all the while she felt Merell watching her, assessing her, passing judgment.

"What *is* it?"

"My school starts on Monday, Mommy. If I don't have the right clothes the other girls'll laugh at me. They won't want to be my friends."

"What's wrong with your clothes?"

"I need a special school uniform. I'm in the Upper Primary now. Remember?"

Johnny's saintly battle-ax sister, Alicia, would never forget something like a school uniform. Roxanne would write it on one of her lists. "I'm sorry, baby, I forgot again."

"Can I ask Aunt Roxanne to take me? We could go tonight. The stores are open until late."

Oh, what the hell.

"Go ahead."

"I love you, Mommy." Merell bounced off the kitchen stool, springs in her legs. "I love you more than anyone in the whole world."

Olivia had painted her sheet, the crib, and herself with the contents of her diaper. Simone backed out of the nursery, yelling for Celia.

"I can't do it. I'm pregnant. I'll throw up."

"Babies is not my job." Sweat shone on Celia's forehead and curled her dark hair. "Johnny tol' me I don't do babysitting."

"This is cleaning. The crib . . . the wall . . ."

Simone watched Celia's expression as she considered the situation. "Start with Olivia, okay. Put her in the tub."

"Who gonna watch her in the tub?"

"I don't know. You, I suppose. You can sit down for a change. It'll be a nice rest."

"I tol' you—"

Simone's almost automatic reaction was to scream and then to cry; but she controlled the impulse because this day had to be a new beginning. A thought flashed across her mind. If this wasn't a new beginning, what was it? An ending?

She tried to put some steel in her voice. "I can't do it, Celia."

"I still gotta vacuum Mr. Johnny's office and then I gotta go to the market."

"Merell's making a list."

"I got my own list." Celia looked at the door to Olivia's room and wrinkled her nose. A half smile dimpled her cheek. "That baby, she made a big mess."

"You knew? You went in there and saw it and then you just left her?"

"Mrs. Duran, I got plenty to do without babysitting."

"I'll give you twenty dollars extra."

"Is not the money—"

"And another twenty if you'll keep her out of my hair for a while."

"Johnny don' like it if the house is dirty."

"You clean six days a week. How can it possibly be dirty?"

"Okay, okay."

Simone hefted the big upright mixer out of the pantry. It weighed more than one of the twins, and she bet the dark-haired woman on television had never tried to lift hers. She set it on the counter and cleared a space beside it. In a cookbook she'd gotten as a wedding shower gift she found a simple recipe for chocolate cake, and she began to look around for the rest of what she needed.

The twins, watching television in the family room, ignored her when she called them; and they complained noisily when she stood in front of the big screen, blocking their view. "Go wash up so we can make cupcakes."

Holding hands, grumbling and giggling, the twins ambled off in the direction of the bathroom next to the laundry room. Their little backs and tangled hair and shuffling barefoot walk looked odd and pitiful to Simone. She wondered what mischievous spirit had been present in the bedroom when she, who had never truly wanted even one baby, conceived two at the same time.

"Mommy?" Merell said. "The baby's crying again."

"Celia's taking care of her."

"I think I know why she's crying. I made a bottle for her when I got up, but she likes cereal and applesauce for breakfast."

Food for Olivia hadn't occurred to Simone. At the moment she couldn't even remember what the baby ate from day to day.

"What did you put in the bottle? The milk has chunks."

"I opened one of those cans of formula."

Merell was all the things Simone wasn't: active, resourceful, responsible. It was a small thing to thank this child, and yet the words jammed at the back of Simone's throat.

Eventually the twins wandered back from washing their hands, their T-shirts and shorts soaked down the front. Simone realized she had been standing in the kitchen doing nothing. Time had passed but she had no idea how much.

"Where's the cupcakes?" Valli asked.

"Go outside. I'll call you when I want you."

"You said—"

"Go."

She sat in the kitchen, reading and rereading the cake recipe, trying to make sense of it. She forgot about her daughters and the print blurred in front of her eyes.

Merell appeared in the kitchen with the baby on her hip. The little one wore clean overalls and her hair was still damp from washing. Merell put her in her high chair and Simone watched her move about the kitchen efficiently, warming formula in the microwave to mix with a packet of oatmeal, humming a little tune Simone recognized as the theme from *Shrek.* Between spoonfuls of cereal and applesauce Olivia smiled and whacked her hands on the tray of her chair. She had three teeth and it seemed as if Simone had never seen them before. Merell talked to her, coaxing her to open her mouth wide.

She's a better mother than I am.

More time drifted by.

The roots of the headache sank between Simone's shoulder blades, the trunk rose up her neck, and the branches spread from ear to ear and throbbed with life. She thought it strange that when she touched the back of her head she couldn't feel the tree-shaped headache under her fingers. Could it kill, a headache like this? Death did not seem so terrible.

For some time now Merell and Olivia had been stacking plastic blocks on the floor of the family room. A book was open beside them.

Merell said, "Franny always gave Olivia a bottle in the middle of the morning when she takes her nap. Do you want me to give it to her in her crib?"

Simone saw that when Olivia wasn't crying, she was pretty: brown eyes and a round face framed by dark hair. Johnny's sisters all had girls who looked like Olivia. But she's mine, I made her, Simone thought. She grew inside me. The pulsing headache receded, and she felt a warmth she recognized as love for poor, usually bawling Olivia. She wanted to do something special for her.

"Let's put her outside. Fresh air will do her good."

"In her playpen?"

"Good idea." She thought of the big wicker laundry basket full of clean sheets she'd seen on the washing machine. "She can sleep in the laundry basket."

Merell looked doubtful. "It's a really hot day."

"We'll put her in the shade, of course."

"What if the sun moves?"

"After we make the cupcakes she can come inside and we'll have a party. I think she's old enough to eat cake, don't you?"

Simone imagined her four daughters gathered at the table with dish towels tied around their necks to keep their clothes clean, their fingers and faces covered with chocolate cake and frosting.

In the deep shade under the avocado tree at the far end of the terrace Simone opened the playpen and put the basket full of clean sheets and pillow slips inside it. Olivia was a small baby and reluctant to explore her world. With encouragement she sat up on her own and rolled over, but she had not begun to crawl and showed no eagerness to stand. The laundry basket was the perfect fit for her.

You're like me, Simone thought, arranging the sheets to prop the baby bottle. She had produced a little girl as tiny and slow-moving as she had been. *You'll grow up just like me.* But Johnny didn't want any of their daughters to be like her. *Stupid and helpless.*

She looked down at her baby and felt herself begin to break under the weight of love and certain failure, more than anyone should have to bear.

Chapter 13

Merell's mother had gone upstairs hours ago, promising to come back down when her head didn't hurt so much. The twins were whiny because there were no cupcakes, but Merell wasn't disappointed. She understood that her mother's intentions had been good.

Merell cleaned up the kitchen, the scattered flour on the counter, and the spilled sugar that crunched underfoot. She put the eggs back in the refrigerator and went outside to play in the tot lot with her sisters. Lunchtime came and went and the twins complained that they were starving, but the peanut butter was gone and though the freezer was packed with frozen meals, Merell was forbidden to use the microwave without an adult. She thought about asking Celia to do it, but the housekeeper was polishing and dusting in the living room no one ever used, and cleaning up Olivia's mess had put her in a sour mood that told Merell she'd better stay away. She hated being bossed around in a language she didn't understand.

The idea of learning Spanish reminded her of school and her uniform. She left a message on Aunt Roxanne's cell phone, begging like a baby.

Merell finally got sick of Valli and Victoria blubbering about how they were starving and called the nearest Domino's and ordered a large extra-cheese pizza. To pay for it, she found her mother's purse in her study and took a ten- and two five-dollar bills out of the wallet.

Several times during the day Merell checked on Olivia. Sometimes she was asleep, but when her eyes were open she seemed happy just to lie on her back playing with her fascinating feet. Merell wondered if Olivia would be smart like she was or more like the twins. Eventually the baby got tired of her toes and cried, but not the screaming cries associated with acid reflux. Merell understood these to be *I'm bored, pay attention to me* cries and put her in the stroller and pushed it around the house and up and down the driveway a dozen times, which seemed to make Olivia happy. Victoria and Valli rode their pink-and-yellow bikes with training wheels. After a while Celia asked Merell to unlock the gate across the driveway, and she drove the Mercedes to the supermarket. She liked to take the big car into her sister's neighborhood and show off. She wouldn't be back with groceries until late afternoon. The twins begged Merell to play school but Merell preferred to hold Olivia in her lap and swing with her. The breeze felt almost cool. She wondered if she should take Olivia into the house where the air conditioner, after going on and off all morning for no reason, now blew a steady, frigid wind. The twins complained that it was like the North Pole. Merell thought Nanny Franny would say that fresh air was the best thing for a baby, so she put Olivia back in the laundry basket, pulling it close to the trunk of the avocado where the shade was deepest. She put on a sweater and in the family room she lay on the couch and read about Harry Potter and his friends. Time always went fast when she was reading.

Victoria ran in from outside screaming, "Baby Libia's all red. And there's bees on her."

Merell had never realized how rapidly the sun traveled across the sky. It had moved out from behind the avocado tree and was shining directly on the base of the trunk where she had resettled the laundry basket. Olivia's bottle had fallen to the side in the basket and dripped on the pile of sheets and pillowcases. Where milk had seeped beneath her head, her fine, dark hair was gluey and stuck to the laundry. Striped yellow jacket wasps, drawn by the sweetness of the formula, crowded on her sticky cheeks and swarmed around her hair and ears. Her cheeks and forehead and the top of her head were sunburned a bright pink, and her eyes were glassy slits between her swollen eyelids. She tried to cry, managing only a dry, cracked sound like a frog learning to croak.

Fear exploded through Merell's body. She waved her hands right into the buzzing midst of the yellow jackets, ignoring the vibrations of their angry bodies against her fingers, grabbed Olivia's wrists, and dragged her up into her arms. The baby's head fell to one side and the wasps swarmed and landed again, some of them on Merell. Feeling their tiny feet on her skin, she screamed and staggered across the terrace to a wicker chaise shaded by an awning.

"Where's Franny?" Valli whined.

"Shut up, I have to think."

Wearing only a white bra and bikini briefs, Merell's mother lay on her back, snoring gently. Awake, she would be no help, but Merell had come to her anyway, not knowing what else to do. Gramma Ellen had driven somewhere without saying good-bye, and she wasn't answering her cell phone. Celia wouldn't be back until she'd spent a lot of money and had coffee with her sister. Daddy was in Las Vegas. Merell tried calling Franny's cell phone but it rang and rang and there was no voice telling her to leave a message at the tone. At the lake Aunt Roxanne had written down her cell phone number and given it to Merell. She had been afraid of losing the paper so she had memorized the numbers on it. Merell left a message telling her to come soon because something terrible had happened and she wasn't kidding. She repeated this twice.

She thought about calling 911 again. The police would come, and this time no one would be able to save Mommy from trouble. The secret Merell held grew enormous inside her. The police would make her confess it and she would be punished, banished to a foster home. But whatever happened to her, it would be much worse for her mother.

On Simone's bedside table Merell saw an amber-colored pill bottle lying open on its side. She replaced the lid and read the label. It was the only word Merell had ever seen that began and ended with X.

Simone sighed and threw her left arm up. Merell stared at her underarm, at the prickles of black hair spiking there. She inhaled the sour scent of her mother's body, repelled and attracted at the same time. Of all her mother's identities—mother, wife, woman—it was woman that fascinated her and filled her mind with questions. She knew—though she could not quite believe—that one day she too would be a woman with breasts and hair in hidden places. But how was she to know the right way to be a woman if no one told her? She loved her mother at the same time she pitied her, understanding that she did not know how to be a woman or a mother any better than Merell. The pity shamed her. She had read many books about girls growing up, and not one of the heroines had ever felt sorry for her own mother.

Her mother did not know how to act like a mother, but her body knew how to have babies anyway. Merell had gone online and seen a photo of a baby's head emerging from a red and bloody wound. She hated to think of this, hated knowing that she had once been part of her mother's body and had entered the world through the secret place between her legs and caused her an unspeakable pain. She laid her hand on her mother's stomach, felt it rise and fall with each inhalation.

Be a boy. Mommy will love you if you're a boy.

Downstairs, the twins stood guard over Olivia on the chaise.

"Libia needs a bath," Valli said.

For once her little sister made sense and Merell wished she'd had the idea herself. With one arm under the baby's bottom and the other around her back, she carried her sister into the house and down the back hall. The house was cold but Olivia radiated a damp, sticky heat. In the bathroom two inches of water stood in the tub and there was more pooled all over the floor where the twins had played earlier. Merell slipped out of her sandals and sat in the tub.

"Mommy's gonna be mad," Valli said. "You can't wear clothes in the bathtub."

"Yeah, Mommy's gonna be mad." Victoria held her hands on her hips.

The twins prattled but Merell ignored the irritation, facing the faucet with Olivia between her legs. She turned on the cold water and gently dribbled handfuls over the baby's head and body, soaking her. Olivia flinched at the touch of the cold water, her eyes popped open, and her arms jerked out, pinwheeling. She began to scream and Merell hoped this was a good sign.

"You're in trouble, Merell. You made Libia cry."

A red plastic cup sat on the corner edge of the bathtub. Merell filled it with water and held it to Olivia's lips.

"She can't use a cup yet," Valli said. "She likes a bottle."

"Go get one."

Merell filled the plastic bottle from the tap and screwed the nipple top tight. She held it against Olivia's chapped mouth, but she seemed to have forgotten how to suck.

Merell's heart sank.

The children turned at the sound of a door slamming and footsteps. Aunt Roxanne called, "Merell, where are you?"

Victoria ran into the family room calling, "Merell did something bad."

Merell cried with relief when she saw her aunt standing in the bathroom door.

"I came as soon as I could."

Immediately, she knew what to do. She knelt beside the tub and the twins hung on her shoulders and pulled on her arms, chattering excited versions of the day's events and blaming Merell for every bad thing that had ever happened. Normally Merell would have defended herself, but she was too relieved and grateful to care how they went on.

"Twins, be quiet. Merell, you tell me."

She stumbled over her words but her aunt seemed to understand.

"Well, the first thing we have to do is cool this pumpkin down."

Celia came home with bags of groceries in the trunk of the Mercedes, and Aunt Roxanne stormed at her for leaving Merell and her sisters alone when Simone was napping. Celia tried to make excuses and Roxanne said she didn't have time to listen.

"I want you to stay here and watch the twins and if my sister wakes up, tell her we've gone to urgent care."

At the hospital the nurses and doctors made a fuss over Olivia, and finally Merell realized that everything would be all right and her knotted stomach relaxed and her hands stopped making fists.

Olivia was given fluids and the sunburn was treated. She had one yellow jacket sting on the back of her thigh. On the examination table in the emergency room she looked pink and peaceful in her tipped-back car seat. Merell thought they would leave the hospital then, but a nurse said they had to wait to see another doctor. This doctor had a clipboard and at first Merell wasn't sure he was a real doctor because his white coat was so perfectly clean and ironed, but his name tag said he was Jerry Hamid, M.D. He asked Aunt Roxanne some questions and watched her face intently when she answered. Sometimes he made notes.

"I'm going to have to write this up," he said, motioning with his clipboard. "This baby was neglected to the point—"

Aunt Roxanne interrupted him, but in a polite way. "Dr. Hamid, I'm not minimizing this, I know a sunburn's serious. But my sister's pregnant and not well. She has four young children, and normally she has help, but today she didn't. She put Olivia outside in what seemed to be a safe place and then . . . She has three other children. It was just more than she could handle. Today."

Dr. Hamid chewed on the end of his pencil the way Merell's teachers said was bad. He had chocolate-syrup eyes with thick lids, and he didn't blink as he looked back and forth between Merell and her aunt. "How did you get involved, Mrs. Callahan?"

"My sister called me at work."

The lie astonished Merell.

"And where is the mother now?" he asked. "Why isn't she here with her baby?"

"She's home," Roxanne said. "She was in no condition to drive so I left her with the other children. . . ."

"What do you mean, 'no condition'?"

"Well, she's upset, of course. Who wouldn't be?"

"She's alone with the children."

"The housekeeper's with her."

"You just told me she didn't have help."

"She didn't. Not earlier in the day."

Dr. Hamid wrote something on his clipboard.

"Look, it was a judgment call on my part." Aunt Roxanne made her voice sound everyday friendly. "I just thought she'd be better off at home with her kids."

She didn't sound like herself when she lied. It was lucky Dr. Hamid was a stranger or he would have known she wasn't telling the truth exactly.

Merell said, "My daddy's in Las Vegas."

"On business," Roxanne said.

"I see." Now Dr. Hamid tapped his pen against the side of his nose. Merell knew he was worried about Olivia. "I want to see this baby again in a couple of days. And I want the mother with her." He drew his phone from his pocket and moved his fingers on the keys even faster than Daddy. "I've made a note to myself that if I don't see Olivia and her mother by Monday next week, I'll file a report with protective services."

In the car Merell asked, "What's protective services?"

Roxanne adjusted her rearview mirror. "An office that looks after children."

"Like foster children?"

"That and other things."

"What other things?" Merell knew her aunt didn't want to answer questions, but she asked again, "What other things?"

"I don't know, Merell." Aunt Roxanne started the car and backed out of the parking space. She turned out of the parking lot onto Torrey Pines Road. To the right, between the trees, Merell could see the flat line of the ocean, a darker blue than the sky. "Child welfare, I suppose. Abuse. Neglect."

"Will I get in trouble?"

Roxanne took her eyes off the road for a second. "You've done nothing wrong, Merell."

"What about Mommy? Is she in trouble?"

"She'll bring Olivia back in a couple of days and everything'll be fine."

Merell didn't know how this could be managed. She would be in school and with Franny gone there was no one to take care of the twins.

"Do you think Olivia was neglected?" It was a heavy-sounding word Merell had never said before.

Aunt Roxanne turned the car off the road and onto a side street. She parked and shut off the ignition.

"What's the matter? Why'd you park here?"

Aunt Roxanne let out a long sigh and closed her eyes for a moment.

"Yeah. I think she was neglected."

"I should have brought her inside, huh?"

"It wasn't you, you didn't neglect her. You behaved responsibly, and that's great because it shows how smart and strong you are. But you're a little girl and taking care of your sisters shouldn't be your job."

"You told the doctor that Mommy's upset but she's not. She's asleep. You didn't tell the doctor about the XX pills."

Aunt Roxanne drummed her fist on the steering wheel.

"You lied."

"It's complicated, Merell."

Complicated wasn't an answer.

Merell didn't want Aunt Roxanne to be like all the other grown-ups in her life, saying things that weren't true or making excuses that didn't explain anything at all. Merell wanted to know *why* Aunt Roxanne hadn't told Dr. Hamid the whole truth and *why* children couldn't tell lies when grown-ups did all the time. It hurt to think about these questions. She didn't like not knowing things and wished she could turn off her mind like a television set or press the double-arrow button and repeat the good times, fast-forward through the bad. She wanted to be the twins' age again, back when she did what she was told whether the rules made sense or not. When she was as young as they were, she had thought that she understood what it meant to be honest, and she had tried hard not to lie even if it meant she sometimes got in trouble for hitting the twins or eating their Halloween candy. Daddy said he trusted her because he could always count on her to be truthful. Now she knew people lied all the time, whenever they wanted to. She felt tricked.

She looked out the car window at the street she had never seen before and her thoughts drifted to wondering what it would be like to live alone in a town where every street was as unfamiliar as this one, where the houses had no numbers, and there were no signs, no helpful people offering directions. Inside every building something dangerous hid, holding its breath, waiting to pounce. Life was like such a town. No street names or numbers, no map or guidebook, nowhere absolutely and positively safe.

Aunt Roxanne held Merell's hands and kissed the palms. It was a funny thing to do, peculiar and tickly.

"Sometimes, Merell, it's best to leave out the details when you answer a question. Sometimes details confuse the truth."

Merell looked out the windshield at the quiet suburban street, empty of people, not even a cat ambling along the top of a wall. She wiped a tear from her cheek and wondered if the people living in the big houses without numbers and with blank, staring-eye windows ever wished they lived somewhere else, far away.

Aunt Roxanne said, "If you and I had told that doctor exactly all the details of what happened today, it would have taken a very long time; and probably he would have understood eventually. But Dr. Hamid doesn't have time for the whole story with every detail. And he might not listen carefully. There's even a chance he might not understand that life is very hard for your mother even though she does the best she can, and we're all trying to make things better. So it was just simpler for me to leave out the details." She looked like she had a stomach cramp. "Simpler and safer."

Merell thought this over a moment, weighing Aunt Roxanne's words carefully. So this was the truth, finally. Lying wasn't a bad thing or a good thing either. Sometimes it was just necessary, the simple and safe thing to do.

Chapter 14

Simone, we have to talk." Roxanne shut the bedroom door and walked across the room to where her sister sat on the bed. Her face was flushed and tearstained.

"Olivia's fine but you have to go back to urgent care before Monday or they're going to file a report." She sat on the edge of the bed. "If that happens, there'll be an investigation."

"You'll come with me?"

"Johnny will go with you."

"No, he won't. He has to work. And I don't want . . . I don't . . ." She hiccupped a sob. "I can't tell him what happened. If I do . . ." She covered her face. "You have to help me, Rox. I swear on my children's lives, I'll never ask you for anything ever again."

Her promise meant nothing. In a week or a day she would forget she'd made it.

"He wants to separate. I'll have my own house and Alicia will stay here and take care of the girls."

"I'm sure he doesn't mean it, Simone." Roxanne felt oddly aloof from her sister, concerned but disconnected, and she knew this was the way it had to be. "Johnny's tired and under a lot of pressure."

"I never should have had any children."

"Stop feeling sorry for yourself."

"They'd be better off never born."

"Get off the bed, put on some clothes, and go downstairs. You don't have to do anything except sit in the family room and make sure no one has a fatal accident. You can do that much. Celia's going to make dinner for you."

"I hate her food."

"Too bad. You'll have to force it down."

"Why are you being so mean?"

"I'm being realistic and I want you to be the same."

Roxanne's choices were clear: she could sit on the bed and hold Simone's hand, on Monday she could give up a day of school and take Simone and the baby to urgent care for Dr. Hamid's approval. She could spend the rest of her life protecting Simone from the consequences of her actions.

No. No to all of it.

"I called Johnny. He's still in Nevada but he'll be home by eight."

"I don't want to see him."

Roxanne wasn't going to follow that line of conversation.

"Merell needs a school uniform. I'm going to take her down to Macy's and get that taken care of."

"What's wrong with me? Why doesn't he love me any—?"

"Johnny loves you, Simone. This isn't about love."

"I just wanted to make cupcakes. . . ."

Roxanne thought of her babysitter, Mrs. Edison, teaching her to read using *The Fannie Farmer Cookbook* as a text, and the way she'd thought that Bakersfield meant a field of bakers. She remembered being five years old, driving north on Highway 99 with no idea where she was going or why; and as if it had happened only the day before, she felt the intense reality of childhood: longing to grow up, doomed to grow up, not quite believing it would ever happen. But it had and it would be just so for Merell and the twins too. Only for Simone was it different. Only she would stay as she was, a little girl in a woman's beautiful body.

"I'll call Franny," Simone said. "I'll say I'm sorry and then she'll come back."

"I already tried the number she left. She's gone."

"Gone where?" As if Franny should have stayed around waiting to be insulted again.

"After we get her uniform, Merell and I will have dinner."

"And you won't tell Johnny? We'll go see the doctor, you and me?"

"I'll come back here with Merell and wait up with you until Johnny gets home."

Simone grabbed a handful of hair, curled it around her index finger and twisted it.

"I'll stay with you and you can explain everything that happened. Then you and your husband can figure out what to do next."

"No."

Roxanne put her hand over Simone's and gently pulled her fingers back, letting the corkscrewed hair unwind. She said, "I'll be with you, Simone, but you must tell Johnny everything that happened today and then you and he will figure out what to do about Dr. Hamid."

* * *

Simone lay on the bed, half-paralyzed with fear.

Alicia.

An arrangement.

A separation.

How many times had she wanted to wake up in a house without the clacketing demands of children? Now she saw that it would be hell: the twins' idiotic chatter, Olivia crying, Merell knowing everything; this confusion was what gave her life a shape. Without it what was the point? What would she do if she had a little house all to herself? Right then she wanted to bring the girls into bed with her, close the door and hold them so tight they couldn't speak. They would lie there together until Johnny came home and when he saw how sweet and peaceful they were he would be sorry he'd made threats.

Before Johnny, Shawn Hutton had loved her.

How strange it was that until last month she hadn't thought of Shawn for years. Or of sailing, for that matter. Now they were both in her mind all the time. Even when she wasn't thinking about them, they were nearby waiting for her attention. Perhaps they had been there all along but she was too busy with children and Johnny to notice.

She closed her eyes and saw Shawn as he was at seventeen. Big teeth, eyes the color of turquoise water, nose always pink and peeling. Such a funny-looking boy but sweet and always kind to her. When he taught her to tie a bowline hitch he'd been patient, going over the steps again and again until she could do it herself and when the next day came and she'd forgotten it, he didn't mind starting all over. He was the sweetest person she'd ever known. Not sharp and impatient like Johnny.

That summer Simone and Shawn had often sneaked aboard the *Oriole* and made love on his parents' double berth. The sheets never felt quite dry and she smelled the bilge, a weedy background stink she didn't mind. One night Shawn said, "My folks'll skin me if they ever find out about this." His words set Simone off into giggles she couldn't stop. Shawn grabbed for her as she ran up on deck. He caught her and held his hand over her mouth so she wouldn't wake the people who lived aboard the boats moored on either side of the *Oriole*. After they made love again he took her home and she crept up to her room, slept a couple of hours, and then at seven he picked her up and they were on the water all that day with his parents and their friends. The way Johnny wanted a son and Roxanne wanted to teach, Simone and Shawn had wanted to sail together.

After the accident Ellen and BJ told her to put sailing out of her mind *once and for all* as if flying free across the water was something she could just forget like the times table. But they kept telling her she couldn't even think about it and so she didn't, not knowing what she did now, that when something is right for you, you must be willing to do anything for it.

She drifted into a sleepy, salty daydream where Shawn and sex and sea mingled together. She dreamed she was flying and woke up after a few moments with the most wonderful idea.

* * *

In a special section of the girls' department at the Fashion Valley Macy's, a wide selection of school uniforms were arranged under their various school crests and flags. Late on this Friday afternoon the department was crowded with excited little girls and their mothers as well as a few blasé older girls shopping on their own, cell phones glued to their ears. Roxanne bought Merell skirts and blouses and, most important, the short cocoa-brown blazer with a gold embroidered Arcadia crest that distinguished the girls in the Upper Primary from "the babies" in the Lower. After their shopping spree Merell threw off excited sparks and the last thing she needed was sugar; but Roxanne took her to the Big Bad Cat in Hillcrest and didn't say a word when she ordered a chocolate milkshake and a plate of French fries doused in melted cheese the color of a Halloween pumpkin.

What a hell of a day Merell had been through. She deserved to have anything on the menu she wanted.

The tables around them were crowded with kids and adults who all seemed to be talking at the same time, trying to make themselves heard over the din of rock and roll from the fifties and sixties played by a disc jockey in a glass booth suspended above the dining room.

"When you were in the fourth grade did you have a best friend?" Merell asked. "I'm gonna have a best friend this year. And I'm going to ask Mommy if I can have a sleepover at our house." She stirred her milkshake with her straw. "You think she'll let me?"

Roxanne would bet her salary against it, and she suspected Merell also knew how unlikely it was. She tried to imagine what changes the next few weeks and months would bring to the Duran family, but it was impossible to know how Johnny would react to the news of Olivia's trip to urgent care. She wondered if Simone's talk about separation and Alicia had any basis in fact or if she'd made it up and then convinced herself it was true. Either way, it was the kind of idea that could send her into a tailspin. Roxanne put her hand on her lap and surreptitiously glanced down at her watch, not wanting Merell to know that she had begun to feel they'd spent too much time away from the house.

Merell pushed away her milkshake. "Daddy's going to be really mad when he finds out about Olivia. They already had a big fight last night after they got home from that dinner thing. Daddy yelled a lot of mean things." She stacked her fries as if she were building a log cabin.

"He said she was useless and she kept crying and saying no, no, no. He's going to be so angry when he finds out Mommy went to sleep and left Olivia outside. Maybe he'll blame me." She looked up from her construction. "He called her a stupid slut and that made her cry even more."

Roxanne sat back. Her entire vocabulary, every word, had gone right out of her mind. She clutched her napkin in her lap, as if it had the power to keep her upright in her chair.

"How did you hear all this?"

Merell looked down and then off to the side of the room where a magician was entertaining a table of little girls in glittery birthday hats.

"Merell?"

"You know the cedar closet in the hall? Where the sheets and blankets are?"

The linen closet was next to Johnny's and Simone's bedroom. Lined with rough-hewn cedar boards, it smelled like the mountains in summertime.

"If I go in there, at the back, I can hear them."

"You have to stop that. What you heard was a private conversation between two grown-up people. People have a right of privacy, even your mother and father."

The magician pulled a chain of pastel scarves from behind the neck of one of the birthday guests. Her giddy shriek made everyone in the room turn to see what had happened.

"That's so lame," Merell said. "He just pulls 'em out of his sleeve."

"Listen to me," Roxanne said, leaning in across the table. "I know that confusing things happen at your house and it probably seems like if you could just listen to what Mommy and Daddy talk about, you'd be able to figure out what's going on. But life doesn't work that way. Grown-up people sometimes say terrible things to each other, things they don't really mean."

Perhaps this explained Johnny's talk of Alicia and separation. He didn't really mean it.

"If you try to make sense of what people say when they're fighting, you'll only get more confused and unhappy," Roxanne said, convincing herself. "I want you to promise you won't eavesdrop anymore."

Merell was quiet. She looked up from her stack of fries. "She does bad things."

"Who?"

"Mommy."

Roxanne picked up one of Merell's fries and stirred it in the cheese before she took a bite. It was like eating cardboard dipped in salty melted plastic. "Is that your secret? The bad things she does?"

Merell nodded.

"Who else knows this secret, Merell?"

"Mommy and Gramma. Nanny Franny. The twins too only they don't know they know it. And Olivia, but she can't talk."

Merell moved her milkshake glass around in the pool of condensation on the table, making the wet spot wider and wider. Roxanne expelled a long breath and waited for Merell to explain.

"We were waiting for Daddy to come home and it was hot so we went down to the swimming pool. Mommy didn't want to go but Gramma said she had to. She said the water would do her good and Mommy said she hated the water and nothing would do her any good ever, and Gramma said she was a miserable excuse for a woman."

Merell's gaze flicked around the room as if she expected the magician to cease his tricks and the children and adults in the Big Bad Cat to lean forward to catch her secret.

"Mommy was crying and Gramma Ellen told her to stop being so dramatic. Mommy said she wanted to kill herself and Gramma said she could drown herself in the pool if she wanted to. No one was stopping her." Merell was silent a moment. She seemed to be playing her grandmother's words over in her mind. "I don't think she meant that. I think she was being mean and making a joke at the same time."

"Sarcastic."

"Yeah." She sipped her milkshake. "They were by the pool and Gramma Ellen was drinking wine and Mommy had some too and Franny said she shouldn't because of the baby in her tummy and Mommy told Franny to shut up because she wasn't part of our family."

"Where were you?"

"Up on the steps. The twins were in the shallow end, in their inner tubes."

"Why weren't you swimming?"

"I was trying to read my book."

Merell squared her shoulders, sniffed, and blinked fast. Roxanne had not realized before how much dignity a child has, the pride that supports a small body.

"Tell me the secret, Merell."

"Olivia started crying and Mommy was walking around with her, patting her back, trying to make her burp because sometimes that helps stop the hurting only this time she threw up on Mommy. Olivia isn't a bad baby. She's a good baby, and she can't help throwing up and screaming because she hurts. It's not her fault." Merell was quiet for a moment and then the secret she'd been holding burst from her as if the words were chased by a nightmare.

"Mommy screamed at her, *shut up, shut up,* and then she threw her in the swimming pool. I saw her sink right to the bottom. It was Franny jumped in and got her."

Roxanne was stunned but strangely, horribly, not surprised by Merell's secret. The official version of what happened that day had never convinced her; but with so much to worry about, she had overlooked the crucial fact that Simone would never have taken Olivia into the pool in the first place. She hated the water. And if Roxanne knew this, then Johnny also did; but like her he had accepted the easiest explanation. It was a kind of willing blindness, a choice not to see what was right before them.

"But Franny was really mad and yelling at Mommy, and Gramma Ellen kept telling her to be quiet and let her think. She said she'd give Franny five thousand dollars if she'd forget what just happened."

The inestimable Franny had taken a bribe. And now she had vanished.

"But you know what?" Merell said. "Franny wasn't even looking at the pool. She was lying on her stomach, reading a magazine. She just turned around when everyone started yelling."

"But you saw all this?"

"Mommy wanted to drown her. That's how come I called 911."

* * *

Simone sent Celia home with two fifty-dollar bills.

"Everything's fine now," she said, glowing with her own

generosity. "I can manage. See you tomorrow, bright and early."

She put Olivia in her chair in the kitchen with a pile of bright orange cheddar cheese crackers and a sippy-glass of grape juice on her tray. Olivia grabbed a handful of crackers and stuffed them in her mouth.

Simone assembled a picnic supper, the twins looking on as she packed potato chips and string cheese and oranges cut in fourths in a cooler bag with blue ice.

"Where are we going?" Valli asked.

"We're going to look at boats."

If Shawn was at the boat shop he might offer to take them out for an evening sail. Simone would like to see the sunset from the water again, but her hopes and dreams did not require that. She would inquire of whoever was in the shop where she could sign up for sailing lessons. She'd pay for ten at a time, maybe twenty. She patted the pocket of her slacks, making sure her credit card was where she'd put it.

If you'd just do *something.*

If you weren't so helpless.

She had to arrange for lessons and be back from the Shelter Island marina before Johnny came home and they had the conversation. She knew he wouldn't be pleased at first. He would say it wasn't safe for a pregnant woman to sail a boat. He'd probably laugh and say she couldn't even throw a ball, what made her think she could trim a sail or hold a course? He'd be surprised when she told him that after more than ten years, she could still tie a bowline hitch.

He wouldn't care. He'd have a fit when he heard what had happened to Olivia that day. The memory rose in Simone's mind like sand stirred up off the bottom of the sea, taking up so much room it was hard to keep thinking about happy things like sailing. And cupcakes. Just that morning she'd planned to make cupcakes and now...Maybe Roxanne would explain to Johnny about Olivia. Simone would listen and nod and she wouldn't make excuses. Johnny would call her terrible names and shake her by the shoulders until she had to squeeze her eyes shut to keep them from falling out of her head. Roxanne would try to stop him but he would push her away. After a while he would calm down and say he loved her and that he was sorry for losing his temper. He'd be happy then to hear that she'd signed up for sailing lessons. The conversation was like a recorded book in Simone's head. And then another, different conversation began. Johnny saying over and over that she had almost killed their baby, and he was sick of her. He didn't want a son, not from her. She was helpless, stupid, he didn't want her anymore.

Johnny might as well have been standing beside her, going at her like a seagull pecking at a piece of bread, repeating the same savage things over and over until she knew she would rather die than listen to any more.

Valli tugged on the leg of Simone's shorts. For how long had Olivia been crying? If they didn't hurry, Shawn would close the shop and go home. They would miss the sunset.

"Go-go-go."

"What about Libia?"

"I'll come back for her."

The twins were adorable in their oversize lifeguard hats and flip-flop sandals decorated with garish plastic flowers. Simone forgot about the conversation with Johnny and sang, "Sailing, sailing, over the bounding main."

In the garage she stood on the landing and looked at her two black cars. It was like choosing between mud and dirt, and at the prospect of driving anywhere in them, her mood deflated again. Why had Johnny ordered both cars in black? If he had asked her, she would have told him she wanted a happy car. A yellow car. An oriole.

She remembered the vintage Camaro. The Yellow Bird was perfect. They would fly down to the marina in a yellow bird and then they would get on another yellow bird and fly across the waves. She would be responsible and make sure the girls wore life preservers.

She removed the key from the hook and opened the door to the vintage garage, remembering to replace the key on the hook afterward, thinking as she did that Johnny would love her if she did all the right things.

"Libia's crying," Victoria said, looking back toward the kitchen.

"I know, I know. I'll get you settled first." She laughed so the twins would see how happy she was, and excited.

Shawn's mother or father might be in the shop. They would be glad to see her and surprised that she had twins. She imagined one of them saying, "Go right aboard the *Oriole*. Make yourselves at home."

She opened the Camaro and checked that the key was in the ignition where it was supposed to be. She pulled back the driver's-side seat.

"Hop in, sailors."

The twins settled in the backseat with their pails and shovels and towels piled between them.

"We don't got our car seats."

"You don't need car seats in a Camaro."

"Where's my hat?" Victoria put both hands on her head and started to cry. "I want my hat."

It had vanished somewhere between the kitchen and the Camaro. "Never mind about your hat."

"I want my hat." Victoria kicked the seat back. "I'll get burnded same as Libia."

"Where's the seat belt?" Valli asked, raising her voice to be heard over Victoria's yelling. "I can't find the seat belt."

It took Simone a minute of searching before she realized that old Camaros didn't have seat belts in the back.

"I want to go in the van," Valli said, pouting. "I don't like this car."

The Mercedes and Cayenne each had its own set of car seats, three of them, permanently in place. Simone saw that this excursion, which had seemed so simple a few minutes before, had become as complicated as making cupcakes. The thought sent fire to her face, and she knew she could not survive another failure. Maybe the Camaro wasn't safe but when she thought of driving one of her black cars she realized she'd rather not go anywhere. But if she canceled this plan... The thought was unbearable.

"We're going to the marina and we're driving this car."

"Why are you mad, Mommy?"

"I'm not mad."

"You sound mad."

"My head hurts." The tree was on fire and had spread its branches all the way around her head, grabbing hold of her eyeballs and squeezing.

"What about my seat belt?"

"We're just going over to Shelter Island. You don't need a seat belt."

"I'm exciting!" Victoria cried, her hat forgotten, and banged her hand against the window glass so hard she hurt herself and started to cry.

Simone watched her cry and a word popped into her head. *Stupid.* Johnny had said Simone was as stupid as a post. Or had she imagined that? Had someone else said it?

"Let's go, let's go, let's go," the girls chorused.

Going back for Olivia, Simone faltered at the door connecting the garages, thinking that the trip to the marina would be so much easier without lugging a baby along. Olivia was strapped into her high chair and there was no way she could fall out of it. Why not just leave her there? Roxanne would take care of her if she and Merell got home first. She'd never tattle to Johnny. He still might find out though. The twins might tell him.

In the kitchen she stopped at the sight of the crying baby, twisted around in her chair and almost facing backward, her crimson face spackled with soggy cheddar crackers. Simone stared, her hands jerking and grabbing at her thighs. Her feet wouldn't move. Time drifted by.

Valli ran in from the garage. "When are we going? I wanna go."

Simone had lost more time. Where did it go?

Valli said, "Did we have lunch yet, Mommy?"

Simone couldn't remember where she had been at lunchtime.

"My tummy hurts," Victoria said and sniffed, working up to another volley of tears.

"Go back to the car. I'll give you some string cheese."

"I don't like—"

"You can eat it or starve."

The twins darted away. Behind Simone's closed eyes,

galaxies spun out dizzying possibilities. She looked at her hands and told them to stop jittering so she could press the release on the strap holding Olivia in the high chair, but the tremor didn't stop and the release stuck so she pulled out drawers until she found a pair of scissors and cut the straps. Still shaking, she lifted her baby's sweaty little body out of the chair and carried her past the Cayenne and the Mercedes into the vintage garage, where she put her down on the carpet at the back.

"How come she's on the floor?" Victoria lay down on the carpet beside Olivia and moved her arms and legs, making a snow angel. "This floor is soft."

"Go back to the car."

"I don't wanna see boats," Valli said. "I wanna watch TV."

"Get back in the car, dammit."

"Can I have some string cheese?"

The logs of white cheese were sealed in plastic and Simone's hands shook too much to open them. She bit the plastic seal and tore at the edge. It slipped from her hands.

"I want cheese, I want cheese."

"Get in the car." She shoved the twins into the back of the Camaro and tossed the cheese after them. "Open it yourself!"

She picked up the baby and got into the Camaro and slammed the door. The Naugahyde upholstery cooled the back of her thighs.

"Mommy, you forgot the food."

The cooler sat on the rug, open.

"I'll buy you hamburgers."

"Yeah," the twins screamed.

I can do this.

"Where's Libia's car seat?" Valli asked.

I must do this.

"She'll sit on my lap." Simone glanced in the rearview mirror and saw the alarmed expression on Valli's face.

"Don't look at me that way. What's the matter with you?"

Simone thought, *I won't drive fast and I'll stay on surface streets.*

In the backseat Victoria and Valli began singing two different songs. One about sailing, one about string cheese. Simone's thoughts jumped like water drops on a hot skillet. She would turn left out of the driveway, go down the Juan Street hill into Old Town, but then what?

Useless.

"I gotta pee," Victoria said. "I'm gonna wet my pants in Daddy's car."

"I'm gonna poop," Valli said.

"I'm gonna poop *and* pee."

"I'm gonna poop and pee and throw up."

The twins collapsed together, giggling.

Too stupid to live.

Simone thought of her daughters' lives stretching out

beyond hers. Like her, they would be foolish, do-nothing women. Time and the world would fly past while they dithered helplessly. The terrible pity of it converged to a single stiletto point so sharp it cut out her heart. She knew exactly what she had to do.

She realized she had always known.

She turned the key and the Camaro's V8 engine roared to life.

The twins squealed and Victoria banged the window again.

The sound of the racing engine cleared the last doubt from Simone's mind as if she had sailed out from fog into bright weather. Where there had been confusion only moments before, now there was calm clarity and on the bottom of the sea every grain of sand was as precisely outlined as if she had drawn it there with a fine-tipped pen.

Valli complained. "I don't like the smell."

"I'm warming up the engine," Simone said, holding Olivia against her heart as she used the lever that reclined her seat back. "This is an old car."

"Smells bad," said Victoria.

"I don't feel good. My head hurts."

"I'm gonna throw up, Mommy."

The twins' voices were sweet and plaintive as the songs of captive birds. Simone closed her eyes and imagined a narrow street lined on both sides with shops full of bright yellow birds in wicker cages. Her fingertips tingled as she opened the cages and set them all free. In the sky their wings lifted and rode the air like sails. Olivia rested in Simone's arms, quiet at last.

This is how a good mother feels. This softness inside.

Chapter 15

March 2010

Prosecutor Clark Jackson was a barrel-shaped man in his forties, his bald head encircled by a curly gray tonsure. On the first day of Simone's trial for the attempted murder of her daughters, he sprang from his chair and strode confidently to the front of the courtroom to deliver his opening remarks to the jury in a sharp tenor voice that was abrasive and compelling at the same time. In the gallery, Roxanne took a deep breath and tried to relax. She'd woken up with a tennis ball in her throat; oxygen could barely get around it.

Jackson frightened her because she knew immediately that punishment was as important to him as justice.

He smiled at the jurors, leading with his teeth. "On behalf of the people of the state of California, I want to thank you for your willingness to serve as jurors in this very difficult and important case. What is decided by you in this courtroom will be seen and read about around the world. But let me put your minds at ease. You won't have any trouble coming to a fair decision. The evidence will show without a shadow of a doubt that Simone Duran is guilty of four counts of attempted murder."

The twins, Olivia, and Claire, unborn.

Looking from Jackson to Simone's attorney, David Cabot, sitting at the defense table on the other side of the bar, and then back at Jackson, Roxanne felt a new presence in the courtroom, an excitement like what she remembered feeling before one of Ty's marathons or 10Ks. Until that moment she had been naïve, not realizing that Simone's freedom and the future of her family devolved to just this: a competition between two ambitious men, with justice moving in and out between them, an obstacle and at the same time a referee.

David said they were lucky to get Judge Amos MacArthur, a big, gruff, exhausted-looking man with a thick head of dark hair and a mustache too large for his face. Though inclined to be both irascible and eccentric, he was a judicial moderate and not likely to be swayed by the high voltage of the case.

Jackson stepped away from the jury box and dramatically pointed at Simone. "The government will show that when this woman tried to kill her daughters she knew exactly what she was doing. She *planned* to murder them. And she was *almost* successful."

Jackson's tenor voice softened, confided. "Ladies and

gentlemen, defense counsel is going to tell you that Simone Duran was insane at the time of the crime. And you're going to want to believe it because you're good people and Simone Duran is a pretty, sweet-looking lady. She doesn't look like a monster, does she?"

Jackson stared right at Simone, encouraging the jurors to do the same. Roxanne saw Cabot reach under the table for Simone's hand.

"Don't let yourselves be fooled. Our evidence will show this is a *dangerous* woman. She is not insane. She has never been insane. She knew what she was doing when she tried to kill her children and she must now face the consequences."

At the end of his short remarks, Jackson resumed his seat, and David Cabot, six feet five with an athlete's natural grace, announced that he would reserve his opening statement until after the prosecution had presented its case. This caused some murmuring in the gallery. Cabot had prepared the family for this departure from the usual order of trial, assuring them that in this case it made strategic sense.

The prosecution's first witness was the SDPD's lead investigator on the case. He testified that he had arrived at the Duran residence just after the EMTs and gave the jury a vivid and disturbing picture of the scene outside the garage. Roxanne did not remember much of what had happened that late afternoon. Trauma did that to some people, the doctor told her when she left the hospital.

Jackson's next witness, a medical technician, told the jury about the girls' precarious condition at the crime scene. At Jackson's prompting, he said that, based on his eleven years' experience, he knew that if Simone and the children had been exposed to carbon monoxide for one minute longer, they would have suffered permanent brain damage. Before Cabot could object, the witness volunteered that Olivia's survival was "a miracle from heaven." Cabot declined to cross-examine these witnesses.

The state's psychiatrist and expert on postpartum depression and psychosis, Gerald Frobisher, took the stand with an unassailable dignity and self-confidence. He was a middle-aged man, thin and elegantly dressed, his shoes polished to a mirror shine. His smoothness disgusted Roxanne. There was a word to describe Gerald Frobisher: *smarmy*. Jackson asked Frobisher what qualified him as an expert, and he responded—taking care, Roxanne noted, to adopt a subdued and modest tone of voice that did not for a moment convince her—listing a daunting number of postgraduate degrees and publications in prestigious journals.

At the end of Frobisher's lengthy testimony, Jackson asked him, "Doctor, will you tell the jury, on the basis of your tests and interviews and in your opinion as an expert in the field, at the time of the incident in question was Mrs. Duran able to distinguish between right and wrong?"

"I am certain she was."

Judge MacArthur glared out over the murmuring gallery.

"On the day she attempted to murder her daughters she was no different than you and me?"

"Oh, well, I wouldn't presume to say that." Frobisher pushed up the bridge of his glasses. "Mrs. Duran was operating under substantial emotional stress, to be sure. She has had several children in a relatively short space of time and almost certainly suffered some hormone imbalance as a result. Additionally, she has a natural tendency to bipolarity, which would have been exacerbated by hormonal surges. But none of this is terribly unusual."

"In your conversations with Mrs. Duran did you uncover some significant event, some clue to what triggered her murderous actions?"

"Well, to start with, she fired the nanny," Frobisher said. "Without the nanny her life became intolerably stressful. Even as simple a task as making cupcakes was too much for her."

"Are you saying that she tried to murder her children because she couldn't bake *cupcakes*?"

Cabot stood. "Your Honor, I have to object to Mr. Jackson's tone here."

Roxanne knew that the prosecution needed Frobisher's testimony to convince the jury that Simone was sane, but Cabot had predicted Jackson would still dismiss any attempt at a psychological explanation, perhaps ridicule it, in order to weaken the defense argument in advance of its introduction.

Cabot said, "Simone Duran's future and the future of her family hangs in the balance today. Sarcasm is unbecoming here."

"Did you intend sarcasm, Mr. Jackson?" the judge asked.

"Certainly not, Your Honor."

"Overruled. Continue, Mr. Jackson, but watch your tone."

"To sum up, Dr. Frobisher, is it your expert opinion that Simone Duran attempted the murder of her children because she was under stress?"

Frobisher turned to look at the judge. "May I elaborate on that question, Your Honor?"

"Be my guest, Doctor."

The psychiatrist shifted in the witness chair and spoke directly to the jury. "Most of us deal with stress pretty well. Our bodies and our relationships may suffer in the process, but we cope. We are very good at coping, as a matter of fact. But Simone Duran has been pampered all her life. She is dependent upon her husband to an extraordinary degree. This last pregnancy—little Claire—and especially the loss of the nanny, was finally too much for her. All she wanted to do was escape the stress."

Jackson asked, "Why didn't she ask for help?"

Frobisher said, "According to Mrs. Duran, she never tried to conceal her problems but she says that nobody paid any attention. She claims no one wanted to help her but that seems far-fetched. Her recall of events is highly selective."

"You mean she lies when it suits her purposes."

"Objection, Your Honor, there's no basis for that question."

"Sustained. Rephrase, Mr. Jackson."

"Dr. Frobisher, from your study of Mrs. Duran does it appear she will lie to protect herself?"

"Most people will alter facts to avoid unpleasant consequences, Mr. Jackson. Simone Duran is no exception."

"So, finally—let's be crystal clear about this—it is your expert opinion that at the time of the crime, Simone Duran knew what she was doing and she also knew the difference between right and wrong?"

"Absolutely. Yes, to both questions."

It was after three on the second day of the trial when David Cabot rose to cross-examine Frobisher.

"There are one or two points I'd like you to clarify for us."

Frobisher sat back and crossed his legs, perfectly at ease in the witness stand.

"First, it would help us if we knew how long you spent in conversation with my client, Simone Duran."

"May I consult my notes?"

"If you must, but can't you give us a ballpark estimate?"

"Well, let's see. The better part of one afternoon. After lunch until about four." Frobisher tipped his chin a little to the right and looked up. "The next day we had a couple of hours and then I believe there was a lapse of a few days and I saw her again for most of one morning."

"Could we say a total of six or seven hours then?"

"Closer to eight."

"That's not very long, Doctor, is it?"

"In this case it was perfectly adequate."

"During your conversations with my client did you discuss her childhood?"

"Yes, of course."

"Why was that necessary?"

"The mind works in subtle and complicated ways. Who Mrs. Duran was at the time of the incident is linked to who she was long before that."

"'Subtle and complicated.' That makes sense. Do you mind if I use that term again?"

Frobisher dipped his head. "Not at all."

"So of the eight hours you spent with Simone Duran, how long do you think you spent talking about her childhood?"

"I couldn't say. We returned to it a number of times."

"Would you say two hours? Four?"

"Altogether? Between three and four."

"Did you discuss her marriage?"

"Of course."

"She and Mr. Duran have been married... how long?"

Frobisher looked down at his notes.

"Never mind," Cabot said with a hint of antipathy, as if he did not think much of a doctor who could not recall the answer to so basic a question. "If I said they've been together roughly ten years would that be close enough?"

Frobisher nodded.

"I'll take that as a yes, Doctor. Can you estimate for the court...? Did you spend thirty minutes talking about her marriage, three minutes for every year?"

"Again, Mr. Cabot, the time was sufficient."

"Sufficient for what?"

"To determine if Mrs. Duran knew the difference between right and wrong at the time of the crime."

"No kidding." David Cabot stepped back and looked at the jury with a surprised expression. "You could come to a conclusion in so short a time? I think that's amazing."

"Objection, Your Honor."

"If you were talking to Mrs. Duran and you discovered something that didn't support your belief that she knew right from wrong at the time of the incident, would you report this or ignore it?"

Jackson leaped to his feet. "Your Honor, Dr. Frobisher is a highly respected professional in his field. Counsel's question is insulting."

"This is cross-examination, Mr. Jackson." MacArthur

frowned over the top of his glasses. "You may respond, Doctor."

Frobisher squared his jaw. "I am a scientist, so of course I kept an open mind until I had gathered the facts."

"Dr. Frobisher, did you question Mrs. Duran about her sexual relationship with her husband?"

"We didn't speak about sex. Sex had nothing to do with the crime."

"But if her marriage was relevant and sex is part of marriage... You talked about marriage but not about sex? I find that a little confusing, Doctor."

Dr. Frobisher's credentials could not be faulted, but Cabot wanted to plant a seed of doubt in the minds of the jurors as to his impartiality and the thoroughness of his analysis.

"Mrs. Duran has been pregnant eight times in ten years, counting the miscarriages. But you didn't mention sex?"

"Mr. Cabot, you haven't laid a foundation for that question." Judge MacArthur sounded cross. "Move on."

"Can you explain to the court *why* sex wasn't relevant?"

"My goal was to determine if Mrs. Duran knew what she was doing at the time of the attempted murder and could tell right from wrong. I didn't have to know the intimate details of her personal life."

"Okay, you didn't talk about sex. Did you talk about

Mrs. Duran's relationship with her sister, her mother, her children?"

"We covered all of that, yes."

"Again, how much time do you remember that taking?"

"I don't know, Mr. Cabot. I do not compartmentalize my interviews. They last until I form a professional opinion."

"Can I assume you talked about the near-asphyxiation itself?"

Roxanne knew David would never say "attempted murder." It was always the *event*, the *incident, the near-asphyxiation.*

"Of course."

"And all of this you did in the space of six or seven hours."

"Between eight and nine."

"Would you call your examination of my client thorough?"

"Yes."

"Would you say it was a comprehensive examination?"

"Limited by time, of course, but sufficient under the circumstances."

"Can you swear you learned the *subtle and complicated* way Simone Duran's mind worked at the time of the incident?"

Frobisher flushed, paused a moment, and then said, "Yes."

Cabot turned to the jury, to Amos MacArthur, and then back to Frobisher. "Doctor, do you believe that you could spend a few hours with His Honor, Judge MacArthur, and say you know him *thoroughly and comprehensively*?"

"Objection!"

"Would you comprehend the *subtle and complicated* way his mind works?"

"I said I object, Your Honor!"

"And I heard you, Mr. Jackson."

"I withdraw the question," Cabot said. "I have nothing further at this time."

On the third day of the trial, after calling several more witnesses, including Celia, the Durans' housekeeper, a social worker, and a number of psychologist scholars who testified that postpartum psychosis was extremely rare and seldom, if ever, rendered a woman unable to tell right from wrong, Clark Jackson called Merell to the stand.

Beside Roxanne Johnny drew a sharp breath. Like her, he had been preparing himself for this moment; nevertheless, hearing Merell's name spoken by Jackson was like a gunshot out of nowhere, an ambush.

Months earlier, when he learned that his daughter would be called as a witness against Simone, Johnny's outspoken rage had provided headlines for all the supermarket tabloids. Emerging from a long pretrial conference with the prosecutor and Judge MacArthur, Cabot told him that Jackson had prevailed.

"She's going to testify. The judge says she's old enough."

"Testify about what?" Roxanne asked. "She and I were together in the garage. Why doesn't he call me as a witness?"

"Goddamn it, Cabot, she's a kid." Johnny stormed across the attorney's office on the third floor of a renovated downtown building. The corner windows overlooked Broadway, eight blocks east of the court complex. "I don't want my daughter—"

"What you want doesn't count here, Johnny."

"Of course it counts. I'm her fucking father. What's Jackson going to do to her?"

"Calm down, Johnny. The judge won't let Jackson get away with anything. He's as concerned as I am about Merell's well-being." Cabot said, "If she were my witness, I'd ask her about the 911 call. I would try to establish a link between what happened at the pool back in July and the incident in the garage. He wants to show a pattern of intent." Cabot paused as an ambulance passed on the street below, its siren screaming. "Jackson knows we're going to say that in the garage Simone didn't know the difference between right and wrong. But if he can convince the jury that just a month or six weeks earlier she tried to drown Olivia—"

"That's a pile of crap!"

Ellen had finally told Johnny the truth about that day. He didn't believe her.

Cabot said, "Jackson will be happy if he can just plant a suspicion of intent in the jury's mind."

Johnny sank onto the office couch, his head down, resting his elbows on his knees.

"Everything will be done to protect Merell," Cabot assured him. "During any prep sessions, there'll be a court-appointed social worker in the room to protect her rights. Jackson's a good lawyer and I wouldn't expect him to try to intimidate her, but just in case, we know there'll be someone with her. She won't be alone."

Johnny resumed his restless pacing of the length of the room, his face twisted in frustration. Roxanne had never seen him this way and his changed demeanor was mildly gratifying after all the times she'd seen him flaunt his power. He was accustomed to getting what he wanted, to having money and influence behind him in every fight; he didn't know how to deal with powerlessness.

Cabot said, "It's an interesting tactic, using Merell."

"Interesting?" A drop of sweat slipped from behind the orb of Johnny's ear. Roxanne watched it move down his neck and disappear beneath his shirt collar. "More like child abuse."

"Jackson's taking a chance. It'll all depend on how the jury takes to her. Merell's not a reliable witness, if you ask me he'll take advantage of that. She lied—"

"She's not a liar," Johnny said.

"She told one story to the 911 operator and another to the police. One of them was a lie."

"She got confused. That's all that happened."

"Whatever." Cabot shrugged and Roxanne thought she saw pity in his expression when he looked at Johnny. "Jackson's going to try to convince the jury that she lied to protect her mother."

"I'll talk to her, we'll get her story straight once and for all."

"No. You won't do that." Cabot strode across the office and stood in front of Johnny. "Sit down and listen to me."

Roxanne thought Johnny was going to argue.

"From this point on," Cabot said, laying down the law in a way that stopped Johnny's objections, "in your house, with anyone in your family, there will be no discussion of anything connected to this case because if there's the slightest suspicion that you're trying to influence the prosecution's witness..."

"You're telling me I can't have a conversation with my own daughter?"

"It's a crime, Johnny." Roxanne sat on the couch beside him and placed her hand on his shoulder. She was startled by the heat of his body and the rush of tenderness she felt. "You could go to prison."

"And if you tamper with a witness you can forget any chance for Simone. If you want her to go to jail for twenty years, that's the way to do it."

"All right, all right."

Roxanne saw that until that moment Johnny had misunderstood the situation. He had believed himself to be in charge, with Cabot operating according to his wishes, but now he had been forced to submit, to bend his will before another's, and it pained him. She saw him grimace.

It was chilly and damp in the courtroom on the afternoon of the third day of the trial when a female bailiff escorted Merell down the gallery's center aisle, through the gate in the bar, and into the witness box.

That morning as she was leaving home Roxanne had seen three crows hunkered on the branch of a canyon eucalyptus. They seemed to be watching the house like a trio of dour monks, menacingly still. An omen, she thought, and not a good one.

Merell looked taller and bonier than when Roxanne had seen her a few days earlier. Her bangs had been cut too short, accentuating the bend at the end of her nose and giving her a slightly orphaned look. Her cowlicky hair was pulled back in what was, for Merell, a tidy ponytail. She wore her Arcadia school uniform, Mary Janes, and knee socks. There was a note of obstinacy in her voice when she swore to tell the truth and stated her name. Seeing her there in the witness chair, vulnerable and yet fierce in the way little girls can be, Roxanne felt something in her chest give way, as if the muscles that held her heart in place were slowly tearing.

"And how old are you, Merell?"

"Nine."

"Where do you attend school?"

"Arcadia Academy."

After every answer Merell squared her shoulders and closed her mouth in the tight straight line so like Gran's that Roxanne found herself hoping that the old woman's spirit was in the courtroom now, giving some of her strength to her great-granddaughter. It was a thought worthy of Elizabeth.

"What grade are you in?"

Merell looked straight ahead, focused on the middle of Clark Jackson's red-and-black-patterned tie.

"Upper primary."

"That would be about fourth grade, am I right?"

"Yes."

"Do they teach you the difference between right and wrong at Arcadia Academy?"

"I guess."

She had to be frightened, but she hid it well. Two days earlier a note had arrived in the mail addressed to Roxanne in the careful penmanship of a fourth grader. It contained one sheet of paper on which was written a single sentence. *I hate him.* There was no return address, no signature. She would not be intimidated by Clark Jackson. She would show him how tough she was. Roxanne wished she could caution her before the trial went further. *Jackson is dangerous,* she wanted to say. *Tread cautiously, little girl.*

Jackson paced a little. "Will you describe for the court exactly what happened in the first week of September 2009, the day you came home from Macy's with your aunt Roxanne?"

Merell was prepared for this question and spoke so automatically that Roxanne thought she must have memorized the words. "We came in the house and I heard a noise like a car in the garage, and I thought someone was stealing one of Daddy's vintage cars."

Jackson led her through details of where and how the cars were stored and maintained.

"What did you see when you opened the door to the garage?"

"I didn't open the door."

Jackson looked at her with mild surprise.

"My aunt Roxanne opened it."

"Very well, continue."

Roxanne guessed that Jackson didn't have children. He tried to sound kid-friendly, but he wasn't convincing.

"There were five cars in the garage, you say. Which one did you notice first?"

"The Camaro."

"And tell the jury what you saw in the Camaro."

For the first time, Merell's confidence faltered. She looked up at the judge.

MacArthur spoke like a kindly grandfather. "I know it's not easy, young lady, but you have to answer the question. This is the law and I can't change it. Go on now, tell folks what you saw."

"The twins were in the backseat."

"The backseat of what?"

"The car. The Camaro."

"What were they doing?"

"They looked asleep."

"And your mother?"

"I don't remember exactly." Merell tugged on her bangs as if she could pull them down to cover her face.

"I think you do remember, Merell," Jackson said.

"Objection, Your Honor, the witness has said she doesn't remember."

"Overruled." The judge looked down at Merell. "Try to answer Mr. Jackson's question, Merell. Do the best you can."

"My mother was in the front seat and the twins were in the back."

"Was your mother alone?"

"I said the twins were there."

"In the front seat. Was she alone in the front seat?"

"She was holding my sister Olivia."

"And Olivia is the baby?"

"Claire's the baby now."

"Your mother was holding the baby Olivia, who was how old at the time?"

"Eight or nine months?"

"What was your mother doing?"

"I thought they were asleep."

"What did you do?"

Merell described how Roxanne had opened the garage door and together they had dragged Simone and the girls into the air outside.

"I called 911 and then I threw up."

Someone in the gallery laughed.

Jackson said, "That was a good picture, Merell. Very clear."

Merell smiled. Tears stung Roxanne's eyes when she saw how needy she was, how at war her emotions were that she should at once hate this man and yet bloom in the light of his praise.

"Do you ever tell lies, Merell?"

"No."

"Oh, come on now." Jackson grinned at the jury. "Everyone lies once in a while, Merell. Do you mean to tell me—?"

"Objection, Your Honor. Is the prosecution trying to impeach its own witness?"

"Withdrawn." Jackson's look at the jury implied Cabot's objection was frivolous. "Merell, let's go back to something that happened back in July, the third week of July. That was the day you made a 911 call. Do you remember that?"

"I guess."

"You, your mother and sisters were around the swimming pool in the afternoon. Your grandmother and the nanny were also there, am I correct?"

"We did that lots."

"Of course. However, I am speaking of the day you made a call to the 911 operator. Do you remember that day in particular?"

"Yes."

"Please tell the court exactly what happened on that day."

Merell squared her shoulders. "I called 911 and said Olivia was drowning."

Jackson said, "Your Honor, I submit into evidence the recording of Merell Duran's call to the 911 operator."

"Noted," the judge said. "Go on. Play it."

Into the silent courtroom came the voice of a terrified child crying, "My mother's trying to drown my sister."

The effect of the recorded message was damning and it spread through the courtroom like toxic fumes. Judge MacArthur rapped his gavel and called for quiet in the gallery.

Jackson asked, "Was that your voice on the recording, Merell?"

"Yes."

"What happened after you made that phone call?"

"The police came."

"And what did you tell them, Merell?"

"I said Mommy had Olivia in the pool and she squirmed and slipped out of Mommy's arms. It was an accident."

"What else did you tell the police?"

Merell fidgeted; even from where she sat, Roxanne saw

the color rise in her cheeks. "I said I made up that Olivia was drowning because I wanted to see what would happen if I called like an emergency."

"Let's get this straight." Jackson sounded perplexed. "You told two different stories, Merell. Which was the truth?"

"Objection, Your Honor. The prosecutor is cross-examining his own witness."

MacArthur pushed his fingers up under his glasses and rubbed his eyes. "Overruled, Mr. Cabot. I'm going to give Mr. Jackson some latitude with this reluctant youngster."

"You told two stories. One of them was a lie. Am I right?"

Merell sat on her hands. "I guess."

"Merell, did your mother try to drown Olivia?"

"No. I told you—"

"Why should the jury believe anything you say, Merell? Maybe you were lying to the police. Maybe you're lying now."

"Sometimes—" She didn't finish her sentence.

"Sometimes what, Merell?"

She pulled her hands up and shoved them under her arms. "It doesn't matter."

"Tell the court what you were going to say."

She didn't speak.

The judge said, "Answer Mr. Jackson's question, Merell. And remember you've taken an oath to be truthful."

"Sometimes . . . there's a good reason to lie."

At the back of the gallery someone laughed softly.

"Would you lie to protect your mother, Merell?"

"Objection, the prosecution is asking this witness to—"

"Overruled."

"Would you lie to protect your mother?"

"No. That would be perjury." Merell sat up straighter and grabbed the arms of the witness chair. "Perjury is a crime, and you can go to jail."

"Bearing that in mind"—Jackson waited a beat—"tell the jury now, did your mother try to drown Olivia?"

The courtroom was perfectly silent except for the sounds of wind and rain.

"No. I only called 911 to find out what would happen."

Chapter 16

The next day David Cabot opened his defense.

Speaking to the jury, he said, "I chose to postpone my opening statement until now because I wanted you to have the opportunity to focus all your attention on what Mr. Jackson and his witnesses had to say. Mr. Jackson wants you to believe that Simone Duran is a cold-blooded murderer and planned to hurt her children." He shook his head as if this idea was impossible to grasp. "When I rest the case for the defense in a few days, you will know how wrongheaded that notion is. You will know that Simone Duran is a loving mother who would never intentionally harm her children."

He stood behind Simone and rested his hands on her shoulders.

"When it's time for you to decide your verdict, you will know all about a condition called learned helplessness. More importantly, you'll know about postpartum depression, a mental condition that afflicts *millions* of women around the world. And you'll understand that postpartum *psychosis* takes a mother's natural love for her children and turns it back on itself. It turns a loving mother into a loving killer."

He let the jury ponder his words. A *loving killer.*

Tomorrow's headline.

"Don't misunderstand me. I think anyone, when they hear that a woman is accused of trying to hurt her children, will feel disgust. Revulsion. It's a horrifying crime that Mrs. Duran has been accused of, the most unnatural crime there is...." Two or three jurors sat forward, waiting for him to complete his thought. "That's why you have to be *insane* to do it.

"So far you've seen and heard the prosecutor's image of Simone Duran. Now I'm asking you to clear any premature judgments you might have formed and start *again* with open minds. In the next couple of days you're going to get to know the *real* Simone Duran. I'm going to call her to the stand and she'll describe the incident in the garage in her own words. One of the things she's going to tell you is that her baby, Olivia, was suffering from infantile acid reflux at the time."

Cabot nodded to his associate at the defense table, who pushed the button of a small recording machine. All at once the courtroom filled with the sound of an infant's piercing cries.

Prosecutor Jackson leaped to his feet, and Judge MacArthur's gavel slammed down; but Cabot went right on talking to the jury, stepping closer to the jury box and raising his voice to be heard over the recorded screams. "More than one witness will tell you that Simone Duran's baby cried like this almost all the time, day and night."

"Your Honor, this is a mockery! What's he going to tell us? She tried to kill her children because the baby wouldn't stop crying?"

Cabot's associate shut off the recording.

Roxanne thought she could hear the judge grinding his teeth. He scowled at Cabot. "You get one chance in my courtroom. No more showboating, or you'll regret it."

Cabot dipped his head apologetically, but he didn't seem overawed.

"With due respect, Your Honor, the jurors can't understand my client's frame of mind unless they hear what she heard every day for months and months. It's the defense's intention to repeat this recording at various times throughout the case."

"Not without my permission you won't! I'll entertain a written motion, Counselor, supporting your use of a recording in this way. Have it on my desk by five this afternoon and not a minute later."

Cabot's associate gathered the recorder and her briefcase and hurried out of the courtroom. Roxanne knew that the motion was already written and ready to be delivered to the judge's clerk.

MacArthur's eyes disappeared beneath his lowered

brows. "The defense is warned. I am not in a patient frame of mind."

Cabot turned back to the jury. "I apologize for that, ladies and gentleman. That's a terrible sound, I know, and I'm sorry it's necessary for you to hear it. But it's essential you understand that the screams of a baby in pain were a constant in Simone Duran's life."

Cabot paused to glance at a paper on his desk. Roxanne felt the jury's curiosity quicken. Several shuffled in their chairs, rearranging themselves to listen more intently. An excited hum of anticipation spiked the crowd in the gallery. To some extent Jackson's prosecution had been predictable in its scope, Merell being the only unexpected witness. Cabot's defense promised not only surprises but drama and some fireworks.

"Now, it may surprise you to hear that I'm not going to contradict all the prosecution's evidence. The defense doesn't dispute that Simone Duran did something crazy."

Jackson jumped to his feet again. "I object to the use of the word *crazy*, Your Honor."

David sighed and dropped his shoulders, looking slightly abused.

"Stay in your seat, Mr. Jackson," the judge said. "I don't know how they do it up in San Jose, but down here lawyers don't interrupt opening statements. Screaming babies are an exception, of course." He looked like he was ready to step down from the bench and take on Jackson, hand to hand.

"But, Judge," Jackson said, "the defense is mischaracterizing the prosecution's case. No one ever mentioned the word *crazy*."

Jackson was whining, and several of the jurors looked impatient. It was not yet noon but in the closed and stuffy room the day already seemed long, and they were obviously fed up with objections, legitimate or not.

"I know you're tired of sitting in those chairs day after day and it's got to be hard to concentrate on expert testimony sometimes. It can be pretty dry." Cabot smiled like everyone's best friend, and Roxanne noted that several on the jury smiled back at him. "Let me tell you a story."

"This court does not look kindly upon fiction, Mr. Cabot. Make sure it's relevant."

"I will, Your Honor, if you'll just allow me a little latitude here."

"Proceed."

"I was an undergraduate at a school in Ohio. Miami University. Named after the Native American tribe, not the city. I had to take a music appreciation course. It was what we called a 'gut course' and I think even my little daughter could pass it. But I was a football player, and football was all I really cared about in those days. To make matters worse, this class met at seven-thirty in the morning and when the prof played Beethoven and Haydn and all the rest of them, I couldn't stay awake, much less distinguish one longhair from another. But I was lucky, I had a girlfriend who was much smarter than me."

"Get on with it, Mr. Cabot."

"Well, long story short, this girlfriend told me what to listen for, and after that, the music made sense to my ear. Knowing how to listen gave me focus so I wasn't just hearing random notes, and thanks to her, I did okay in that class. Now, ladies and gentlemen, for the next couple of days I want you to focus your listening in the same way. The testimony you're going to hear will make more sense to you if you listen for the answer to a question. This question is the key to this trial and your verdict. We know that Simone Duran tried to hurt her daughters. I'm not going to argue about that. But the important question is *why. Why did Simone Duran try to hurt her daughters?*"

He walked to the defense table, but he didn't sit down. Standing behind Simone, enunciating carefully, he said, "*Why* did she do it?"

The following day the defense began calling to the stand the promised experts and authorities, including Dr. Omar, Olivia's pediatrician, who testified to the unusual severity of the baby's acid reflux and the fact that there was, essentially, nothing to do but hold her and walk her and love her until she outgrew the condition and stopped screaming. Under cross-examination the psychiatric experts never wavered from their conviction that Simone suffered from postpartum psychosis at the time of the attempted murders, and that it had rendered her totally unable to distinguish right from wrong.

The defense's final expert was Dr. Barbara Balch, a dignified, large-boned woman with bright blue eyes and a neat cap of white hair. She assumed the witness stand with poised assurance, placed her handbag on the floor beside her chair, smoothed her skirt, and looked up, ready to begin. She told the jury that she had been an obstetrician initially but became a psychiatrist specializing in postpartum syndromes when she realized that, following the births of their eagerly anticipated infants, many of her patients who should have been happy instead fell into a deep despondency.

"I discovered, Mr. Cabot, that many, many women begin motherhood feeling as though they've been cheated. Pregnancy itself is an immense physical challenge, but there's always the promise that at the end of nine months there'll be a sweet, adorable baby who will make it all worthwhile. The truth that's rarely spoken is that a newborn is generally neither sweet nor adorable except when sleeping, but then a newborn wakes up every two hours, hungry and yelling. Even an orderly household is turned upside down. And for what? A seven-pound tyrant who cries at all hours and keeps its parents from getting more than an hour or two of sleep at a time. And even in the most egalitarian home, it is the mother who bears the brunt of this tyranny. Hormonally, she's still hooked to this baby. It cries and her hormones go into alarm mode."

The woman who owned a copy shop seemed ruefully

amused by Dr. Balch's testimony. Roxanne remembered from voir dire that she had four children, now grown.

Dr. Balch said, "The recorded screams you played for the jury were what Simone heard every day and night starting almost as soon as the baby Olivia was brought home. And to make things more difficult she became pregnant again when Olivia was less than six months old. Much, much too soon."

"Why did this make the situation more difficult?" Cabot asked.

"You and I hate the sound of a child in pain. It's the normal reaction but it's a mental and emotional reaction. For Simone it was also physical because she and baby Olivia were still chemically bound to each other."

Cabot asked her to explain what she meant.

"A pregnant woman goes through system-wide hormonal changes, we've talked about that. What most people don't realize or think about is that all the major organs—heart, kidney, liver, the whole internal life-support system—have to shift position in a woman's body to make room for the growing fetus. Pregnancy alters a woman's body forever and in ways that can be extremely upsetting, and while it is entirely possible to conceive just a few months after giving birth, it's not particularly healthy. In primitive societies where this is routine, women are either dead or physically aged by the time they're forty."

"So it was physical changes that caused the postpartum psychosis?"

"Not at first. At first she would have been merely depressed. And while PPD—postpartum depression—is so common that we might even think of it as normal, I would call Simone's situation—physical and emotional—a kind of perfect storm. From the beginning of her first pregnancy she was headed for disaster."

"And what do you mean by disaster, Dr. Balch?"

"Psychosis."

Dr. Balch told the jury that because societies do not encourage a new mother to be honest about her negative feelings, PPP was almost always a hidden condition until a crisis occurred. "Despite what most people believe, PPP is actually fairly common. It has been estimated that one or two in every thousand cases of postpartum depression will develop into full-blown psychosis."

"How many babies are born every year in this country, Dr. Balch?"

"Roughly four million."

Cabot looked at the jury. "That's a lot of thousands. And for every thousand, there will be one or two children with a psychotic mother?"

Jackson stood up. "Objection, Your Honor. These numbers are very general and Dr. Balch has offered no scientific support for them. Without substantiation—"

"Dr. Balch is an expert in this field. And her statistics represent real mothers and children. When you think of the number of babies born every year in this country alone—"

"We take your point, Mr. Cabot," MacArthur said. "I'll allow the testimony, but from now on, stay away from the math."

"Doctor, considering all the mothers and babies in the world, why don't we hear more about women killing their children?"

"My colleagues and I *do* hear. But these are deeply disturbing stories and most people would prefer not to know about them. Every day," Dr. Balch said, "infants are born in back alleys and abandoned buildings to girls who have hidden their pregnancies from their families and friends. They leave their babies in Dumpsters or in the bus or outside a church and go back to school. Every day babies are smothered and tossed away. For every one we hear about in the news, there are hundreds that go unfound, unnoticed."

"That sounds like murder, not psychosis."

"It is murder caused by a profound state of psychosis."

Outside the courthouse walls, the rain and wind seemed to have stopped for a moment as if to acknowledge the thousands of babies born unwanted.

"Earlier you said that Simone Duran's condition was a kind of perfect storm. What did you mean by that?"

"Postpartum depression can be progressive," Dr. Balch said. "In the case of Mrs. Duran, she has suffered from severe depression with sporadic mania since adolescence. Following the birth of her first daughter, Merell, her symptoms became more intense."

"How was that different from her usual mood disorder?"

"During our conversations she revealed to me that she has never believed Merell was her child, but stopped talking about it because she saw it made her husband think there was something wrong with her mind. She was deeply depressed for the better part of a year and with every subsequent pregnancy—including the many miscarriages—her depression worsened. But, clinically speaking, the seeds of her psychosis were sown in her childhood."

"Objection. Speculation."

David Cabot addressed the bench. "Judge, for purposes of this testimony Dr. Balch has had extraordinary access to my client's entire life history."

"Overruled. But I want to hear some substantiation."

Dr. Balch turned in her chair and spoke to the judge. "I did an extensive medical history of Simone Duran and conducted more than a dozen interviews with her doctors, teachers, and family members. I administered a number of tests, including a standard IQ test, and compared the results to those she took periodically throughout school. She scores on the high side of what I would call a borderline mental disability. Additionally, she has an attention disorder and a severe depressive mood disorder complicated by periodic mania, grandiosity, and narcissism. Because of all these factors, the family has protected Simone. She has been cared for and sheltered all her life. She never learned to take responsibility for herself or anyone else. About the only thing she's ever learned completely is how to be helpless."

Judge MacArthur scowled at the people whispering in the gallery. Their stares burned into Roxanne's back.

Cabot said, "Explain what you mean, Doctor. How does a person learn to be helpless?"

"Well, to start with, it has nothing to do with IQ. There are plenty of people with IQs no higher than Simone Duran's who have families and jobs and function as responsible and productive citizens. However, due to a particular set of circumstances in her family, Simone was kept from being accountable by the people who loved her most. They thought they were helping her, but they were really teaching her to be helpless."

Like pages in a book, examples of Simone's helplessness turned over in Roxanne's mind. She couldn't balance on a bike so she rode on Roxanne's handlebars. She forgot how to program her phone so Roxanne did it for her. She lost her glasses and Roxanne read most of *Jane Eyre* aloud and helped her write a book report. *Carry me, carry me.* At age six she would not walk from the town house to the corner. It was easier to pick her up than to listen to her whining.

One way or another, they had carried Simone all her life.

Dr. Balch explained that at its most severe, learned helplessness was characterized by extreme passivity and dependency, a sense of inferiority and powerlessness, and was most frequently associated with women who were physically abused and seemed powerless to escape their abusers.

"The syndrome applies in Simone Duran's case equally as well, although her case is extreme and quite unusual and has its roots in her infancy." Dr. Balch leaned forward, speaking intently. "Children learn competence by trying and failing and trying again until they succeed. Simone was rarely given this opportunity. As an adult she had no confidence that she could take care of herself or her children. Treated as helpless all her life, she had come to believe that she *was* helpless. And near the end, she saw—believed she saw—that she had transferred her inadequacies onto her daughters. With the exception of Merell, whom she did not believe to be her own."

"And you have arrived at this conclusion how? Reading school reports? Medical records? What else?"

"Since December she and I have met for two hours twice a week."

"After all these hours of consultation, can you tell the jury what it was that pushed Simone Duran over the edge into a psychotic state?"

"It was cumulative, of course. In a period of just eight years she'd had four children and several miscarriages. When she learned she was pregnant yet again and with another daughter, she could bear it no longer. But the final blow to her sanity occurred when her husband said he would bring his sister into the house to manage the children and so on."

"Most women would be glad for the help," Cabot said.

"But this wasn't hired help, this was someone who would not receive a salary. Her sister-in-law would take over her position. It meant an end to the role from which Simone took her identity. In a very real way, she would cease to exist. Faced with the possibility of annihilation, she suffered a total break with reality. Her mind snapped."

"And when her mind snapped was Simone Duran able to distinguish right from wrong?"

"Oh, my goodness, no. Absolutely not."

Jackson asked, "Dr. Balch, is *snapped* a clinical term?"

She smiled. "It is not. It is, however, descriptive."

"Did Simone Duran know what she was doing when she 'snapped' and tried to kill her children?"

"Not as you and I would know."

"But she knew?"

"She was delusional, Mr. Jackson."

"But she knew."

"She knew what she was doing but she didn't know it was wrong."

Chapter 17

The next morning Cabot called Simone to the stand.

Watching her sister, Roxanne's response was an empathy so intense it drove out self-awareness. She became Simone as she rose from the defense table and passed before the jurors in the box. She became what they saw, an ugly curiosity, a freak, a fascination. It was Simone who took her seat in the witness chair, who blinked too fast and licked her lips, but Roxanne felt everything with her. She was aware of her face, of each feature separately huge and horrible, something to stare and point at. She longed for a dark burka in which to hide herself.

"Simone, you've recently given birth, have you not?"

"Yes."

"You'll have to speak up, Mrs. Duran," the judge said.

"Yes."

"A daughter named Claire?"

"Yes."

"Where is Claire now?"

"She's in a foster home."

"Why is she there?"

"I was told it was because our home isn't a healthy environment."

Roxanne tried to read the jurors; she was always trying to read them. She even dreamed about them at night. The copy-shop owner sat with her head tilted to one side. Did this mean she was curious about Simone, that her mind was still open? The man beside her looked half-asleep. It appeared that as far as he was concerned, the case was sewn up and decided.

"And your other daughters? Where are they?"

"With my husband. And my sister-in-law."

"Is that Alicia?"

"Yes."

"Where do you live now, Simone?"

"My mother and I have an apartment."

"Do you see your children?"

From the gallery Roxanne saw the tears well in her sister's eyes.

"No."

"Do you miss your children?"

Simone began to weep. "I thought I was doing the right thing. I didn't want them to grow up like me."

"And would that be so bad?" Cabot asked gently. "What would your daughters be like if they grew up like you?"

"Helpless." Simone mumbled her words. "Trapped. Useless."

"On that day, Simone, why did you tell your twin daughters you were taking them to the marina?"

"Because that's where I meant to go."

"Why didn't you take one of your other cars? You had a Cayenne SUV and a Mercedes sedan in the other garage, did you not?"

"The other cars were just...ordinary. And gloomy-looking. But I knew we'd have fun in the Camaro."

"What was the color of the Camaro?"

"Yellow."

"Did you often have fun with your girls, Simone?"

"No."

"You never took them to the zoo or the beach?"

"Not by myself."

"Why was that?"

She shrugged. Like an adolescent, Roxanne thought.

"I couldn't take care of them by myself."

"Why not?"

"I don't know. I just couldn't. It was too much for me."

"But you decided to go alone with them to the marina? What was different about that day?"

Simone's brow creased with irritation, a look that was familiar to Roxanne. It meant she was sick of answering questions. "I wanted to sail again. When I was sailing I wasn't helpless."

"Were you going to rent a sailboat?"

The silence following Cabot's question lasted so long, it seemed like Simone wasn't going to answer it at all.

"I was going to sign up for sailing lessons and Johnny would see that I did know how to do something. I wasn't useless."

Roxanne felt Johnny tense beside her. She leaned a little toward him, pressing her shoulder into his. She made sure it was a small move that even the couple sitting behind them would not notice.

"But you didn't go to the marina. Why not?"

"It was too hard."

"What do you mean, 'too hard'?"

"Olivia was screaming and screaming and I couldn't open the string cheese."

Simone's hands twisted in her lap as if trying to open the plastic packaging.

"I couldn't do anything right! It was too complicated. There weren't any seat belts in the backseat and Olivia was still screaming and the twins kept asking questions. I lost track of time."

She looked around as if she needed to be reminded of where she was; and then she continued, breathlessly, speaking to herself now and not the jury. The crowded courtroom, utterly silent except for the sounds of the rain, seemed transfixed.

"I couldn't make my thoughts line up straight. I was trying to think but it was just words and words and words. And my head hurt like someone was holding it with two hands and squeezing.... The twins wouldn't do what I told them, they wouldn't just, wouldn't just...be quiet, just for two minutes so I could think. I loved them but they were stupid and silly like me and there was nothing I could do about it. What was the point?"

Roxanne wondered if Simone was aware of the tears running down her pale cheeks. One of the retirees on the jury took a tissue from her purse and dabbed her eyes discreetly.

"What happened next, Simone?" For a big man, David Cabot had a surprisingly gentle voice.

"I got in the front seat and I shut the door and in like a second, all the confusion went away." She looked at David, wide-eyed. "I knew what I had to do. I *knew*."

Clark Jackson leaped from his seat at the prosecution's table and charged to the witness stand; in his eagerness to get down to it, he was up so fast that he almost collided with David Cabot returning to the defense table. He stopped midway between Simone and the jury and faced her as if he were spokesman for the twelve people seated behind him. And then he said nothing, just looked at Simone as if she were a specimen. Roxanne couldn't see the look on his face; but she could imagine it as clearly as if it were being directed at her.

"Isn't it true, Mrs. Duran, that you told your girls you were taking them to the marina because you wanted to hide the truth from them? Because from the beginning you intended to gas them?" Jackson snapped his fingers. "Oh, yeah, I forgot! You were helpless, weren't you? You were just doing what a voice—"

"Objection," Cabot said. "Bullying the witness, Your Honor."

"Sustained." The judge frowned at the prosecutor over his narrow glasses. "Mr. Jackson, it has been a long day and my fuse is short. Make sure you don't light it."

"Sorry, Your Honor." He paced a moment before going on. "So you heard a voice—"

"Stop saying that!" Simone stood, her face scarlet. "It wasn't a voice and I didn't *hear* anything. I just *knew* what I had to do."

"Sit down, Mrs. Duran," said the judge.

"If you didn't hear a voice, Mrs. Duran, how did this so-called knowing come to you? Was there a thunder roll? A flash of lightning?"

Cabot had told Roxanne he was going to let the prosecutor take as much rope as he needed to hang himself. He called Jackson a bulldog who would push too hard if given a chance. He might make Simone look more pitifully helpless than Cabot ever could.

Jackson asked, "Do you think God was talking to you, Mrs. Duran?"

Simone slammed her hands over her ears. "No one talked. There wasn't a voice. I just *knew*."

Jackson's shoulders slumped as if cross-examining Simone had worn him out. Shaking his head, he walked back toward the prosecution's table.

He's finished, Roxanne thought, stunned with relief.

And then he stopped and turned back.

"Mrs. Duran, in July something happened at your home that made your daughter, Merell, call 911. Will you tell the jury what happened that day?"

"Merell already told you."

"Now I'd like to hear it from you."

"I was in the pool with Olivia, the baby. She fussed and twisted out of my arms." She turned a little so she could address the jury directly, sounding confident now, no longer helpless or confused. "Merell was up on the steps, she didn't see what happened, not clearly anyway. She called 911 to get attention."

Her testimony was too pat.

"Merell always wants to be the center of things."

The first train of storms had moved east. Rain still fell intermittently, but through the courtroom's smeared windows Roxanne saw patches of blue sky and occasional flashes of sunlight. More wet weather was forecast but for the moment the world beyond the courtroom looked brighter than it had in several days. However, sunshine and blue sky were not enough to overcome the malaise of testimony-fatigue hanging over the courtroom when Johnny took the stand at the end of the second week of trial.

Looking out at the gallery from the witness stand, his eyes were lost in deep bruises of fatigue, and—most telling of all to Roxanne—he didn't smile. This was Johnny Duran stripped of gloss, of ambition and charm, Johnny bared to his core.

Cabot asked, "Mr. Duran, you met Simone when she was eighteen. What was she like then?"

"Beautiful. Feminine."

"What do you mean by feminine?"

"Not aggressive or pushy. She didn't have a lot of opinions."

"And you liked that."

"I'm traditional. I like women who act like women." Johnny spoke without affect. "She let me take care of her, and when I talked to her, she paid attention. There was never any feeling of competition between us."

"She needed you."

"You could say that."

"When did you first realize Mrs. Duran was prone to depression?"

"One time, before we were married, her stepfather told me she had these...spells. He didn't use the word *depression*. He said she was fragile and didn't handle stress well."

"What was your reaction?"

"I wanted to take care of her." Roxanne heard a hint of belligerence.

"When did you begin to realize your wife was more than simply delicate or fragile?"

Johnny looked at Simone with an expression Roxanne thought was tender. "She had these quirks."

"Can you give us an example?"

"She never wore sandals or went barefoot. She told me she didn't like people looking at her feet."

"Was something wrong with her feet?"

"No, nothing. She had this broken toe that kind of stuck out at a funny angle but it was barely noticeable. She said it wasn't really her toe. She said she broke her own and the doctor sewed someone else's on in its place."

"What did you think when she said that?"

"I assumed she was joking."

"What changed your mind?"

"After we were married she always wore a sock on her right foot. In bed. All the time. She was ashamed of that little toe."

A woman to the right of Roxanne whispered to the man beside her. There were whispers all around.

They think she's crazy, Roxanne thought. *Good.*

"Were there other little 'quirks'?"

"Before Merell was born the doctor, the nurse, even the tech who read the ultrasound images, everyone said she was going to be a boy. When she wasn't, Simone got it in her head that Merell wasn't really our baby. It was like the toe thing. At first I didn't get that she was serious. But she wouldn't touch Merell. She let her lay in the crib all day, so my mother had to come in and help. And then after a while she seemed better and all she could talk about was getting it right next time."

"Getting it right? What did she mean?"

"We both wanted a son."

"How many miscarriages did your wife have after that?"

"At least four. Maybe five."

"That's a lot, isn't it? Were these short-term miscarriages?"

Johnny rubbed his forehead. "One of them was far enough along she had to go into the hospital. And a nurse told her it would have been a boy. It took her months to get over that one."

"What happened after the twins were born?"

"Like with Merell, she wouldn't take care of them. She started staying in bed most of the day."

"A year and a half later, Olivia was born. She had infantile acid reflux. What was that like?"

"She screamed. At night especially. No one got any sleep."

"What did you do then?"

"Walked her."

"For how long?"

Johnny shrugged. "I don't know. Hours. From one end of the hall to the other. Sometimes I fell asleep but I kept walking."

"Did Simone walk the baby too?"

"She tried. At first. And then she got so she'd just cry every time Olivia started up. Sometimes I'd go downstairs and wake up the nanny but she had to be with the kids and Simone all day.... It was easier for me to do it."

"Mr. Duran, is this what you heard?"

Cabot's associate pressed a button on a tape recorder and a baby's screams filled the courtroom. Johnny flinched. Inadvertently, Roxanne put her hands over her ears.

"All right, Counselor," boomed the judge, "I said you could play it ten seconds. That's it!" He rapped the gavel and declared to the noisy gallery, "I'll clear the courtroom if I have to."

"What did you do to help your wife cope?"

"I hired a nanny and a housekeeper, we got a vacation house where she could relax. I built an apartment for her mother so she'd be nearby. For a while I employed someone to cook for us, a personal chef. A whole week of meals was delivered every Monday morning when she was pregnant with Olivia. It wasn't junk either. It was good food, lots of vegetables. Nutritious."

Johnny glared at Cabot, daring him to contradict. Then he seemed to realize that he sounded defensive. He sat back and his voice cracked with weariness. "I let her stay in bed all day and I never said a word against it. I bought her two new cars because I thought it might make her want to go out. She used to have a few friends. But..."

"But what, Mr. Duran?"

"She was like one of those walking ghosts. A zombie. She didn't care about anything, she didn't *do* anything. Half the time I came home and she was still in her nightgown and she wouldn't know what time it was. She wouldn't even take a bath, for chrissake."

"The night before the incident did you threaten to bring your sister Alicia into the home?"

"What was I supposed to do? I was at my wit's end.

The nanny was gone and my mother-in-law was off doing something. I couldn't leave her alone with the children."

"How did Simone respond to this idea?"

"She panicked. She didn't like my sister."

"Why not?"

"She said if Alicia stayed she'd never leave."

Cabot turned to the jury and paused in his questioning, letting Johnny's testimony take hold.

"Did you at any time seek advice regarding your wife?"

"I talked to her doctor and my mother and sisters and they told me a lot of women get depressed after miscarriages and babies. They all said the same thing. She'd get over it."

"In fact Simone's condition grew worse. But you still didn't go to a psychiatrist or a therapist. Why is that?"

Johnny crossed and uncrossed his legs.

"When I was growing up we didn't take our problems outside the family. If it was medical, that's different. This was . . . personal."

"Did you fear the doctor would make the situation worse?"

"Yes."

"Mr. Duran, I want you to tell the jury *how* you thought a doctor might make your family situation worse."

A moment passed.

Johnny cleared his throat. "Way back, when she was having miscarriages, a doctor gave her some pills."

"Did they make her less depressed?"

"I don't know."

"Your attention was focused somewhere else, wasn't it?"

Johnny stared at the wall at the back of the gallery. Roxanne knew there was a clock over the door there. She imagined him watching the seconds tick by.

Cabot said, "Your Honor, will you instruct Mr. Duran—"

"You don't have to instruct me about anything," he said, straightening. "I'll say it. I'm not a hero here. The pills made her cold in bed. I didn't like it."

Behind Roxanne a woman whispered something that sounded like "Bastard."

Cabot had told the family that in a case involving violence to children, the jury needed to assign guilt but not necessarily to the defendant. They needed someone to blame and Johnny had been assigned that role.

"Did you ever think about not having any more kids? Using birth control?"

"I wanted a son."

"Did Mrs. Duran object to the lack of birth control?"

"No."

"She was compliant? Submissive?"

"I guess you could say that."

"And you didn't want that to change, did you?"

"No."

Johnny sat before the jury, exposed as Roxanne had

never seen him. The pride he had taken from his wealth and powerful friends seemed now like a pitiful attempt to compensate for a profound insecurity. From this day forward there would be no more invitations to golf and tennis with his pals in high places, and no seats reserved for him at the mayor's table. The chief of police would not return his calls. He had answered David Cabot's questions with unflinching honesty, and given the jury—the press and public—someone to despise instead of Simone.

Cabot sat down. "I have no further questions, Your Honor."

During his cross-examination, Clark Jackson again brought up the 911 incident. "The attempted drowning of your infant daughter, Olivia."

"Objection, Your Honor! The incident reports have been put into evidence. There's no mention of an attempted drowning. Prosecution is trying to mislead the jury about what happened that day."

"Sustained. Jury, you will disregard Mr. Jackson's last question."

Johnny blurted, "How many times do you have to hear this? Merell made that story up. She likes attention, she likes to try things out."

"Come on, Mr. Duran, you weren't there. You didn't actually see what happened, did you?"

Johnny sighed. "No. I wasn't there."

"Does Merell love her mother, Mr. Duran?"

"Yes, of course." He looked at Simone. "We all love her."

"Have you talked with Merell about what will happen if her mother is found guilty?"

"No."

"I'm going to ask you a question and I want your opinion as this girl's father. Do you think it's possible that she would lie to protect her mother?"

"Your Honor," David Cabot said, "Merell Duran is not on trial and Johnny Duran has not been offered as an expert."

"True." Judge MacArthur removed his glasses, examined the lenses, and handed them off to his clerk to be wiped clean. "Nevertheless, he is the girl's father and I'm going to allow the question."

"Mr. Duran, would Merell lie to the court if she thought it would keep her mother out of jail?"

"No," he said. "Of course not."

Jackson didn't move for a breath. Then, although addressing his comment to Johnny, he looked at the twelve men and women in the jury box. "Maybe you don't know your daughter as well as you think you do."

Chapter 18

Judge MacArthur recessed the trial until Monday morning, when the jury would hear summations.

Roxanne went straight home and locked the front door of the bungalow. She apologized to Chowder, but there would be no walk that day. Ty came home after dark and was accosted by a pair of reporters who leaped from their cars parked in front of the house, but on Saturday he and Roxanne avoided attention, sneaking away early. They drove to the Laguna Mountains and were rained on as they hiked the trail to the old mine. They lay in the grass by the side of the trail and let the rain come down on them until they were soaked and chilled and ran the half mile back to the car, laughing, to warm themselves up. On Sunday Ty built a fire and came back from Theo's Bakery with chocolate croissants and *The New York Times*. Between them they read every page, even the wedding announcements with their hopeful photos. That night they watched the entertainment channel and talked about celebrity shenanigans as if they were a couple with nothing more dramatic than Hollywood gossip to occupy their minds.

It seemed a long time ago that Roxanne and Ty had argued over Simone. Though she still felt close to her sister and during the trial she had sometimes experienced extraordinary waves of empathy, the calamitous truth exposed by Simone's crime had severed the breathing line that had connected the sisters. It was no longer possible for any of the family to pretend that Simone's meany-men were trivial. No matter how they might try, they could not be deluded into believing that she was like other harassed mothers, the women Roxanne saw pushing overloaded carts in supermarkets and shepherding children in and out of vans and cars.

There was nothing Roxanne could do for Simone now except love and stand by her. And yet she did not feel completely free, could not deny that she felt culpable. She had been her sister's caretaker because, from the age of nine until she met Elizabeth, she believed she had no choice in the matter. Some responsibility for what happened in the garage belonged to her. The certain knowledge of this was a cramp in her heart that took her unexpectedly, cutting off her breath with its intensity. She didn't bother complaining to a doctor. She never complained to Ty. She knew the cause.

On Monday Roxanne didn't hear much of Jackson's and Cabot's summations. Sometimes a particular word or intonation snagged her attention, but she had been sitting in the same seat in the gallery long enough, heard enough to know that neither the most bumbling nor the most eloquent summation could save Simone.

However, near the end of David's summation, his words finally managed to make her listen.

"Simone Duran did not hear voices. She did not suffer hallucinations. But at some point on that hot September day she became delusional in her conviction that the baby she was carrying, the twins and Olivia, were all doomed to be as helpless and profoundly unhappy as she was. She 'knew' the miserable destiny that lay ahead for her daughters and she 'knew' what she could do to stop it and she 'knew' it was the right thing to do."

Roxanne held her breath.

"It wasn't rational, this *knowing.* It was terribly wrong, but it couldn't be debated because it filled her mind and there was no room for any other thought. When she turned the key in the ignition of the yellow Camaro, she could not *distinguish* right from wrong and under our system of laws, that inability makes her not guilty."

Judge MacArthur scowled down on the murmuring gallery and tapped his gavel.

"No matter what you decide in this case, Simone Duran will not go free.

"Usually when a person is found not guilty, she can walk out of the courtroom and never look back, but this case is different. When you find Simone Duran not guilty by reason of insanity, she will *not go free*. She will immediately be incarcerated—locked up—in a hospital for the criminally insane. And she'll have to stay there until a panel of doctors determines she is no longer a danger to herself or others.

"And, ladies and gentlemen, let's be very clear. This might never happen. She might be locked up for the rest of her life."

Cabot's words grabbed Roxanne and shoved her against the chair back.

Cabot said, "So, let me remind you of the question I asked you to focus on when I made my introductory remarks. Why did Simone Duran try to kill herself and her daughters? I think you have your answer."

Cabot stepped back from the jury box. For the first time Roxanne saw the toll the last two weeks had taken on him. On his drawn face he wore an expression of sadness and resignation as much as if Simone were his wife and he was about to say words that described her.

"Simone Duran tried to kill her daughters because she *knew* it was the right and loving thing to do." He let the words sink in. "She did it because, at that moment, she was insane."

The jury was out for four days. The call came from David Cabot's office when Roxanne and her students were in the middle of a civics lesson. She went to the back of the room and called Ty. There was no point trying not to be heard. Every kid in the classroom had turned to watch and listen.

"They've decided."

"I'm on my way," he said.

She shut her cell phone and pressed the school intercom to contact the front office. Students, faculty, and staff at Balboa Middle School had been waiting and planning for this moment. The school's head secretary had arranged for someone to be sent to substitute in Roxanne's class at a moment's notice.

Roxanne turned to tell her class she had to leave them and saw that every child's eyes were fixed on her. She stared back at them, her mind just then a blank. She wasn't going to pretend that nothing was going on. As Elizabeth had said, for her students the semester had been a long lesson in how the country's legal system worked. They had their opinions, of course; and she had heard them discussing Simone's guilt or innocence in the halls and huddled around their desks before class, going suddenly silent when she came near. Some claimed to be sympathetic although she never quite trusted declarations of support from children who depended on her to promote them from eighth to ninth grade. Other students—most, she suspected, though she did not know for sure—had strong feelings against Simone. They were young enough to imagine themselves as helpless victims. On the last day of the trial a girl had told her, "I like you, Ms. Callahan, but what your sister did was evil. She's gotta go to jail or else every mother be killing their babies."

As she gathered her purse, coat, and umbrella she heard a voice from the back of the room. It was Ryan.

"Good luck, Ms. Callahan."

A girl in the front row smirked. "Yeah. Good luck."

The rest of the class said nothing. The sub came to take over for Roxanne, and they watched her go.

On her way out of the school she stopped in Elizabeth's classroom and they stepped into the hall to speak privately. On the other side of the room's partly open door there was the kind of perfect and total silence that would normally mean trouble in a roomful of adolescents, but in this case meant that every child was listening hard.

"Are you going to be okay?" Elizabeth asked. "Do you need someone to drive you? If the taxi's not here..."

"The office called one for me. It's out front now. Ty's meeting me in court."

Elizabeth hugged her. "I'm praying for you, honey."

"Not me. Simone."

"Yeah," Elizabeth said. "Her too."

It was raining again and traffic downtown was backed up at all the lights. David Cabot had promised Roxanne that he and Simone wouldn't go into the courtroom until she was in the gallery beside Johnny, but how long could he stall? A block from the courts she paid the driver and got out, running the rest of the way without opening her umbrella.

She found Ty in the crowd outside the courtroom and they entered together, taking their seats beside Johnny in the already full gallery. Looking down she saw that Johnny's trousers were wet halfway to the knees as if he'd waded through a flood to reach the court in time. She grabbed his hand and held it as Ty was holding hers.

Roxanne heard the door behind her open, the voices of reporters calling out a gabble of questions. The door slammed shut, and as Elizabeth's classroom had been preternaturally quiet, so was the gallery. Two sets of footsteps came down the center aisle. Simone and David stopped beside Johnny. Johnny stood and Simone automatically went to his embrace, neither of them making a sound.

Roxanne realized how much she had missed her sister. Her thoughts went back to the last time they'd had fun together, sprawled on the grass in the side yard. They'd laughed about Shawn Hutton and talked about sailing. Perhaps that conversation marked the moment when the fatal shift began in Simone's mind. She had reminisced about flying across the water and then she climbed a tree and for a few moments remembered how it felt to be brave and free.

"I love you," Roxanne said, not caring who in the gallery heard her.

Simone's eyes reddened but did not fill with tears as they once had so easily. She turned away and went with David Cabot to the front of the courtroom to await the verdict. Roxanne clutched Ty's hand and held her breath.

The bailiff called the court to order and Judge MacArthur entered, his robes billowing behind him. He banged his gavel once and spoke to the gallery before he sat down. "Ladies and gentlemen, in a minute the jury will take its seats and the verdict will be read. I'm going to say something right now and I want you to hear me. Every one of you."

For some reason his hair, his eyebrows, and his mustache looked more alarmingly bushy than ever.

He said, "I realize feelings run high in a case like this, and no matter how the verdict goes there are some among you who won't be happy. I'm telling you right now, keep your opinions to yourself. This courtroom is not a circus tent and this trial is not an exhibit for your amusement."

She wanted Judge MacArthur to stop talking; at the same time she hoped his harangue would go on, and they would never have to hear the verdict pronounced against Simone.

"I have directed the officers of this court that anyone who makes an inappropriate public display will not be permitted to leave the courtroom until I say they can go. I hope that's clear because I'm not in the mood to be patient this afternoon." He turned to the clerk of the jury. "Call them in, please."

The jurors entered in the same order they always did,

those seated at the far end of the jury box first. Roxanne scanned each one's face, searching for some sign the verdict would be not guilty by reason of insanity. N.G.I., David Cabot always said. The copy-shop owner had chewed away her lipstick but the college student had taken the time to reapply hers. Bright red. The retired accountant had misbuttoned his jacket.

All but the copy-shop owner sat down. David had predicted this woman would be the jury foreperson. He was a smart attorney and he'd given Simone a strong defense. A flutter of hope brushed over Roxanne.

"Have you reached a verdict?" Judge MacArthur asked.

"We have, Your Honor." She handed a folded piece of paper to the bailiff, who handed it up to the judge, who read it without a flicker of emotion and passed it back.

"How do you find?"

The foreperson rubbed the heel of her hand across her mouth before she spoke. "On the charge of attempted murder, the jury finds Simone Duran not guilty by reason of insanity."

Roxanne cried out and covered her face with her hands. Johnny ran toward the front of the courtroom. Despite Judge MacArthur's warning, the gallery erupted.

Chapter 19

August, Three Years Later

Ty would accompany Roxanne if she asked him, but she preferred to go to St. Anne's Hospital alone. And he preferred to stay home. He liked the daddy time with their son, Liam, who was eighteen months old, a towheaded boy who collected roly-poly bugs from under rocks and slept with a pink velour spider.

She appreciated having a few hours alone before she saw her sister; and afterward the long return drive allowed her time to resettle her emotions and focus on her family as she wanted to, not forgetting Simone, but putting her in a corner of her mind where she was no longer Roxanne's first concern. Roxanne calculated that she'd traveled the winding road to St. Anne's thirty-three times; and at the current pace of Simone's therapy, it seemed likely she would drive it that many times again. Lately she had begun to wonder if her sister might never return to her family.

During the first several months of her incarceration Simone had seen no visitors, and when the ban was lifted she sent word through Dr. Lennox that she wanted to see Roxanne. The reunion was less awkward than Roxanne had feared. For two hours they sat in the hospital's recreation room and played Monopoly. This was what Simone wanted to do; and Roxanne, remembering their weekend at the lake cottage, was struck by how like the twins she was: misering over her money, squealing with delight when Roxanne landed on one of her properties, and grabbing for two hundred dollars every time she passed Go as if Roxanne wanted to keep her from having what the game owed her.

Before each visit Roxanne spent time with her sister's psychiatrist, Dr. Lennox. Sometimes she thought he had become her doctor as well as Simone's. She sat in his office, and as always in the beginning, she was tense and wary of his questions. Today he began by telling her what she knew already.

"Simone is angry."

"No kidding."

"She says you all ruined her life."

Roxanne's first instinct was resentful and defensive; but her protest went unspoken because she couldn't blame her sister for being angry. Dr. Balch had testified, and

Roxanne knew, that along with Ellen and BJ and Johnny she had done her part to stymie whatever self-reliance might have struggled inside Simone. In Roxanne's mind her sister's thwarted longing to sail had become symbolic of all the roads and byways she had not been allowed to explore, the trips and falls her family had protected her from, the disasters large and small that were a necessary part of growing up.

Liam had been walking since he was ten months old and fallen a hundred times. Ty encouraged him to run and climb; and when he took a tumble, Roxanne, hearing his cry, wanted to scoop him up and put him in a bubble where nothing could ever hurt him. Instead she kissed his sore knee, applied Band-Aids when needed, and let him go. Sometimes it took every ounce of her will to do it.

Johnny visited Simone when she invited him, which was not often. Once on their anniversary he had come, and she had turned him away. Afterward he sat on the stone bench in the visitors' garden and wept as he never had, not even during the trial or after the verdict. Simone said she loved him, but Dr. Lennox said she might never go back to him. She feared being lured back into their dance of submission, helplessness, and control.

Dr. Lennox said Simone and Roxanne also danced. "Simone won't stop dipping and spinning until you do." His voice was kind and quiet, but Roxanne thought he was scolding her so she turned her deaf ear and watched the birds at the feeder outside his office window. It was interesting, perplexing: something about St. Anne's and Dr. Lennox brought out her stubbornness.

Johnny still worked long hours, but he spent every free moment with his five girls. Olivia and Claire were charming little creatures, close as twins in their looks and sweet ways. Valli and Victoria remembered the day in the garage; but their memories didn't hold together. Soon they would slip apart, disintegrate like threads of cheesecloth.

To Roxanne it seemed Merell had, in lying to protect her mother, sacrificed her innocence. She was almost a teenager now, a bright, wild, and unpredictable girl, sensitive as a hot wire. Her teachers complained that she was unmotivated, secretive, and unreliable. They wished that she would make friends. Johnny talked of sending her to boarding school in Monterey, but Ty and Roxanne had convinced him not to and wanted her to live with them for a while. They had a roomy second story, a guest bedroom with beautiful windows.

Two years ago, when Johnny announced his plan to build a new house on the beach in Leucadia, Ellen had stayed behind in the city and bought a town house near her office in Little Italy, where there was always something going on. She had a wide circle of friends, and her real estate business was a small but thriving concern specializing in homes considered difficult to sell.

In his office Dr. Lennox told Roxanne, "Simone still feels as helpless as she did the day she first came to St. Anne's. She's stuck and that's why she's angry. She's like a little girl in a woman's body, and she knows that until she grows up, she's never going to leave this hospital."

Though Lennox was a superior doctor and highly professional, he spoke to Roxanne in a commonplace way, friend to friend, in a language they both understood.

"You've been a good sister, but now it's time to take the next step." Dr. Lennox leaned forward across his desk, fixing Roxanne with his gray eyes. "I can't tell you what goes on in your sister's therapy, but I can tell you she's been very brave. And she knows that she won't be able to go home without your help."

A flash of anger. "You're saying it's up to me. Again?" She liked Lennox and trusted him, but there were times when her patience with the whole therapeutic regime ran out. "Why is it always up to me? She's the one who put the girls in the car and turned on the gas."

"She trusts you. There is no one in the world she loves more than you. You can help her, Roxanne. If you're willing."

Lennox knew too much about Roxanne: she'd been too candid, giving him an advantage. Over her thirty-three visits to St. Anne's she had talked about the house in Logan Hills, the Royal Flush, and the reason for her deafness, going to Gran's, and coming back. Now she regretted every honest word she had ever spoken to him.

"Why are you doing this to me? What gives you the right to use me? Haven't I been used enough?"

Dr. Lennox dipped his head, as if in agreement. "When you were brought back from Daneville, how did you feel about being put in charge of your sister?"

How do you think I felt?

"It didn't matter." Ellen had abandoned her once and she would do it again if Roxanne did not do as she was told.

"Why didn't it matter?"

She wanted to stand up and walk away, drive back to San Diego and to hell with St. Anne's and Lennox and her sister.

"How do you feel now? This minute?"

"I want her to get better, of course."

"That isn't a feeling."

All right: I hate her and I hate you. Are those feelings? I want this sister off my back! And I want to go home to my husband and boy and never come back to this place. Is that enough feeling for you?

"Roxanne, what would happen if you were to tell your sister how you felt back then, how you still feel? How you've felt all along?"

"She knows I love her, Dr. Lennox."

"I am not talking about love."

Outside the window, against the background of blue sky, a boldly marked yellow bird bent its head at the bird feeder hanging from the eaves.

After her visit with Dr. Lennox, Roxanne stood in the lobby at St. Anne's and watched Simone come toward her wearing blue jeans and a tank top. Her tender prettiness was entirely gone. She had lost more than twenty pounds, and in the flimsy top her clavicles protruded like a necklace of bones. Over the years her eyes seemed to have grown larger and darker. They dominated her face in a way that was raw and unattractive. Her hair—she still hated washing it herself—hung lank and drab. Dr. Lennox believed that somewhere in the labyrinth of Simone's history there must be an explanation for her aversion to fresh water.

"Shall we walk?" Roxanne asked, linking her arm with Simone's.

St. Anne's was a sprawling hacienda-style building with thick cement walls and a tile roof and grounds landscaped with desert plants. In the summer the temperature was often one hundred degrees or more; most patients, visitors, and staff preferred to be indoors, where air-conditioning kept every room a mild eighty degrees. Simone and Roxanne preferred to be outdoors and truly private. They walked the gravel path through the beavertail cactus and ocotillo to the top of Anne's Hill. At the crest there was often a breeze and a square of shade under a ramada. The view was across the arid mountains and up to the ridge where a Native American tribe had erected hundreds of windmills.

The wind blew Simone's hair off the nape of her neck, revealing a collar of freckles from a long-ago sunburn.

Simone said, "Remember those pinwheel things we had when we were kids?"

One day before Roxanne started school, the babysitter, Mrs. Edison, took her around the block to a fair at Logan Hills Elementary where she met Mrs. Enos, the brown-skinned, orange-haired first grade teacher who gave her a silver pinwheel. On the way to Gran's she held it out the window of the Buick and watched it spin like the windmills.

She could have told this to Simone, described the teacher she had liked so much and how frightened she was to be taken away from her home and abandoned to the care of a grandmother she hadn't known she had. Instead, she talked about their mother.

"How is she?" Simone asked.

Roxanne tipped her head from side to side, and they smiled. Dr. Lennox once said that having a sister was what made having a mother bearable.

"She's happy these days," Roxanne said. "The business is going like gangbusters. Big bucks."

"I guess she's over missing BJ."

She had never told Simone that BJ gave her money in appreciation when Simone became engaged to Johnny. She had kept the inside and the outside of her life a secret from her sister because a good sister must protect, must not be angry or unhappy or confused, never resentful or rebellious or reluctant. A good sister was orderly in her thinking and knew how to take charge of any situation.

She played back Dr. Lennox's words. *In Simone's world the only feelings that matter are her own. That makes her a child. That keeps her a child. Tell her the story of your life. Let her know what it felt like to be Roxanne. Let her grow up.*

She had never told Simone about the house in Logan Hills and the night she almost burned it down. She hadn't described standing on a stool to wash dishes or covering their mother with a blanket when she passed out drunk on the couch. Simone didn't know that their mother beat her ear with a rubber sandal until it bled. And she didn't know that Roxanne was brought back from Gran's because Ellen feared she would hurt Simone too.

This is what Dr. Lennox asked her: "You gave up your childhood to protect your sister. How does that make you feel?"

Blood rushed in and out of her heart, the valves opened and closed and her pulse kept time. *I will be abandoned. I will be beaten.* Her heart would cramp and then explode; blood and bones would fly out in all directions.

Someone will hold my little sister's head beneath the bathwater to stop her crying or grab her by the heel and throw her in the swimming pool.

This is what Dr. Lennox told her:

"Simone was brought up to be helpless and you were brought up to be afraid, to be on guard and watch for threat. But there is nothing to fear anymore."

Her heart beat against the prison of her ribs.

Roxanne asked Simone if she had remembered to put on sunscreen.

Roxanne told her she was too thin.

Caretaker and charge, helper and helpless. Both of them frightened by life. Roxanne was as much trapped in her roles as Simone was in hers.

Along the ridge, the windmills turned; somewhere a yellow bird took to the air, sailing the sky like a ketch in blue water. Roxanne was sitting on Anne's Hill with her sister. The only sister she would ever have. She held the key to their past; it would open the door to their futures.

"When I was younger than the twins, there was a place across the street from where we lived, a bar called the Royal Flush. Mom and my dad would go there at night and leave me alone." She pulled Simone down on the bench beside her and forced herself to speak. "One day I almost set the house on fire."

The wind was up, tearing through their hair. There was lightness in Roxanne. Another puff of wind and she would fly, she and her sister would both set sail.

"That was the night Mom beat me with a rubber sandal. That's why I'm deaf in my left ear."

She spoke and Simone listened.

Letter from Gran

Roxanne left her grandmother and the ranch when she was nine years old. From then until Gran died seven years later, she and Roxanne exchanged regular letters. Sometime after the events of the story, Ellen Vadis came upon a cache of old letters and among them, apparently overlooked and still sealed, was a letter to Roxanne from Gran, written near the time of her death when Roxanne was a teenager.

My dear girl,

First time I saw you, I couldn't believe there was so much determination in one little kid. Such a small, waifish package, long legs and bony knees and with something hopeful about you, despite your sad eyes, as if from early on you had decided to view life from the sunny side no matter what. At the time, all I could think was that you looked like an orphan in rubber go-aheads, your hair a rat's nest of brown tangles. Neglect was written all over you and it almost broke my heart, though it's true, I didn't want you and I was angry that your mother had the gall to drop you on my porch with just a couple of days' notice. I put you in her old room and for the first week you left off watching from one window or another only when I called you to meals.

You must have been with me a month or so when I fixed a roast chicken supper with mashed potatoes and gravy and gave you the job of shelling peas. Before then, the only peas you'd ever seen came out of a plastic bag. You couldn't get over how wonderful it was that they came packaged in their own green shells. I told you what I thought, that God takes care of the good things on earth. You asked me what God looked like and that was the start of it, three years of you asking questions and me trying to figure out the answers. One thing for sure and it gratified me, a child who asks questions is a bright child. The more questions, the better.

It used to rile me that Ellen went off and left you, never looking back, but you still thought she was someone special. She was always selfish, your mother. She put her own pleasure ahead of whatever anyone else wanted. I blame your grandfather's leaving for that. She loved her daddy like crazy. There was jealousy between us on that account though I'm ashamed to admit it now. He just turned his back on her and went off to live a life that suited him better, and she blamed me. I can't speak to whether it was me who drove him away; too much time's gone by. All I know for sure is, he hated the ranch, the never-ending work, and I can't blame him for that. We were just kids when we got married, and being young, it's hard to see the value of land and trees and fruit compared to parties and dancing and all that glittery business. But after he was gone, I gradually learned there's comfort in work, a kind of peace and a gratification there's not a man on earth can give you.

You were a hard worker, Roxanne; you knew how to listen and follow directions and you always seemed to take some pleasure from a job well done. You had my orderly ways bred into you, I suspect, and that's not a bad thing. First grade, spelling was your favorite subject, probably because there was a clear right and wrong about which letters went where. Plus you liked to memorize: the states of the union, presidents of the United States, the names of every flower in the garden. You knew them all.

Summer mornings you'd come downstairs in your shorts and T-shirt and the big shoes I made you wear to protect your feet from the pointed stuff that's always lying around a ranch, even a well-tended one like mine. You never wanted me to make you breakfast. Come to find out, no one had ever fixed pancakes or even fried an egg for you before I did. After eating you'd clear the table without being asked and then you'd write out your daily list, sounding out the words you couldn't spell. You said the list was your plan for the day. Back then your biggest chores were gathering the eggs and feeding the hens, and I had a kid-size rake so you could keep the big coop tidy. You enjoyed that work, I know you did; and you liked drawing a line through the items on your list.

You even played in an orderly kind of way. In your bedroom there were a half dozen old dolls from your mother's time. You set them up on chairs and played school, teaching those dolls everything you were learning. And then you'd read them stories, sitting up on your bed with them all nestled around you like the family you wished you had. You were the dearest thing.

For me, the years you lived at the ranch were the happiest of my life. I felt like God had given me a second chance to be a mother. See, I know I failed Ellen; and maybe I should have told her that. Maybe it would have made a difference between us. But all my life I've been too full of pride for my own good. Never could say I was sorry or ask forgiveness. When your grandfather came to see me the last time, I should have right out told him I loved him and wanted him to stay. But I could see in his eyes that he was already far away and I wouldn't humiliate myself. Didn't even cry. He wanted to say good-bye to Ellen, but I told him he had no right and he begged me with tears in his eyes. It shames me to say it but I took satisfaction from those tears.

With you, there was only one thing that worried me. Right from day one, I saw that you were accustomed to put yourself second, to give yourself away taking care of whoever needed you most and made the most noise about it. Your mother saw to that, I suppose. When she came back for you, I knew she had another baby girl back in San Diego and she couldn't manage her any better than she could you. I wanted you to stay with me, but she had her plans and as always Ellen came first.

You're a big girl now, practically a woman, and every day I wonder what kind of young lady you've turned out to be and if you ever think about the good times we had here on the ranch. Remember Pablo Salazar and his family? They still pick for me every August. And the boy, Raul, who taught you to swim in the irrigation canal, he's an accountant over in San Jose now. Your dolls are all lined up on the bed, still waiting for you to read them a bedtime story. I kept your pony until he died. Just fell asleep one afternoon in the sun and never woke up. I hope to go as peacefully. It won't be long now. The doctors have me on plenty of painkillers but seems like I can still feel the cancer growing in me. One day it'll get so big it'll drive the soul right out of my body.

LETTER FROM GRAN

Think of me sometimes, Roxanne. Be good to yourself and grow up strong. Find someone who loves you for all you're worth, which is a whole lot. And always remember you were my girl, Roxanne, and in all my life, I never loved anyone more than you.

Note from the Author

My Mother's Postpartum Depression

I was twelve when my sister, Margaret Ellen, was born, plenty old enough to know that since the coming of this baby girl, our family—and by that I mean our mother, who was the heart and core of us all—had problems. My nine-year-old brother, Kip—a worrier even then—was alert to the change too. I can still see the look he gave me over the cereal boxes at breakfast when the atmosphere between our mother and father was so thick we could barely breathe.

Postpartum depression affects the whole family.

Then, as now, words like *adaptable* and *enthusiastic*, *curious* and *playful*, described our mother. True, she had her moods. Mom told me they were unavoidable. "The blues are part of being Irish and there's nothing you can do about it," she said. "There's nothing like a good boo-hoo." She wept because my father was himself and not the man she'd dreamed he was, because plans fell through and dogs died and because she was separated by thousands of oceanic miles from her parents and all but one of her sisters. She loved the old Victorian songs she and her sisters sang around the piano, the maudlin ballads of diaspora and death at an early age. When I was little I'd ask her to sing "Lilac Trees" and we'd both finish up in tears. It was a family thing.

Despite these floods, I remember my young mother as bright-hearted and, above all, resilient, which she had to be in a family where we were often *stony* (one of several terms she had for being out of money), always struggling. Most of the mornings of my childhood I awoke to the sound of her lovely soprano voice singing up from the foot of the stairs: *Patrick, Michael, Seamus O'Brien could never stop sighin' for sweet* Molly O / *Every morning, up like a sparrow and out like an arrow just leavin' the bow.*

The singing stopped when Margaret Ellen was born and a dreadful shadow fell over our home. I remember opening the front door after school with a wariness that was completely new to me, an uncertainty about what lay on the other side. Mostly, everything slowed down as my energetic mother was overcome by a debilitating lassitude that transformed her in my eyes. My father—never one to pick up on the nuances of human behavior—was in way over his head; but I'm sure he never sought the help of a doctor or priest. Seeking advice for so private and shameful a problem as a wife undergoing a *nervous breakdown*—the all-purpose catchphrase for any emotional distress—was anathema to our family. In those days we—like almost everyone else—kept quiet about personal problems.

It was the time of the cold war, and after Margaret Ellen was born my mother became obsessed with the threat of a nuclear holocaust. She wrote a letter to the president, which doesn't sound like much of anything today, but back then it was a big deal, audacious even. Out of respect, the letter had to be typed, which meant taking our ancient typewriter out from its place under the stairs, replacing the ribbon (a dirty, entangled job), finding the change to buy the right kind of stationery because one could not write the president on any old piece of paper. And then getting the words right meant typing, tearing up, typing over again and again until a perfect page was written.

My last memory of my mother's postpartum depression is of being upstairs in my bed on a school night, hearing the sound but not the words of an argument from downstairs: Mom crying, begging to be heard, to be understood; Daddy trying with all his heart, but failing. I got up out of bed and opened my bedroom door. Across the landing, in pajamas and barefooted like me, Kip stood in his doorway too, that worried look on his face. Without speaking we crept down the stairs and sat beside each other. I remember being frightened for the first time ever, aware of fault lines running through the foundation of my life. After a little while my father—wearing one of his much-washed white undershirts, baggy-kneed corduroy trousers belted so they gathered a little at his slim waist—my sweet, overwhelmed, intellectual father to whom the appearance of fracture lines must have come as a shock as well, stood by the stairs and spoke to us. I remember exactly what he said, the precise words: "*Don't worry, kids. Your mother and I aren't getting a divorce.*"

Until that moment, the possibility of divorce had never occurred to me, but hearing the word in my father's Iowa voice put it into my personal vocabulary, where it remained until many years later when I heard my mother say it.

And then, as suddenly as it had come, my mother's postpartum depression was gone. I don't remember that she sang to us in the morning after that, but she probably did. I probably don't remember because at the time I wished with all my twelve-year-old heart that she wouldn't sing *at all, ever.* In a seventh grader's world, a mother's songs were meant for babies. Afterward my mother bore no scars that I could see, but I think they were there. Decades later she and I were standing in line at the supermarket, reading the tabloid headlines. One caught her attention: *Mom throws self and baby out of seventh-story window.* My mother shook her head and said, "Poor woman. I know just how she felt."

Postpartum depression is like standing on a window ledge over a black hole, frozen in place, unable to do anything but look down into the swirling darkness. In the pit, every mother sees something different. My mother saw nuclear annihilation, the world and all she loved destroyed. Though we were spared her vision, my brother and I and our father, too, saw a reflection of that horror on her face and heard it in her voice. We felt her fear, and a shudder ran through our world, rocking it to its foundation.

—*Drusilla Campbell*

Reading Group Guide

1. Many themes run through *The Good Sister*. One of these is codependency, the kind of unhealthy relationship that can tie friends and family together in knots of emotional misery. In large part *The Good Sister* is about Roxanne's attempts to establish an independent life apart from her sister. Why is this so difficult for her? What obstacles real and imagined stand between her and this goal?
2. Roxanne loves her sister and feels responsible for her, and Simone is excessively dependent upon Roxanne. Is Roxanne also dependent upon Simone? In what ways? What events from each of their childhoods led to this enmeshed relationship? When and by what means might it have been terminated much earlier in their lives? Why didn't that happen?
3. Although she feels her mother abandoned her by leaving her with Gran, Roxanne has many happy

memories around the three years she spent at the ranch. It has been said that our memories both sustain and burden us. How is this true in Roxanne's case?

4. *The Good Sister* is the story of four generations of women, each of whom has been abandoned in some way. How does the theme of abandonment run through the story and influence the lives of the characters?
5. Merell slips into and out of rooms like a little ghost, unseen by the adults around her who are too much involved in their own lives. Roxanne was unseen by her mother except in her role of caretaker. Simone is slipping from depression into psychosis and Merell believes she is the only one who sees her mother's pain. Is it true that we often do not see clearly the people closest and most important to us? Why is that?
6. There are two "good sisters" in this book: Roxanne and Merell. How does Merell's development mirror Roxanne's? How do we see the pattern of behavior playing out in Merell in contrast to Roxanne?
7. Do you think there is often one sibling who does everything possible to make the family happy and peaceful? If you were in Roxanne's shoes, would you have stopped your life to help your sister in need?
8. Elizabeth believes that we sometimes serve as "angels" to the people who need us. Have you ever known this to be true?

9. Roxanne knows that without Elizabeth's friendship she might never have found the courage to move away from home and take the first steps toward an independent life. Was it Elizabeth's example that enabled Roxanne or something else? Is it possible that we look for in friends those qualities we know or sense are lacking in ourselves?

10. While postpartum depression is quite common, postpartum psychosis is—blessedly—rare and does not occur in women who are not psychologically damaged in some way. Dr. Balch says in her testimony that in Simone's case, a "perfect storm" of factors was involved. What were those? And does knowing *why* Simone tried to kill her children help you to feel sympathetically toward her?

11. Did reading *The Good Sister* make you think of real mothers in the news who endangered or killed their children because of postpartum depression, such as Andrea Yates? Do you feel sympathy toward them, or do you see them as monsters? Do you think the media treats these women fairly? Do you think there is still a stigma against women suffering from postpartum depression in society?

12. Simone is torn between her fear of life and her longing to regain the feeling she had when she sailed aboard the *Oriole*. How do these conflicting desires play out on the day she decides to take her daughters to the marina on Shelter Island?

13. We apply the adjective *good* to being a mother and sister. What does it mean to be a good mother, a good sister?
14. Johnny thought Simone would be a *good* wife. What caused him to make this egregious misjudgment? Is it possible that with no children or perhaps only with Merell, Simone might have lived up to his expectation?
15. Throughout the book Roxanne represses her anger, but in the final chapter Simone's psychiatrist tells her it is time for her to be brave. What does he mean? What does he want Roxanne to do, why is this difficult, and why does he believe it will help Simone?
16. Will this family ever be whole again? What forces work in its favor and what pulls against it?